A CASE OF
ACCIDENTAL
INTERSECTION

A CASE OF
ACCIDENTAL
INTERSECTION

By W.S. Gager

*Martha -
Become Infatuated
with Mitch Malone!*

W.S. Gager

Oak Tree Press   Springfield, IL

Oak Tree Press

Oak Tree Press books may be purchased for educational, business or sales promotional purposes. Contact Publisher for quantity discounts.

First Edition, June 2010

978-1-892343-70-3

LCCN 2010928506

■ DEDICATION

For my grandparents who showed me that old doesn't mean dead.

■ PROLOGUE

He felt a twinge of guilt that Dominique Pewter would die. She was a pretty girl who he had watched grow up. But today was the day Dominique had to die. He made the decision.

Dominique was putting together the truth and he couldn't have that. He had been skimming millions from Dominique and she was demanding a full accounting. Worse yet, she wanted to work in the business. He would not answer to some upstart, spoiled kid. This was not a job for the faint of heart.

He'd been covering his tracks for the past couple of years. He thought it would be hard for the business graduate to find the skimming. The ten million he had in the Cayman Islands would be enough. He smiled when he thought of taking that money right after the accident knowing it would never be missed. Add that to the business expenses he had been padding for years and depositing that along with the ten million.

He hadn't expected she'd want to see the books since her parents had died three years ago. He wondered if it was just curiosity or if she'd been suspicious. He couldn't think of anything that would have tipped her off. He'd tried to convince her to get some experience somewhere else and then come back and take the reins, but she was adamant.

"I owe it to my parents to continue their legacy in the furniture business," she'd said. Dominique could have lived, if she had wanted to work anywhere else. Now she would die.

■ CHAPTER 1

A twisted piece of fiberglass stuck in the dirt along the side of the road. A rearview mirror the color of cherry-red lipstick had busted off the wreckage and landed some fifty feet away, along the centerline marking the do-not-pass zone.

Firefighters, EMTs and policemen huddled around the still-turning belly of a cement truck that had mowed over the top of something but was itself undamaged. The realization hit me with horror. The mirror belonged to a car pinned under the orange and white girth. It now looked like an octopus with jagged sheet-metal legs protruding in all directions, rather than a fancy sports car from a showroom.

I moved in the direction of a woman pacing and wringing her hands. I pulled out my ever-present small digital camera and snapped a couple of shots of the wreckage. Then one of the woman who clearly showed the magnitude of the scene without any words needed. I slipped the camera back in my breast pocket.

"I'm Mitch Malone with the *Grand River Journal.*" I held my hand out to shake hers. With the other hand I pulled my narrow notebook from the back pocket of my jeans and flipped it open. I tugged the pen from the spiral band at the top with my mouth. I grabbed the pen from my lips. The contact of warm flesh made the woman pause. She looked from the wreckage that had mesmerized her. As her eyes focused on me, she settled somewhat.

The woman was short, compact and old, still wearing an apron tied around her ample hips.

"I never heard such a noise as when that there car. . ." the woman paused for a moment trying to come to terms with the twisted metal that had originally been designed for speed. "I was in the house and heard the truck's brakes lock up. I've gotten used to the noise with all that roadwork going on. I was just turning back to my dishes." A shaky hand rose and smoothed a strand of gray hair ruffled by the slight breeze. Her hand shook and I didn't know if it was from age, illness or the accident.

"The ripping, tearing…it screeched until I wanted to put my hands over my ears. I could feel my home shake, the dishes clinking in my sink." The senior adjusted her shirt and fiddled with the hem that had pulled out from under the apron. "Then it was dead silence, eerie like all the sunshine had been taken from the day. I thought that was bad enough." She lifted the bottom hem of her floral apron and stared at it.

"Then the screams started."

I nodded to the woman, hoping to keep her talking. This was good copy, even if I'd happened along the catastrophe by chance. I'd been to see a pint-sized friend and was returning home via a more scenic route when I came upon the accident. I'd had a great afternoon tromping through the woods with my former roommate, Joey.

The accident scene crushed my happy memories much like the truck had crushed the car. I went from leisure-time pursuits to award-winning journalist in less than a turn of the cement truck, even if it was a Saturday afternoon of my weekend off.

"I looked out, scared to see it and called 9-1-1. I went to help, but couldn't figure out where to go. I followed the screams, but couldn't get under the truck. I don't get around too well any more. I'm eighty-three and have a bum hip."

I nodded again to keep her talking, scribbling in my own form of shorthand.

"I saw a car leave and thought what terrible people they must be to leave an accident and not help, but I looked at the wreckage again and knew there was nothing I could do. I felt so helpless. The screams turned to sobs. I called to her, but she didn't respond to me. She kept saying, 'Ashley, Ashley, I'm so sorry.'"

The woman stopped abruptly and shook her head. Her next words were a whisper. "Then it was quiet, dead quiet." She stopped and ran a hand through her graying hair, pulling wisps of it from the bun. She took a deep breath before continuing, trying for a normal tone.

"It seemed like the longest time until I heard sirens in the distance and the police finally arrived. I've been standing here since."

"They haven't left with anyone?" I wanted to know if anyone could survive such an accident. I doubted it, but wanted to know the number of people in the car.

The roar of the Jaws of Life broke above the cacophony of other noises and stopped our conversation. I looked toward the truck, its orange and white tank still spinning. Its optical illusion added to the flashing lights looking more like a carnival ride than the carnage it was. Firefighters in their heavy coats pushed blankets into small crevices under the giant wheels.

The mechanical whine of the spreader strained as the full weight of the heavy truck was forced up by the miraculously simple Hurst tool. I wondered if it was made to lift the tonnage of a fully-loaded construction vehicle. Scurried movement danced around as supports were inserted to stabilize the vehicle for emergency workers to get to the victims. The pitch increased again, but this time a blade-like pincer made contact with metal. It only lasted for a second. The cuts sounded like a bolt cutter snapping a chain.

Shouts and the bustle of movement ensued before the Jaws again revved and pierced the afternoon with its cry.

EMTs stood off to the side, waiting for the tool to allow them to get to the victims. Their faces were pained, tense, doubting they would have any work to do but always hoping for a miracle.

I looked at the older woman. She had tears running down her face. "Do you think they're alive?"

I could see that she wanted to believe they would be alright. I didn't want to tell her I thought the odds were long that anyone could survive a crash like this one.

I patted her shoulder feeling awkward. I rationalized that if I offered slight comfort, I might get better quotes.

The Jaws started again. I let out a breath, relieved I didn't have to answer. We continued our conversation between the Jaws and the beeping of a second cement truck. It backed up to the first to unload the heavy burden of cement that must be close to its permanent state.

"I was at my kitchen sink. I couldn't believe it. Another dark car leaving in such a hurry." Again she stopped, stared at the rush as the EMTs moved in with neck braces and backboards.

I continued to note each of her observations. Some didn't make sense and her comments were in no particular order—Ramblings of an old lady who should be baking cookies, not watching the mincemeat of a high-end car.

"As I rushed out, a man was just walking away. He just left." The ambulance backed up close to the wreck, blocking our view. "How could this happen?"

I didn't have an answer.

"I was at the kitchen sink which faces the road. It just shot across into the intersection."

I could see my companion was going into shock, stuck in the repeating horror playing in her mind. "Why don't we go back to your house?" I said. "I could use a glass of water."

"I'm sorry. Where are my manners?"

I offered her my arm and assisted her across the yard to her back door next to the garage. I wasn't sure what I was doing. Reporters weren't supposed to become immersed in the stories they covered. They were unbiased observers covering the facts. Not helping little old ladies back to their homes before hysteria set in.

I wasn't thinking about being a Boy Scout earning a merit badge, but I wanted as much info as I could get. She needed to get her mind off the carnage before she couldn't function at all. I put my notebook in my back pocket.

"I looked when I heard the brakes and saw that car, red like candied apples. You know that color? The car shot across the intersection."

I opened her screen door. She stopped at the threshold and looked back. Her eyes registered horror and I was willing to bet she was seeing the accident and not the current rescue operation.

"There was somebody standing on the far corner. The accident plum made me forget. That's why I was looking out the window. I was trying to figure out what he was doing. He was walking up to the two girls in a car and they didn't look happy about it. It seemed odd. I thought maybe he was one of them perverts or something giving those girls a bad time."

I looked at her wondering if she had lost her mind or was simply confused. Could the occupants of the car been fleeing from someone? We crossed into a small mudroom with hooks on the wall for jackets and then into a cheery yellow kitchen. A green, gingham-checked valance hung across the window above the sink, matching the fruited wallpaper along one wall. In the homey kitchen, it didn't seem possible that there was an ulterior motive to the crash. I had to stop seeing what wasn't there. This was an accident, plain and simple, but it would be good copy. I had the quotes to prove it.

I wanted to probe to get more details but knew it would bring nothing now. She was bouncing from subject to subject with no connecting dots. She needed normalcy.

"Is that coffee brewing?"

"Oh, yes. I put it on. . ." she stopped to think a moment. "Would you like a cup?"

"Yes, please." I moved to the kitchen table and pulled out two seats before I sat, waiting.

She shuffled to the stove and grabbed the pot. It was a silver percolator that must have been a hundred years old. She grabbed two mugs from wire hooks under the upper cabinet and brought all three to the table. She poured each mug to the brim with a dark brew and then replaced the pot on the stove burner before sitting beside me.

I figured this cup would either be delicious or horrible from the age of the pot. I burned my tongue and quickly set the cup down to cool. My hostess wrapped her short, compact fingers around her cup, but I doubted she felt the earthenware's heat. She, again, was off into space.

She started as if shocked, jolting the cup and sloshing the coffee onto her fingers. She wiped them on her apron.

"I'm sorry. I don't know where my manners are. Would you like cream or sugar?"

"Black's fine. Thank you. It's delicious." I hadn't tasted a drop yet.

"Elmer took his coffee black, too." She rose and went to the refrigerator and took out a carton of half and half and poured a dollop into her cup. I watched the cream swirl. She returned to the table with a spoon from beside the sink and stirred.

"Elmer?"

"Elmer was my husband. He passed on two years ago."

"Elmer was a lucky man to have married a beautiful woman like you." I watched the color return to her checks. I flirted with her as I took a swig of the coffee. I needed to get back to the accident, but realized I didn't even know her name to quote.

"Elmer always liked his coffee thick, he called it."

I nodded.

"Said those newfangled drip coffee pots were a waste of money. A good percolator got better with age."

"He was a connoisseur of coffee." I needed to get her off the sainted Elmer. I didn't need his name, I needed hers.

"I'm sorry but I never got your name." I was back to business and pulled the notebook back out.

"Goodness gracious. I can't get over that wreck." She glanced out the window. The EMTs were now half under the cement truck and the police had begun labeling car parts with numbers for photographing.

"Elmer always said people drive too fast. Wouldn't drive over forty miles per hour. I miss our long drives to the grocery store."

I fidgeted. I only needed her name and I could be on my way. "I'm sure you were a handsome couple, Mr. and Mrs...."

"Dobson. Mr. and Mrs. Elmer Dobson."

"Right." I wanted to gnash my teeth. Didn't this woman have any identity outside her husband? "And you?"

"Elsie. Elsie Dobson." She thrust her hand out and I took it.

"Nice to meet you, Elsie. Is that E-L-S-I-E?" She nodded. "D-O-B-S-O-N?" She again nodded. Great. I could leave now.

I took another mouthful of the coffee and appreciated its heat jolting me into action. Elmer was right. This coffee had character. Someday, I might have to get me an old percolator.

I stood, pushing my chair back as a knock sounded at the door.

"Goodness gracious. More guests." I looked over my shoulder and saw a uniformed officer standing there. It was Deputy Derrick Smothers.

Now I knew my day was going downhill. I had a great relationship with most officers in the city police and county sheriff's department. Every department had a few bad apples. The sheriff's department's worst, in my opinion, was on the other side of Elsie's screen door. My day had just taken a nosedive.

■ CHAPTER 2

Elsie let in Deputy Smothers and offered him a cup of coffee, but he declined.

"Did you see how the accident happened?" The officer spied my reporter's notebook on the table and frowned. Derrick and I didn't get along well.

"Why yes. I was just telling…" she paused and was embarrassed to have forgotten my name.

"Mitch Malone," I supplied to ease her distress.

"I was telling Mr. Malone about it."

The officer's brow furrowed deeper and a hard edge glinted in his brown eyes. I could see he wanted me gone, but I wanted to hear her official version of events. I wasn't willing to accommodate Derrick, never had and that irked him.

"I was just finishing up the lunch dishes and I heard the screech of brakes. Those trucks are always releasing them before they make the turn and I was tired of them. I looked up and saw the sports car shoot into the truck's path and then," Elsie paused and I could see her searching for how to describe it. I glanced at the cop but he wasn't writing anything down and his eyebrow was raised in speculation.

"Disappeared. The red car disappeared." From the wreckage I knew what she meant and thought it was a great description of the truck going over the car and squishing it, but I could see the cop wasn't impressed with my source's mental faculties.

"I was standing here doing dishes, watching the birds at the feeder there." Elsie then related the accident again for the officer, but these reactions were more emotional than factual. Most officers would appreciate my notes but Derrick wasn't one of them. He was cocky and arrogant. I wasn't going to help him climb to a higher position. He was one of the shoddier kinds of deputies who enjoyed the power the position gave.

"Elsie, I need to get going and gather some more information." I finished the last dregs of the cooling brew. "Thanks for the coffee. Elmer was right."

Mrs. Dobson flashed me a beautiful smile that must have been the one Mr. Dobson fell in love with. "You're welcome, Mr. Malone. Come back again."

Her cheery smile was a perfect counter to Derrick's scowl. My work here was done.

As I left, I looked ahead of me at the accident scene. The pavement was fresh from the current roadwork Elsie complained about. The center road markings were fluorescent yellow and without age against the smooth inky-black surface. The edges of the road were level with newly-sculpted embankments and straw covered the mulch to stabilize them until the new roots formed. Enough delaying, I had a job to do and it wasn't assessing the landscaping. I focused my attention to the fancy sports car being torn limb from limb by the Jaws of Life. I felt like a morbid groupie waiting for an autograph from a star outside their dressing room, but no beauty would be walking away from this accident.

It looked like the EMTs were struggling to get underneath to the bodies. I couldn't believe anyone could survive such wreckage. The slow urgency of their movements said volumes. Work on the other side of the vehicle was even slower, methodical. The emergency worker's shoulders were slumped but worked to free what could only be a body.

I snapped a couple photos of the backboard coming out. They didn't show whether the victim was there or not. I also took photos using a wide angle to set the scene. I would find the photos invaluable to describe the scene to readers when I was back in my cubicle.

The corner behind the wreckage was in full bloom of bright red tulips in the May sunshine. I focused in and snapped shots of the dark police car with the first sign of spring. The flowers looked too normal for what would surely ruin at least a couple families' spring and summer.

I walked back to a deputy who was writing information on a clipboard.

"Hey, Mitch. Nasty wreck."

"Yes. Any idea what happened, Hank?" I looked at his clipboard that had an intersection pre-drawn. A driver's license clipped to the top.

"Not yet. Just starting to take all the measurements." Hank Baldwin was a deputy I hadn't worked with much but had never had a problem with his easy-going manner.

"Bubba's really his given name?" I asked, reading the license.

"It takes all kinds. I feel bad for the guy. Doesn't look like there was anything he could do." The deputy nodded to a copse of trees on the opposite side of the street. "Yes, Bubba Gentry was the driver."

Bubba wore a navy uniform with a red name tag with white lettering. I was too far away to read it. The man was pacing and it looked like he was talking to himself. I headed in his direction.

I was about ten feet away. His back was turned away from me and he hadn't hit his end point to return in my direction. "Bubba?"

He turned and I noticed a beer gut giving him a pregnant protrusion and his name tag clearly read, "Bubba."

"Who wants to know?" His tone was surly and I would guess this hadn't been one of his best days.

"I'm Mitch Malone with the *Grand River Journal*..."

"Great. Now you're going to plaster all over the paper that I've had a drunk driving arrest and there'll be all kinds of hintin' about being drunk now. I'm sober. I haven't touched the stuff in five years. You can print that."

I pulled out my pad and started writing. "I will." Bubba looked at me like I had grown three heads.

"You'll print what?"

I finished writing his quote to put in the article and answered him. "That you haven't had a drink in five years and that wasn't the cause of the accident."

"You will? I ain't ever heard of a reporter printing the truth before." He took off his baseball cap and ran his hand over his greasy hair, further messing up a serious case of hat head.

"Most newspaper reporters try and print the truth, but they are only as good as their information." I paused. I could see Bubba's eyes were clearly glazing over with my attempt at education. "Can you tell me what happened?"

"Should I be talking to you?" He cocked his head to one side and gave me the once over.

"You don't have to. I just want to make sure I get both sides of the story. From what I heard, there was nothing you could do. Just wanted to hear it from the horse's mouth, so to speak."

"Oh, okay. It wasn't my fault. I'm awful sorry those girls got hurt. I tried to stop. I just didn't have time. They just shot out in front of me. All I keep seeing is that girl and her big brown eyes. The look of horror on her face. The scream."

I watched his face screw up and then harden. I would not want to mess with Bubba. I bet he was a mean drunk. But he was sober and he got himself under control. The tears he was fighting so hard to keep in stayed behind his lids.

"I know you couldn't. That's what other witnesses said." I leaned in, grabbed his shoulder and squeezed. I breathed in and all I smelled was really bad body odor, none of the sweet smell of alcohol leeching through his pores as the stress of the day pushed him to a breaking point.

"Did you see anyone? Did the car brake at all?"

"I don't know. I just keep seeing that girl's face. That face is going to give me nightmares. I don't know if I will ever forget."

I couldn't assure him that he would. I couldn't think of anything to say. We both looked back at the wreckage.

"I've never had an accident with my truck. Mabel and I have been together for five years. I got her just after I went on the wagon. They kept talking about replacing her but I wouldn't hear of it. I knew she had lots of good years left in her."

"Mabel?" I couldn't follow what he was talking about. Was Mabel his wife, his girlfriend? Was he losing it?

"Yeah, Mabel, my truck. She was something special. I'll bet my company totals her out and takes the money. They wanted to replace her with a truck with a higher capacity, but I wasn't ready."

"Mr. Gentry?"

We both turned and a deputy in a brown uniform called from the road.

"Yes."

"I'd like to take your statement now."

"Okay." He lumbered down one side of the ditch and up the other side to the deputy on the edge of the road.

He never looked back. I hoped the tragedy wouldn't drive him back into the haze of alcohol addiction, but lots of times it does. They just can't get over the feeling of despair. I doubted even alcohol would ever dull the image of the brown eyes burned into his memory.

I found myself on the opposite side of the accident from Elsie's house. I took a few photos, then jumped the ditch and moved further down the road. I hoped Bubba didn't beat himself up too much. There was no way he could have seen the car coming. From this direction, the road was a blind drive.

I walked back noticing that the machines cutting the wreckage had stopped their whine. The accident was beginning to wind down. There was no urgency. A double fatality. No one would ever know what really happened. The girls were distracted and didn't see the truck. Another senseless accident by a preoccupied driver.

Then there was a flurry of activity. The emergency worker closest to the passenger-side of the car waved his arms and yelled.

"We have a pulse."

■ CHAPTER 3

The antiseptic smell of the hospital put my nerves on edge and I wished there was a way to get the information I needed without going, but I knew there wasn't. I hated hospitals.

Elsie Dobson's great quotes about the accident had released my inner demon to get as much information as I could. The police wouldn't release the names of the victims until tomorrow afternoon after the next of kin were located. If I wanted any kind of condition on the girl who survived in tomorrow's newspaper, I would have to be at the hospital to see it firsthand.

So I chased the ambulance from the scene. Only one ambulance came in hot with the lights and sirens. I followed right on its heels. The other ambulance hadn't even loaded the second victim and was waiting for the medical examiner. The accident had one fatality and one close to a fatality, judging by the pinched facial expressions of the professionals

From my experience, this accident was as bad as it could get. The only thing worse was when small children were involved, but from Elsie's description, I didn't think so. The fact that they were both young adults, maybe even teenagers, was bad enough.

I wound my way around the information desk at the hospital, acting like I knew where I was going. I did for the most part. I wanted to get back to the emergency room nurses' station to get the scoop on the victim. Federal health privacy laws prevented the hospital from giving me anything but a person's condition, which was usually classified as critical, serious, fair, or treated and released. I wouldn't even get that until the person was admitted and I had his or her name. I suspected this victim was critical, but I wanted to know what the injuries were.

Was it possible someone could survive that crash without months of surgery and rehabilitation?

I hoped so, but I had lost my optimism in happy endings a long time ago. Most of my stories ended in death and dismemberment. That's just the way the world worked. I printed the worst news. I shouldn't be taking this accident so personal or examine my feelings too closely. This was like any other story I covered. I was an unbiased observer. Period.

As I entered the emergency room corridor, the EMTs had just snapped out the wheels of the gurney. The victim was strapped to a board on top of the stretcher. Bits of long blonde tresses that weren't matted in blood blew in the soft breeze from the automatic double doors. The hair was the only distinguishing feature peeking out from bandages in varying shades of red. A heavy collar encased her neck, keeping her face from moving and causing further injury.

Both legs were in stabilizing splints and her arms strapped to the backboard. It was hard to believe a young woman was underneath all the padding and bandages. My view was obscured as a doctor in a white coat approached and everyone disappeared behind the door to treatment room three.

I could imagine two young girls out enjoying the first days of spring in the small sports car, having fun, catching up from being away at college, laughing at events and people they had met. Their distractions of friendship and conversation had cost them dearly, one with her life. I needed to find out what the cost was to the other for my story.

I waited. A nurse casually walked down the hall. A technician in blue scrubs carrying what looked like a plastic dishpan with a special handle protruding on top went into another treatment room and exited a few minutes later. Another nurse glanced at me. I avoided eye contact and she continued with her reports.

The white-coated doctor, now with brown spots on his pristine attire, ran a hand over the top of his short military style hair cut. "CAT scan, x-rays, intracranial bleeding, pressure on the brain, possible internal injuries." The doctor detailed the medical issues facing his newest patient to the charge nurse.

The nurse working on her reports jumped to her feet at his arrival, a question in her eyes.

"We almost lost her. We're stabilizing her now. We need a neurologist and orthopod notified for emergency surgery."

"Yes, doctor."

"See how much AB negative blood we have. Check to see if we can get more. She will need at least four to five units, possibly more."

He returned to his patient.

I had my answers. She was critical and not likely to survive. I debated what to do next. I should have left immediately but I didn't. Hospitals made me nervous but I fought the urge to flee. I could have returned to the accident scene and talked to the reconstruction expert but I knew I would get more information if I waited until he returned. He didn't like to be interrupted during his initial investigation. I was mentally piecing together my lead for the next day's edition.

I was struggling with how to adequately describe the sheer force exerted upon the car to flatten it like a pancake. By now I was back by the door leading to the waiting room and the public entrance beyond.

"You let us in. My little girl's in there." The loud demanding tone came from the waiting room and brought me to full attention.

"Ashley, Mommy's coming. You'll be all right." This voice was higher pitched but filled with desperation, barely banked.

The charge nurse hurried through the outer doors to lend support to the lobby volunteer.

When the nurse opened the door, I could hear a calmer voice. "Please, calm down. Let me see if I can find her. The sooner you calm down, the sooner I can help you. Ashley? What is her last name?"

"Albanese. Ashley Albanese." The deeper voice clipped.

"I don't have an Ashley Albanese admitted." The volunteer's voice was firm.

"The police came and said she was taken here from an auto accident." The woman's voice broke off and I heard her start mumbling. "Hail, Mary, full of Grace…"

The authoritative nurse's voice broke in. "Please. Have a seat. As soon as the doctor is available, I will have him speak with you. Our first priority is the patient."

"Yes, yes. Take care of our Ashley. Where is she?"

"Let me check. Please have a seat in the waiting room."

The charge nurse reappeared and called to the EMTs who were coming down the hall from the bowels of the hospital with coffees.

"Ben, Sam. You have any identification for your victim?"

"A twenty-two-year-old white female. There were two girls in the vehicle. One didn't make it. We didn't have time to get identification. We were afraid we would lose her." Sam looked at Ben and shrugged – a gesture of acceptance. "We didn't think anyone would survive but she had a slight pulse and we rushed her here."

"A family arrived looking for Ashley Albanese."

"That was one of the names we heard. I don't know. Maybe the family can make an ID?"

The charge nurse entered treatment room three. Within moments she came out and shook her head. Her features couldn't hide her belief that the girl would not survive and she wasn't looking forward to talking to the family. She straightened her back, took a deep breath and schooled her features trying to look impassive.

She went to the waiting room and I heard muffled conversation punctuated by a wail, which I assumed was the mother.

"We want to see her," the deep voice said.

"The doctors are with her now. Please be patient. Maybe you can see her before she goes to surgery."

"Pray for us sinners now…" the mother's voice chanted.

The door opened and the nurse returned. The automatic double doors at the ambulance entrance also opened and Deputy Derrick Smothers shuffled in, adjusting his brown sheriff uniform as he went. I snarled to myself. I didn't want to tangle with Derrick here. I wasn't allowed behind this side of the double doors.

"Hey, beautiful," he said to the charge nurse who blushed even though she was old enough to be his mother. "What's up with the accident victim?"

"Do you have a name?" Her back-to-business attitude brought the deputy up short and his jaw clenched.

"How many accident victims you have in here tonight?" Any trace of flirting was gone in the hard voice.

"I have a protocol to follow, deputy." Her voice hardened as well, which brought a smile to my lips. The meeting earlier today was mild for us. Derrick was smart and mean. He would pay me back when no one else was watching. I'd had run-ins with him at scenes in the past couple of years when he was only on crowd control. He was the kind of man who shouldn't be a cop. He had refused to allow me access to an accident scene for no other reason than he could. I'd never forgotten. He had graduated from traffic stops to investigative work.

"Ashley Albanese."

"I've received no confirmation of the victim's identity."

"Well, unless you have another victim brought in then that is who I'm looking for. Is she going to make it?"

"I'm not God. That is out of my hands," the nurse said crossing her arms in front of her, irritating Derrick further. "You have any identification?"

The deputy consulted his clipboard and read. "One Ashley Albanese and Dominique Pewter were in an accident. A red sports car believed to be a Victory Red Chevy Corvette convertible." He stopped reading than added: "Although there was not much left of it to be sure," he smirked as he looked down at the clipboard and continued: "The car was owned by Dominique Pewter, who was believed to have been driving. Her passenger, Ashley Albanese, was transported to Mother of Mercy Hospital."

"Ms. Albanese's family is in the waiting room. The doctor is prepping the victim for surgery." The nurse turned to depart when Derrick grabbed her arm.

"Has she said anything?"

"Not that I know of." The nurse pulled her arm away and went behind the desk.

Without even a thank you, Derrick headed for the waiting room and paused when he saw me leaning against a wall by the door. I tipped my finger at him in mock salute. I waited for an attack but after glancing around for witnesses, he continued wordlessly. I was surprised. Maybe he was taking anger management classes.

I moved closer to the door. I didn't want to eavesdrop on the family during their distress but I wanted to hear how Derrick handled them. I didn't need any more information. I just wanted to dislike Derrick more with his brutal methods.

To my surprise, he was solicitous.

"My name is Deputy Derrick Smothers and I'm investigating an accident. Can you tell me what your daughter, Ashley Albanese, was doing tonight?"

"She went out with her friend, Dominique Pewter." The voice was the one I associated with the father.

"Do you know what they were doing?"

"Dominique and Ashley had just graduated from the University of Michigan. Dominique was going to work for her family's company and purchased a new car to celebrate. She took Ashley for a test drive."

"Do you know how I can reach Dominique's family?"

"She doesn't have any. Her parents were killed three years ago in a car accident. She was an only child. She spent holidays with us. Now, how is Ashley? Can we see her?"

"You will have to talk with Ashley's doctors. I don't know. There isn't any extended family we can contact for Dominique?"

"No, just her guardian, Seth Lynch. There is also a CEO. He runs Dominique's family business, Herman Steel Designs."

"Thanks. I hope your daughter is all right," Derrick said, completing his interview.

"How is Dominique?" the mother's voice asked.

"I'm not at liberty to discuss that."

I peeked through the double doors to the waiting room and watched the deputy leave through the sliding doors to the outside parking lot. I slipped through and watched the family. There were at least five of them in varying sizes. Each had a dark head and dark eyes. It wasn't hard to see they were all related.

I couldn't see how a blonde fit in. My curiosity was piqued. I moved forward.

"Hi, I'm Mitch Malone from the *Grand River Journal*. I don't want to intrude, but I came across the accident by chance. Would you mind talking with me?" I gave them my best boy-next-door charm.

"Do you know how our daughter is?" the mother asked.

"No, I'm sorry. You will have to talk to her doctors."

"Do you know what happened?" The tallest man stepped forward who I assumed was the father. He fit the voice.

I didn't want to tell them they didn't expect their daughter to live, let alone the car was crushed. They would find out eventually. I wrestled with these questions every day. What could I tell them that would give me the personal information I needed?

"I came upon the accident. It happened on Lake Drive by Vista Point. Do you know why they were there?"

"No. But they were taking the car for a test run. That is a beautiful drive," the mother said. "We used to take the kids out there to the beach when they were little."

"A test drive, huh?"

"Yes. It was Dominique's gift to herself for graduation. The girls looked so beautiful in their caps and gowns. Two peas those two have always been. How's Dominique?"

"I don't know. Two peas, huh? So they were both dark haired like you?"

"Oh, no. Dominique was blonde. Ashley was dark haired, but for graduation, Dominique gave her a spa treatment. Ashley decided to go blonde and see if they had more fun," her mother said, a smile curving her face as she remembered.

"Shocked us. I wasn't so crazy about the blonde. She didn't look like one of us anymore." The disapproval was hard to miss in Ashley's father's voice.

"So they were both blondes in the pretty red car?" The dad took offense to my tone that I hadn't realized was derisive. He stood straighter.

"Dominique was rich, but she never acted rich. This car was the first big ticket item she bought for herself," a brother, who was only a few inches shorter than his father, added with eyes that said I can take you, if you say anything bad.

The information about Dominique's parents dying in a car crash made me think of my own parents' death. That dark time when I was angry at the world. I don't remember the first year, except I wanted to die. After that I started to rejoin the world and had started college. I felt a strange kinship with the dead girl.

Ironic that just when she was starting to live again after the crushing grief she would then die in a similar death to her parents.

"Yes, Dominique didn't spend money at all. She was conservative. But we shouldn't talk about Dominique. She wouldn't like it," the mother added.

"I'm sorry, I don't mean to pry," I said, knowing that line usually gave people permission to keep talking.

"You're with the newspaper, Mr. Malone?" the father asked.

"Yes, Mr. Albanese."

"Please, call me Tony."

"Thanks, Tony." I pulled out my notebook and wrote down his name. "You have a beautiful family.

I could see his chest puff up. He was proud. "Yes. This is my wife, Angela." I shook hands with the petite woman.

"My son, Anthony Jr. We call him AJ. My daughter, Amy, and our baby, Amanda."

"You are all As," I said.

"Yes. When I met my Angela, I knew it was fate." He looked at his wife. They were clearly still in love and could read each other's thoughts by the small smile they shared.

Any reply was broken by the double doors opening and a doctor in blue scrubs walking in. "Are you the family of Ashley Albanese?"

The mass of Albaneses rushed forward.

"How is she, doctor?"

"My name is Dr. Stuart Ward. I'm a neurosurgeon. We are stabilizing her for surgery. Her most serious injury is to her head. Pressure is building from bleeding and swelling around her brain. We'll go in and relieve the pressure. If we don't, she may suffer brain damage. She may have already. There is no way to tell. While she is in surgery, we will set her arm. We don't know yet if she has any internal injuries. It doesn't appear that way from our initial assessment. She is bruised and battered."

"What are her chances?" Tony asked, pulling his wife into the circle of his embrace.

"Will she be all right?" her mother echoed, her eyes filling with tears.

"We don't know. We need to get the pressure released and then assess its function. We'll induce a coma to give the brain time to heal itself and monitor her progress. The injury is in the front of her brain.

Prognosis can be good for these types of injuries. However, she may never regain consciousness. The brain is tricky and there's no way to know the extent of the damages. We'll do our best." He attempted to smile reassuringly at the end.

"When will we know?" Mrs. Albanese said, reaching to pick up the youngest child who tugged on her housedress.

"We will be starting surgery within the next half hour. The surgery will take two to three hours. We will install a tube to continue drainage after surgery to keep the pressure off. After recovery, she will be placed in ICU to allow the maximum amount of monitoring should any problems arise. I may know more after surgery. You can wait in the surgical waiting room on the fourth floor."

"Can we see her?" the deep voice cracked at the end.

"I wouldn't recommend it. She is being prepped for surgery and not conscious."

"Thank you, doctor." Tony reached around his wife and shook the doctor's hand. The doctor retreated behind the doors.

The family had forgotten all about me as they hurriedly headed for the elevator to take them to the surgical waiting room. I was glad I didn't have to face them after the crushing news.

I slipped back through the double doors, attempting to take a shortcut to my car through the emergency room entrance. The light alerting staff to a problem went on in treatment room three. I was pushed aside by a nurse and the emergency room doctor I'd seen enter the room earlier.

"What's the problem?" the doctor asked.

■ CHAPTER 4

I didn't hear an answer to the doctor's question. I heard vital signs from two voices that didn't sound good.

"She started coming around," a nurse said. "I asked her if she knew where she was. Her name and what day it was. She just kept repeating 'Ashley, Ashley.'"

"Ashley, can you hear me?" the doctor asked.

Another nurse entered and while the door was open, I heard a weak voice say: "I'm sorry, so sorry."

"Ashley." The doctor's voice was sharp, insistent.

"Her pressure is dropping, doctor."

I hadn't meant to eavesdrop in the treatment room but was drawn by the flurry of activity. I was just outside the open door and couldn't help but hear the exchange. I could never print any of it, but I firmly believed more information, even if you couldn't use it, added a human touch to a story.

Could this accident and miracle of survival be turned into a double fatality? I grimaced, glad the family had gone to the private waiting room and I didn't have to witness their distress. I just printed the news. I didn't get involved. I had more to do on my story. The crisis in the room seemed to have passed and the doctor walked out, wiping his brow. I could see the nurses monitoring vitals and injecting something into an IV.

I walked to my black Jeep SUV and headed the six blocks to the police station, turned right and went another half dozen blocks and another left and six more blocks and I pulled into the lot parking in the "Employees Only" spot at the Grand River County Sheriff Department.

The modern building had a brick façade and a rounded wing off to the left that housed the prisoners in the Grand River Jail. As I was heading for the building, my karma must have been good. A uniformed deputy was just leaving through a steel door and held it open for me. Usually, I entered through double glass doors at the front, but being late in the day on Saturday, the lobby was locked. I entered a hall that lead to the sheriff's office on the far end but also held the conference room, break room with vending machines, and a briefing room. I heard voices coming from down the hall.

I was heading toward the break room. I was hungry and figured a quick cup of coffee out of a machine would hold me.

"Bob," I hailed as I walked in. "Just the man I was looking for." I knew Bob Johansen craved coffee and never drank it while at a scene whether it was an accident or crime. The minute he walked into the office to do his reports, he took the java intravenously.

"Mitch, isn't it a bit early for you to be checking in? It's still daylight?" The crime scene specialist dropped coins into the slot and punched a red button for coffee with sugar.

I glanced at my watch and realized it was early. I usually didn't make my rounds until ten-ish. It was barely past dinner. Then I remembered my changed hours. The new city editor wanted me to work a normal work week, Monday through Friday, eight to five, as if that would work on the cop beat. I didn't want to get into that here.

"Great observation. That's why you're the detail man and I just write it up."

"Yeah, that's a laugh. Whatcha looking for?" Bob hit the button again.

"What happened at that accident today out on Lake Drive?"

"Damned if I know." Bob shook his head then scratched the balding spot near the back. "None of my measurements make any sense." He stared at the machine, gave it a push and hit the coffee button a couple more times in agitation.

"Wish you'd been there, so I could bounce some ideas off." Bob's spare tire was barely contained by his Oxford shirt pushed against the machine. He bent over to look at the cavity where the cup dropped from.

"I was there. Came upon it after a little R and R this afternoon."

"Really? What was your take on it?" Bob again hit the coffee machine, this time moving it a couple of inches.

"Little red sports car pulled out in front of cement truck."

"Yes, that's what I thought at first but the measurements don't make sense. There aren't any brake marks before the stop sign on Vista Point where the red car pulled out until impact. There are tire marks on Lake Drive where the cement truck tried to stop. He was nearly to them, hence why the truck all but ran over the top of the car."

"So what's the mystery?"

"The sports car should have brake marks start behind the stop sign until the point of impact. It's like they didn't try to stop, but witnesses said the car was stopped at the sign before pulling out."

"They were going too fast. Isn't that normal, especially in accidents with young drivers?" I was being sarcastic and received a dirty look from Bob.

"For the speed needed to create the impact, they needed to be going faster than just pulling out unless the driver floored it from the stop."

"That could have happened." I rationalized.

"I don't know, Mitch. I'm not ready for any of these findings to go public. Just looking for your take on it. I guess what I'm not looking for is a cup of coffee out of this lousy machine."

I glazed over a minute remembering what the old lady had said that afternoon.

"You got something?" Bob squinted his eyes taking a closer look at me.

"I interviewed the neighbor who saw it from her window. She said a guy was bothering the girls." I moved to the coffee machine and with my left hand, hit it along the side. The cup dropped down and started filling with the steamy brew.

"Did you know the dead girl is loaded?" I asked, rubbing my thumb over my fingers for the age-old symbol for money. "Could be motive?" I reached in and handed the cup to Bob.

"Thanks. I hadn't heard yet. Who?"

"The lone child of the founders of Herman Steel furniture dynasty."

"The Pewters?" Bob took a sip of his coffee.

"Yes, why?"

"I wrote the report for the accident that killed the owner and his wife. I had some concerns about that one as well but got some heat from the corporate executives to release my findings so the company could get back to business. I didn't have anything specific at the time. Just would have liked more time." He stared into his cup, thinking back.

"Must be a family of terrible drivers," I joked half-heartedly. I was already thinking it was a bit of a coincidence. I never believed in coincidences especially when there was money and lots of it.

"What can I print?"

"How about keeping it simple for now? Sports car pulled into the path of cement truck."

"Okay, but let me know if you turn up anything else. Think the department will let you keep going?"

"I'm not sure. I don't have anything concrete but I'm going to keep looking at it."

"The cement truck had lots of concrete," I said, deadpanning.

"Good one." Bob didn't laugh and I figured my play on words was a bust.

"I'll check back with you tomorrow and see what, if anything, you've found."

I fed a dollar into the coffee machine. After it filled without incident, I realized it was still set for sugar. I passed the cup to Bob on my way out. "Here, have another cup on me." I figured it was the least I could do for my lame joke.

■ ■ ■

I entered the *Grand River Journal* newsroom which seemed brighter than usual but it could be that the sun was still high in the air. I didn't usually see it until after the sun had set. The newsroom was a mass of cubicles circling the editor's domain in the center. I wound my way to my cubicle and fired up my PC.

I connected to the newspaper's digital morgue and found a cache of stories on the Pewters, pillars of the community. It seemed the wealthy couple had gone to a Christmas party and their chauffeur fell asleep at the wheel, hit a culvert and the couple drowned in a drainage ditch upside down. I found another story from the next day with funeral arrangements and another with a vice president assuming the helm of the company. He expressed grief for the son of the founder who made the small furniture maker into an international conglomerate.

I searched under the company name Herman Steel and saw a recent article stating profits had been just short of expectations for the past eighteen months in an industry that was booming. Did the man who took over not have the right touch or was it the result of the death of the founder?

I started reading a profile on the CEO, Bertram Switzer, who was named to fill in after the accident. Born in Grand River, educated at Michigan State and went to work at Herman Steel. He worked his way up through the administration, taking over when the founder died.

"I was deeply saddened by the death of my mentor," one quote read. Another read: "Herman Steel is poised for great growth and profits."

Not a lot of emotion there, but a lot of focus on money.

My next search was on the dead girl, Dominique Pewter. Not much in the newspaper's morgue. A birth announcement twenty-two years ago, then her graduation, which I was surprised to see, was from a public high school. She was at the top of her class. The next name stopped me.

Ashley Albanese! The two friends had graduated together at the top of their class from a city high school. It was dated four years ago. They had both just graduated from college, the mother had said. Childhood friends starting out on their professional lives that took a terrible turn with a cement mixer.

The last entry was her listed as the lone survivor in her parents' obituary. So much for a debutante. No society photos, no brushes with the law. Just a smart girl who had faced a tragic loss. Paris Hilton could take some lessons from Dominique but it was too late for that now.

My heart went out to the debutante. I felt badly for a girl with a promising future to be cut short. Oddly, I felt attuned to what must have been a lonely couple of years. My own parents had been killed in an auto accident when I was in high school. She probably was just starting to not feel guilty for surviving.

Ashley's mother said Dominique purchased the car as a present for her own graduation. She didn't have any family left to buy her a graduation present. It was her declaration that her mourning period was ending. I remembered mine. I didn't have the money to buy a new sports car, but I did buy a new couch. Okay it wasn't quite the same but it was close. I felt strangely in sync with the dead girl.

I closed the web browser with a determined click of the mouse. This was going nowhere fast. I couldn't think about the parallels between us. I was a reporter and I had to remain neutral. No feelings were allowed although I could play up the tragedy. That would add to the story. I jotted down the highlights of what I had found.

"What's got you in so early?" a voice said behind me.

I turned and saw the new city editor in the entrance to my cubicle. Neil Speilman was trying to be everyone's best friend. I hadn't figured out how to tell him I didn't have best friends, didn't want a best friend. I was a loner.

"I can't help it if the news just drops in my lap, even on a vacation day." I tried for my best earnest expression. I struggled to like the new editor although he made it difficult. He'd changed my hours and habits which I knew wouldn't work. I hoped it would only take a week to get that message across, but that was Monday's problem.

"Whatcha got?" the editor chuckled, slapping me on the back like I had made the funniest joke.

"Local furniture heiress killed, her high school friend in critical condition from an auto accident off Lake Drive."

"You don't mean Dominique Pewter?" His graying blond hair fell over his eyes.

"One and the same, why?" I was surprised. Neil had moved to Grand River a month or so ago for the job and wasn't that familiar with locations, companies and the local movers and shakers yet.

"In Sunday's business section we're running a profile on her graduating from business school to return home and take over the family business." He pushed the blond hair back that had fallen forward as he leaned into my cubicle. I could see the excitement in his eyes and knew I was in trouble. The last time I saw that look, I had been moved from nights to days.

"Really? That must have ticked off the high and mighty CEO who had to work his way up through the ranks. Any chance I could pull from the profile?"

"I can do one better. We'll run the profile as a side bar to the accident and play it across the front page. I'll call the business editor in to rewrite it with her death." Neil turned away but his words still drifted to my ears. "That'll piss him off. Maybe I should put him on the night cop beat."

The words froze me in mid-story. The nights belonged to me. I was the man of mystery. What was with this new editor guy? Was he out to make everyone miserable? I needed to straighten him out, but not tonight. Let him have his fun. I turned back to my computer.

This time a genuine smile crossed my face. I didn't much care for the snooty business editor any more than I did the new city editor. Thought he was better than everyone and only worked a nine to five day, period. He lorded it over everyone else who would listen to the pompous ass. I'd never had to work with him much being we were night and day literally. I could wait a week to go back to nights if that meant the business editor would get a week to see what it was like in the trenches and not at the three-martini lunches. Then we would have to switch back.

"Mitch, don't just sit there, get to work. Any art?" The city editor was back in my cubicle and I hadn't moved, thinking about how my schedule was going to take some work to get back to my solitary existence.

"I snapped a few shots. Let me take a look." I'd forgotten about my camera work at the scene. It all seemed so long ago now. The adrenaline was wearing off and today's early start registered its toll.

I pulled the camera out of the pocket of my standard-issued leather jacket and plugged it into my computer to start the automatic download.

The editor walked back towards the inner sanctum, as we reporters jokingly called it. He looked over his shoulder. "Maybe when you're done, we'll grab a cup of coffee."

I closed the connection to the morgue and got down to writing my story, ignoring the invitation. I didn't want any more contact with the city editor than I had to. Something about him made me think of a used car salesman. Once they thought you were ready to make a decision, they never left your side. I didn't have time to dwell on that. I had a story to write:

Furniture heiress Dominique Pewter was killed Saturday after just picking up her new sports car from the dealership.

Pewter, 22, was heading south on Vista Point Drive and pulled onto Lake Drive into the path of an oncoming cement truck, which crushed the car.

Fire rescue personnel worked for thirty minutes to free Pewter who was pronounced dead at the scene. Her passenger, Ashley Albanese, 22, was listed in critical condition Saturday night at Our Lady of Mercy Hospital where she was undergoing surgery.

Albanese's family said the pair had taken the red Corvette out for a spin to celebrate their college degrees. Pewter was scheduled to begin work Monday at Herman Steel and begin her training to take over the furniture giant as her family legacy.

Pewter was no stranger to tragedy. Her parents were killed in an auto accident in February three years ago.

"She was such a nice girl. She was best friends with our Ashley," Angela Albanese said about her daughter's friend.

I heard the electronic tone that signaled the download was complete and I opened the photo program and looked at my shots. They brought the horror of the accident back again. They would be perfect for an attention-grabber in Sunday's paper. My best one was the photo of the mirror lying in the middle of the road in sharp focus and the blurred outlines of the cement truck, the police and fire vehicles beyond.

I picked the top three and emailed them to the photo department and city editor.

Hoping that would keep Neil at bay, I went back to my story and included the quotes from Elsie Dobson and generic accident details from the accident reconstruction specialist. I spent a few more minutes polishing the prose and then sent the story to the city editor.

I wandered to the coffee machine and got a cup to thwart the need to go with Neil. I glanced through Saturday's paper to kill a few minutes. Before I hit the classifieds, the city editor called me over.

"Any chance you can update it before the morning edition's deadline?" Most days the newspaper was an afternoon edition, except for the Saturday and Sunday editions which were delivered in the morning.

"The only thing would be if the passenger died in surgery and that's a real possibility with the extent of her injuries."

"I'll have the night editor call and see about an updated condition unless you're going to stick around, we could do dinner?"

"I'll call with an update," I compromised. For some reason I didn't want anyone getting an impersonal condition for a story that reminded me of my own dark days. I also didn't want dinner with the editor. His buddy-buddy ways had me back-pedaling without a reason why. The night editor, Ken Clark, was a good friend, but this guy just rubbed me wrong, the way he forced the friendship.

"Great, call before eleven."

"Right," I said, annoyed that I was being treated like a first-year reporter who didn't know the deadlines. I did do this job twenty-four, seven. This was my first vacation day in years and suddenly I was an amateur again. Editors!

Because the newspaper's parking lot was nearly empty on Saturday, I'd left my car. I didn't pay to park at my high rise. I just left my vehicle at the newspaper or the police department for easy access. I walked to my condo, still enjoying the late afternoon warmth. After a couple hours of sleep, I was wide awake. Something about working the night shift didn't make it easy to sleep during the dark hours.

I needed to update the condition of the accident victim. I could call the public relations person from the hospital, but I decided against the impersonal touch. I grabbed my leather coat, put my notebook in my back pocket and left my apartment. I walked the six blocks to the hospital in the opposite direction from the newspaper. My pace was brisk, not wanting to linger in the nippy air that returned after the setting sun. The dark shadows of the sidewalk gave way to the brightly lit exterior of the six-story medical facility that took up four city blocks. I wandered to the west side and moved to the emergency entrance, the only doors that would be unlocked in the after-visiting-hours evening. I nodded to the uniformed guard at the entrance who kept the peace when wild nights of fun took a wrong turn.

I slipped around the information and intake desk and glanced at the myriad of people, in the yellowed fluorescent light, waiting to be called for treatment. A couple stood bouncing a softly-muffled crying baby. A teen was cradling a limb I was sure was broken from its odd angle. Another man pressed a crimson-stained cloth to his leg.

I walked around everyone and slipped out into the main hall and to an elevator bank that would take me into the bowels. Hospitals reminded me of everything that had gone wrong in my life, but that didn't mean I didn't know how to get around in them. I knew the ICU well. The elevator was open and waiting and I punched in four.

As the doors slid open, I was surprised to see the hall rather dark. I walked toward the lighted ICU area. I was both sorry and relieved to see the Albanese family in the family waiting room just outside the double doors to the patient's rooms. I stood at the waiting room door trying to gauge their mood. The parents perched on the edge of a Naugahyde couch, holding hands but ready to jump to their feet at any intrusion. The daughter was staring out the window and the son was paging through a magazine but I was sure that none of the images or words was penetrating his consciousness. The youngest was asleep in another chair. She was the only one at peace.

I hated to intrude on their pain. What was I thinking? I had a job to do and talking to grieving families was what my job on the police beat was about. I stood straighter and crossed the threshold of the room. All four heads turned in tandem in my direction with hope in their eyes. I could tell the minute my identity registered, my lack of information apparent.

"Sorry to bother you. I just wanted to see how your daughter was doing?"

"Bless you, son, for caring," Ashley's mother said, standing and walking over to me. She patted my cheek and I felt like the worst kind of traitor.

"She survived surgery but they induced a coma and she won't be conscious until at least tomorrow," the family matriarch said.

"That's good," I said inanely.

The silence got oppressive. I knew I should say something but I couldn't think. It was painful to watch the family.

"Have the police said anything?"

"An officer stopped by and asked a few questions, but didn't say much."

I was saved from further conversation by a nurse entering.

"One of you may go and see her but you can only stay for five minutes." The woman talked in an Army-drill-sergeant tone that meant she wouldn't allow any slackers.

The family looked at each other, silently debating the single visit. I slipped from the waiting room and disappeared down the dimmed hallway to the elevator. Double doors blocked passage to the hallway on the other side of the elevator. It was dark and contained the surgical unit.

While I waited for the elevator, I heard an ill-placed, squeaky sound that put me on full alert because it was so out of place in the quiet hum of the hospital. I looked around but the hallway was quiet. ICU was behind me and the surgical suites were on the other side of the elevator. Must have been an emergency surgery. It sounded like the tread of a dress shoe on the polished tile.

The elevator dinged to signal its arrival. I entered and hit one. For reasons that left me baffled, I slipped back out just as the doors were closing and moved into the shadows next to doorway leading to the stairs by a four-foot fern.

After a few seconds, a shape emerged from the shadows by surgery and slid toward ICU.

■ CHAPTER 5

The form hovered in the shadows. I heard muted voices and assumed the visiting minutes for Ashley were over and the rest of the family was looking for a report.

I realized the man was listening at the door to the ICU unit. With the door cracked, excited voices could be heard from the waiting room. Was he a boyfriend who didn't want to intrude? Another member of the Fourth Estate who wasn't above eavesdropping for a story? I wanted to know. I didn't want to get scooped by the weekly rag or TV parasites. This had been my story from when I had first driven across it on my only vacation day in half-dozen years. I wasn't going to let a trashy rag of a paper spoil my exclusive by listening at the door.

The elevator dinged its arrival and the shadow jumped and turned toward the elevator, allowing me to take in the front features in the dim light. It was the face of the profile I'd read earlier. Burt, no, Bertram Switzer, that was it. What would the CEO of a Fortune 500 company be doing lurking outside the ICU? Why didn't he just go in and talk to the family? I couldn't imagine, but he slipped back down the hall and entered the dark surgical wing.

When the elevator opened, a lab technician exited carrying her basket of syringes and vials. As she walked past, I slipped back into the elevator. The minute the doors opened on the ground floor I bolted for the nearest exit. My dread and uneasiness of the medical monstrosity propelled me out.

As I left the brighter lights of the hospital behind me, I opened my cell phone and hit the preprogrammed number for the city desk.

"Mitch here."

"About time. Thought you had overslept or forgotten." The familiar voice of the night editor, Ken Clark, soothed my jagged nerves and runaway imagination.

"Have I ever overslept?" I glanced around making sure I wasn't being overheard or followed. "Ashley Albanese's condition is still critical."

"Give me a second while I call up the story." I heard the click of the keyboard and the whisper of his voice as he read, looking for the place to plug in the information. "Okay, got it. Anything else?"

"Not tonight. I'm saving it for my follow-up," I said, only half-joking. I could feel there was more to this story. Mitch Malone was on the trail of something fishy.

After a little small talk, I ended the connection. I continued down Ottawa Street toward my condo, the accident scene haunting my thoughts. I had the feeling I had missed something. Tomorrow was a new day. I'd go over all my notes and see if I couldn't piece together what was niggling at my brain.

■ ■ ■

I woke the next morning less than refreshed with weird dreams dancing in my subconscious. Little red sports cars, cement trucks and strangers swathed in black swayed in my mind, twisting and turning, giving me little rest or reprieve.

Dreams of mayhem and murder didn't happen to Mitch Malone. I never took my work personally and never let the blood and guts that sold newspapers be more than just the written prose I excelled at. I had to get my act together.

I showered quickly and dressed for the day in casual attire of jeans, T-shirt and leather jacket. It was Sunday and typically a day I spent on my apartment, doing laundry and other household tasks, whipping it into shape from a week of neglect. I was antsy and not interested in mundane chores. Almost against my will, I found myself snagging the keys to my Jeep Cherokee and heading out the door, grabbing a notebook and pen on the way.

I pulled up my collar as I hiked the few blocks to the paper, wondering where the sunshine from yesterday had gone in this gray day. Spring was a fickle time in West Michigan. Yo-yoing back and forth between warm and cold, light and dark. It suited my mood. I was pretending carefree, but couldn't shake the darkness from the day and night before.

Doughnuts. I needed doughnuts and coffee to get my brain functioning. The best place for that was Donna's Doughnuts located a half a block from the paper and my car. The smell of fresh baked goods immediately settled my mood in a more positive direction. I headed for the front counter and sat at a stool. Before I could unzip my jacket, a cup was in front of me and I felt the steam rise. I raised my eyes and nodded to the waitress.

I was a regular here and received exceptional service. Donna's also was a great source for information in the political scene. I didn't care about that today. I wanted comfort food and Donna had the best.

"Long John with custard," I told the waitress. "Better make it two."

Without a word she was off. The place was busy this morning but then again it was Sunday, a day when most people had more time on their hands than usual. The waitress returned with my order and I took a bite, letting the baked goodie melt in my mouth. If there were doughnuts handy, the world couldn't be a bad place.

After the first doughnut disappeared, I slowed and took a few sips of hot coffee. Snatches of conversation hit me. "Hope they don't close up now." "We need more companies like that, not less." "Can't believe a company rests on some spoiled girl."

I realized they were talking about the accident that killed Dominique Pewter. I listened, enjoying that my story had spurred talk. I was an anonymous customer at Donna's but that didn't mean I didn't get a thrill when people talked about things I wrote.

"Another senseless accident with a distracted young driver," said a voice filled with authority. My appetite was gone. I signaled the waitress and got a bag for my uneaten doughnut and a to-go cup of hot coffee. I figured I would need more of the liquid caffeine. Anything to keep me from analyzing why that lone comment had stunted my appetite.

Thinking of things that needed to be done today, there were groceries to fill my cupboards, laundry, cutting out my clips from the week's newspaper. None held any appeal as I reached my Jeep at the newspaper.

I wasn't sure where I was going, but I knew I would end up at the accident site. It was my subconscious pulling from my dreams. I headed to the accident scene, not sure what I was looking for or why I needed to revisit it, but I did.

I don't know what I expected to see ten minutes later in the light Sunday morning traffic, but cars calmly flowing from all directions seemed wrong. Didn't they know someone died and another was hanging on by a thread? Why was I obsessing about this? I had covered lots of fatalities and never felt the need to revisit the scene or even remember the location. Maybe it was because I felt a kinship with Dominique Pewter. Okay, I wasn't insanely rich or in the lineage of any industrial dynasty, but we did have many things in common. We'd both lost our parents during college. We both survived the loss and had come out of it to follow in our chosen career paths. Okay, we didn't have that much in common, but she still called to me. I couldn't figure out why her joyride was eating at me.

I'd followed my instincts to some pretty big stories in the past. I wasn't going to ignore it now. I pulled over on the shoulder of the road just down from Mrs. Dobson's house. I got out and checked to make sure my camera and notebook were in their proper places. I wasn't sure what I was looking for but I was willing to look on my own time. I snapped some general shots, hoping the camera would show me what I missed.

The only telltale signs of the carnage from yesterday were the darker black streaks on the road caused by the petroleum in the asphalt being liquefied by the friction from hard braking tires burned blacker on the pavement where the cement truck locked up its brakes. I walked over to the ditch and saw the gouges from metal searing the new pavement. The etched valleys continued as the car left the road but became deeper as the gravel and sand mixture moved to absorb the assault. The car was pushed deep into the yielding shoulder of new construction instead of flattened against the unforgivable roadway.

It was eighteen hours ago. The automobile's wheel marks were clearly visible in the soft earth. That must have been the reason why Ashley was able to survive. The car was pushed down instead of squished like a Frisbee. I took a couple of photos of the hole. The car must have been raised straight up to get out and leave such perfect indentations. I wanted to jump in and feel what it must have been like trapped in the dirt with the truck on top.

I only could imagine the noise and horror for Ashley. I wondered if Dominique died instantly. Then I remembered what Elsie Dobson had told me. The wail she had heard. "Ashley, I'm so sorry." Maybe Ashley had been knocked unconscious and Dominique didn't die right way. Only long enough to apologize to her best friend. Boy, would that make a great human interest angle to follow up the accident. What would it have been like to be trapped in a car and watch your friend die, apologizing with her last breath. I needed to get to the hospital and see if I could get any information out of the girl that survived. This would be a great story.

"Tragic, isn't it?"

I nearly jumped out of my skin and into the hole in front of me. Bob Johansen stood behind me, a quirky smile on his face that said, "Gotcha."

I grinned. "I'll get you for that one." I held out my hand and we shook.

"What are you doing out here, Mitch?" I watched the breeze pick up a few hairs that Bob combed over the top of his bald head and made them fly up in the slight breeze.

"I don't know. I was just drawn back here. I could tell you I was looking for a follow up, but that really isn't true." My honesty surprised me. I usually only joked with my sources, never confiding. Even though I had a great angle, I wasn't that thrilled with writing it. There was something else about all this that bothered me, but I couldn't figure out what it was. This just wasn't a joyride gone bad. I needed to deflect his attention from me.

"What brings YOU back here?"

"Same thing. I told you my data just didn't make sense. I'm trying to get a clearer picture. I fed my data, measurements, road conditions, et cetera into my computer. The result didn't make any more sense." Bob reached up to smooth the wayward hair strands back into place.

"What did the program say?"

"It said Dominique failed to stop, running the sign and was hit by the cement truck. Witnesses said she stopped."

"Could she have been distracted and just pulled out in front of the truck?"

"That's not what the measurements say. A certain amount of forward motion was needed for the impact on the driver's side, although there are no brake marks from the car." Bob scratched his head where the hairline met the bald top, messing the comb-over he'd smoothed only moments before.

By mutual consent, we didn't saying anything else as we walked around the hole toward the stop sign.

Traffic had cleared and I stood where a car would idle at the stop sign. I could clearly see in both directions. The construction didn't block any visibility, certainly not a cement truck which was twice as tall as an ordinary car and very orange.

Bob stood on the shoulder watching me puzzling out what happened. I couldn't print any of it unless I attributed to a source like Bob, but I still wanted to figure it out for myself. I liked to pit myself against cops and investigators. I was good at coming up with plausible explanations of who was the insider who planned a bank robbery or where a suspect might be hiding when they ran. I was the police's secret weapon. I reported crime for the newspaper, but also had a hand in solving it. Many of the boys in blue recognized it and gave me more access than other reporters.

I looked around and nothing was coming up the street from behind me. I backed up to see how far I could go until the view from the left was blocked by the house on the corner. I had backed up a dozen or so steps when my back foot slipped out from underneath me. I must have looked like a cartoon character that had just ran over marbles. My feet were going a mile a minute but I wasn't going anywhere. Then, I went down, hard on my keister.

Laughter greeted my ears. Bob had witnessed the show. I put my hands down to push me back up. I recoiled from the sliminess on the road. I turned to look at my backside and anything that had touched the pavement was a dark spot on my clothes.

"What do you make of this?" I held out my hands for his inspection.

"I think it was a hell of a show." He shook his head, trying to control his laughter, his comb-over flopping in the breeze.

"Funny one," I replied drolly. "Seriously, there is an awful lot of some slippery substance, maybe oil, on the pavement. Was it here yesterday?" I looked and I was a good two car lengths behind the stop sign. Did it have anything to do with the accident?

Bob walked onto the road and bent to examine the six-foot-diameter puddle. He went to his car and came back with some swabs and Ziploc baggies. He photographed the spot before taking his samples and one of my backside, which I was sure I would live to regret later.

"I didn't sample this far back from the corner. I didn't see a reason to," Bob admitted sheepishly. "I'll have to re-examine the car and see if it is missing any fluids and whether this is oil, transmission or brake fluid."

"Could she have slid on this into the intersection?" I was still trying to get my dignity back and re-establish my credibility. "Could this be evidence?"

"Evidence of what?" Bob asked.

I didn't know, but something told me this wasn't a simple accident. Maybe because there was millions in inheritance. Just another piece of a puzzle that had more loose ends than connections. I just didn't think this was an accident but wasn't sure I wanted to share that with the reconstruction specialist because I didn't know why. It was just a hunch. If I voiced it, Bob might think I'd lost my perspective.

I gathered what was left of my oil-soaked dignity and walked to the corner and headed in the direction that the truck had come from. The road took a gentle curve away, and the cement truck would not have had a lot of time to stop once the car pulled out.

I walked the path of the cement truck, noting where the brake marks started until it stopped over the top of the sports car in the ditch just down from the stop sign where the Corvette pulled out.

"Come up with anything?" Bob swabbed more oil.

"No, other than the truck had little to no time to react."

"Tell me something I don't know."

I went back to my car and felt uncomfortable with my oily clothes. I routed around in the back until I found an old towel and put it over my cloth seats to protect them from whatever I had sat in. The day had gone from partly cloudy to mostly cloudy with big gray cotton balls filling across the sky. I thought it might rain and any evidence here would be gone with it. I looked at Elsie Dobson's house and wondered if she was in better shape. If a good night's sleep had calmed her nerves from the carnage she witnessed the night before. I bet that woman had spunk when she wasn't haunted by images. I wondered about the late Mr. Dobson and if he had been as happy as she had. I wondered if I ever would find someone I couldn't live without.

I angrily grabbed the waxed bag from Donna's, upset with my thoughts. I liked my life. Pulling out the leftover doughnut, I bit into it to distract my wayward thoughts. I started the engine and dropped the gear into drive, pulling out faster that I had anticipated. I'd better watch out for cement trucks. The sun peeked through a small opening and I took that as a sign that all was right in my world.

■ CHAPTER 6

I returned to my apartment and thanks to my fall, I tackled the laundry first, putting my jeans in. I was sure it was useless and the jeans should go right in the trash, but I had to try. Should have followed my initial inclination. The jeans never made it to the dryer. I did three other loads as well as vacuumed, then decided I needed clean sheets while I was at it. Busy work. That was all I was doing, but it kept me from thinking. It was mid afternoon before I decided I needed food. There was nothing in my cupboards.

I grabbed my jacket and keys. I needed to move my Jeep from the condo visitor slot. Time to move it before the condo association sent me another letter. The last letter said either pay the parking fee or my vehicle would be towed. Being a good investigative reporter, I knew the letter stemmed from the neighbor across the hall who hated me. I was sure it was she. The woman followed my every move from her peephole. She always frowned when I was coming in and she was going out. She didn't approve of my lifestyle.

As I was leaving, my offending neighbor was coming out of the elevator carrying two bags of groceries. She usually had a little cart she pulled when shopping. I wanted to walk by her, but thought maybe if I buddied up to her, she wouldn't complain about my car parked below. I reached for one of the bags. For a minute I thought she was going to fight me for it, then acquiesced. She moved the other one closer to me and I grabbed that as well. I reversed my direction and followed her. She opened her door and held it for me.

I had never been in her condo. It was filled with a lifetime. Furniture was arm to arm around the perimeter and a small table was crowded in near the kitchen. It had both a tablecloth covered with clear plastic and a crocheted doily in the center held down by a sugar bowl and salt and pepper shakers. I set the groceries on the table and turned to leave.

No words were exchanged. I heard the door shut behind me and the deadbolt click into place. I kicked at the floor on my way to the elevator. Not even a thank you and she thought I was the horrible person.

There was no redemption. I jumped in my Jeep and headed for the Burger King near the police station. A couple of black and whites were in the lot so I decided against the drive-thru. I ordered a chicken sandwich, knowing their burgers couldn't compete with my gourmet taste in ground beef. I took my dinner and headed to their booth.

"If it isn't the man who can't get away from an accident," said one of the cops.

This pair had been on the force for a number of years and had never been promoted to other units, either by their own wish or lack of ability. I didn't know which. They were friendly and didn't hate me on sight.

"Yes. Go figure. My first weekend off in years and I run across a nasty one. Now I'm off to the hospital to check on the condition." I raised my hands palms up in a 'what is a man supposed to do' gesture.

"Your name all over the front page is a tough one to feel sorry for," the other cop joked.

I raised my sandwich and bit into it. As I chewed, I asked, "Anything going on today?"

"Been quiet. That's why we can both stop for dinner."

I nodded and took another bite.

Talk turned to baseball and if the Detroit Tigers could keep their good start going through the rest of the season. I had my doubts.

I finished my sandwich, fries and Coke and we all three rose in unison to leave.

We nodded to each other at the door and went in the direction of our vehicles. I headed to the hospital. I wanted to see if I could get anything out of the victim in the accident. I was sure somebody had taken her statement. I wanted the color for my follow-up.

I went the same way I had the night before. The sun was shining in the window next to the elevator where I had hid the night before. The surgical unit was still empty but not dark as sunlight filtered in along the hall. I stepped toward the waiting room and peeked in. The Albanese's were still holding vigil. Mrs. Albanese had her head bowed and I watched her progress through two beads on her rosary. No one noticed me, so I moved on to the doors of the ICU unit. On the other side of the doors was a unisex bathroom and a drinking fountain. All of a sudden my mouth was parched. Must be from all the sodium in the fast food dinner.

I pushed open the door and satisfied my thirst. The nurse at the desk checking the bank of monitors looked up when I entered and looked down as I drank. As I stood, I glanced around. The first room was in front of me. It said "A. Albanese" on tape on the outside. The room was dark with a green glow from the monitors above and behind her. Her head was twice the normal size and wrapped in white gauze.

A tube protruded out the far side of her head. She looked like an alien from a sci-fi movie. The gauze wrapped under her chin and separate bandages were over her nose. Her skin was black and blue. The blanket was pulled up to her chin as if a mother had put her to bed. I thought of Mrs. Albanese and knew she had done it, and not a nurse.

The roller on an office chair squeaked. The nurse was heading in my direction, so I turned and walked out the doors. I knew I wouldn't get anything from that victim today. My story on surviving a horrendous accident would have to wait. I still needed to do a short follow up for Monday. I debated about going into the paper or doing it from my laptop at home. Normally I wouldn't hesitate to stop at the newspaper and pound out the copy. Now with the new editor, I didn't want to get trapped with him. He always wanted to be buddy-buddy. Go to dinner, hang out. Mitch Malone didn't hang out. I opted for peace and quiet and did my story from home. It was my day off and I had to report to Neil Monday morning. That was soon enough.

■ CHAPTER 6

I walked into the newsroom Monday morning, trying to quietly make it into my cubicle before becoming the center of attention. Lately, I couldn't get any peace. Neil interrupted me while I was out on a story via my cell phone or by the man himself while I was trying to pound out my story.

"Malone, is that you?" I looked up and connected with his small dark eyes framed in the equally black square frames. He looked like he had two small bull's-eyes on his face.

"Yes…master." The last word said in a whisper, but I was definitely feeling like a slave with an unreasonable overseer.

"What do you have?"

Neil always wanted a verbal report of my stories. He could never just wait five minutes until I had a draft down and read that. No, he assailed you for details before your butt could even get within a hemorrhoid of the seat.

I dragged my feet in his direction ready to snap to attention and feed him my report. As I moved forward, the scanner squawked and I wanted to jump, ready to make up anything plausible from the female dispatcher to get me out of here. I would run home and work on my story from my laptop. Anything was better than a verbal recitation without the benefit of my notes.

"Well, I'm waiting. I don't have all day. I do have a newspaper to put out."

"Burglary suspect arrested possibly linked to the crime spree in the East Town neighborhood last weekend." I was mentally combing my notes for details to add because he would have a question.

"Gang members?"

"Don't know yet until arraignment when his rap sheet will be released."

"Okay, get it done. I want you following this and if he is a gang member make sure you reference the newest crime in the gang piece."

I turned and headed to my cubicle to get to work. I just wasn't happy covering the crime beat these days. I wasn't the man of mystery. Neil was going to be the death of me. I now understood what most henpecked husbands felt like and knew I needed a divorce. I had all the hassles and none of the perks.

Once left alone, I finished my six-inch story on a minor string of uneventful burglaries that was only getting covered because it happened in the publisher's neighborhood. That was okay, I could live with that type of favoritism. It was the constant attention that was drawing thin.

My goal for today was to finish this up and try and do a follow-up on the accident victim and avoid Neil at all costs. I was used to working weekends but now I was strictly days. I liked my nights and freedom to work. However, working the day had its perks. It gave me access to the bigwigs at Herman Steel to find out what the dead debutante was like. Let them wax wonderfully about her for my follow-up and then I could put this case to bed. It was consuming way too much of my time.

■ ■ ■

"Mr. Switzer will be with you in a moment." The leggy assistant ushered me into an office with a view that stopped me in my tracks. It didn't surprise me when I was led to the top floor. I expected as much when meeting with the CEO of one of the largest furniture makers in North America and maybe even the world.

One wall of the office was a bank of windows. The building was located in the suburb of Grand River called South Gate, near the airport. The award-winning Herman Steel building was easy to spot from the air because of its unique pyramid shape. According to my research, the building was the brain child of the dead girl's father shortly before his death, ironically enough, in a car accident.

Donald Pewter didn't live to see it completed.

From the windows on this sunny and cloudless day, I could see the outline of the downtown hotels and office buildings along the river. The windows on the opposite side of the hall had to have an excellent view of the airport, only a mile away.

I had already spent a couple of hours at the newspaper on my new eight-to-five schedule. I hated this schedule. Going to the cop stations this morning for news was a waste of time. None of my sources were in. They had already hit the sack after working all night. I would not be popular if I started calling them at home for details on minor incidents. I opted for less cop news. Neil needed to know his plan didn't work. I belonged on the night shift. It was too bright during the day and the newsroom was full of people. It was hard being the man of mystery with full sunlight shining in the window. My best work was done in the shadows. Couldn't Neil see that?

I knew the answer was no. He was perky in pink today with a button-down shirt and gray pleated wool pants. What male in their right mind wore pink? I was still puzzled by the accident, annoyed I couldn't make sense out of it. That and Neil made me grouchy.

Because of my night schedule, I didn't do the human interest stories after the initial accident story. Those were passed on to someone on days and I would go to the next big crime. Now I was on days and following up with the human interest piece on the accident victim, one Dominique Pewter. I wasn't disappointed being assigned this follow up. I just didn't want to make it a habit. I wanted to ask the CEO why he had hid at the hospital.

"Mr. Malone?"

I jolted. I had been caught wool-gathering by one of the most important men in the West Michigan business world, Bertram Switzer, CEO of Herman Steel. I turned from the panorama and held out my hand. "Mitch Malone from the *Grand River Journal*. Thank you for seeing me on such short notice."

I took the measure of the man. He was wearing a dark pinstripe suit, custom made, white shirt, and a light blue paisley tie. His black tasseled loafers, probably handmade, held a shine that could rival many mirrors.

He nodded and his brown hair didn't move.

"My sincerest sympathies on the loss of Dominique Pewter."

"Yes, such a tragedy. She was about ready to join us in the business world. We will miss her spirit." He pointed to a pair of overstuffed brown leather chairs tucked in a corner by the left side of the window bank. I took a seat.

"I wanted to get some information on her for my story. She doesn't have any family, does she?"

"No, such a tragedy. Her parents died several years ago and there are no other close family members. It feels like I've lost a part of my family." He crossed his legs, leaning back in a relaxed fashion. He had to be in his sixties. A father figure for Dominique? Was that why he was at the hospital?

The last part of his statement didn't ring true to me, but I continued. "Can you tell me what Dominique was like?"

"She was a lovely girl. Graduated at the top of her class at the University of Michigan. She could have gone anywhere to school, but she wanted to go to her father's alma mater." He clasped his hands and rested them lightly over his crossed knees.

"Did she have any interests, charities?"

"Dominique was concentrating on school. Her trustee handled all her business decisions since her parent's death."

"Her trustee?" I interrupted.

"Yes. Seth Lynch." His voice was hard, clipped. He paused. "This is just such a tragedy." He shifted in his seat slightly, possibly from grief and a touch of anger. Was he angry the girl died or was the anger directed at Seth Lynch?

Again, the perfect note of sincerity, but it rang false. I couldn't pin down why. It was as if my Spiderman sense told me there was more. I was trying to create a tribute to one of the wealthiest women in Grand River and he gave me syrup and no substance. I tried again.

"What was she like?"

"A woman who had tragedy in her life and chose to move past it. She was going to begin working here today as a matter of fact." He shifted his weight, pulling up the other leg to rest on his knee.

"What were her duties to be?" Maybe if I talked about the job, he would warm up.

"She was starting out in our business at an entry level. She was going to learn the business from the bottom up, was being groomed to take over one day."

"I understood she was taking an office on the top floor." I connected eye to eye.

"Well, yes." Switzer coughed, breaking eye contact. "Her office was on this floor, but the work she was going to do was entry level work. You can't walk from a dorm room into a multi-billion dollar business and expect to take over. I was going to guide her." His tone was haughty.

This was not going well. I was trying to do a memorial and he was giving me nothing, the stuffed shirt. How could I get him to open up?

"Tell me about the company. Is it doing well?"

"Oh, yes. We are weathering the bumps in the market but aren't anticipating any red on our balance sheet. Our new line of ergonomic furniture is taking off and will be the must-have office pieces for corporate America as generation X & Y start making decisions on what the working environment of the next twenty years will look like."

He warmed to his subject, boring me with his highly-rehearsed ad copy. I let him go on bragging on the new line and what it would mean to the company. When he paused to take a breath, I cut in.

"What happens to the company now that Dominique is gone?" I leaned closer to him and poised my pen over my pad, ready to take down every word.

Switzer looked down at the pad, licking his lips.

"Well, she was not the only stockholder. We are a privately held company and have insurance and contingencies in the event of a major stockholder's death." He grabbed both lapels of his suit coat and tugged them straight.

"How much stock does she own?"

"Sir, our financial information is private. We are not publicly traded. I am not at liberty to disclose that information." He looked at his watch. "You will have to excuse me. I have another meeting. Good day."

He rose, walked to the door and opened it. I debated about asking him why he was at the hospital. I decided to wait. Before I launched an attack on a powerful man, I needed more information. He may think he pulled one over on me, but Mitch Malone was on the story. He'd better beware.

I took my time closing the notepad and joining him at the office's entrance. "Thank you for your time."

He nodded. I had barely crossed the threshold when the door clicked behind me. I smothered a smile, knowing I had finally gotten to something close to Bertram's heart—money and who would be running the company.

Looking up, I noticed the assistant watching.

I couldn't see the legs anymore behind her desk, but she had shoulder-length brown hair. Upon closer inspection, she was a little older than I first imagined. She looked up with a question in her brown eyes. I gave her a big smile. Might as well start cultivating sources now. I knew I was going to need them.

"Hi. Mr. Switzer had an important matter to attend to."

"Oh," she responded and consulted a computer screen tapping a few keys. She wrinkled her nose, tilting her head.

"I think it was something that just came up." I smiled indulgently.

"That happens more and more these days. With his cell phone, I don't know half of what he's doing, but he expects me to keep track of those calls." She sounded cross and I wondered if I could butter her up for some information and attribute it to company sources.

"I was looking for information to do a nice tribute on Dominique. Did you know her?"

"Not really. She had been coming into the office when she was home on breaks from college. She seemed nice, but we didn't talk about anything but business. She was eager to learn."

"We got interrupted before I could ask Mr. Switzer what Dominique would have been doing for the company." A good reporter knew when he had to stretch the truth.

"She was going to take over. It has been quite uncomfortable for the last couple weeks since she announced her desire to run the company at the last board meeting."

My shock and disbelief must have been all over my face.

"I was there taking notes when she announced it to the board of directors. When you own fifty-one percent of the company, you can be CEO whenever you want."

"I guess so. Must be nice to be rich. I can't imagine Mr. Switzer was happy about that." I widened my eyes, going for that same innocent look.

"No he wasn't. He thought it was too soon, she wasn't ready. But his vice president of operations was livid. He nearly had a coronary at the meeting and I thought Dominique was going to fire him on the spot. He got himself under control, but…" she stopped talking and turned away from me. "I won't be able to reschedule that appointment for you."

She had gone all cold and professional, just when it was getting good.

"Good morning, Mr. Frasier," she said addressing a rather small man with dark hair, small dark eyes and a hawk nose walking from the elevator.

"This is Mr. Mitch Malone from the *Grand River Journal*. He is working on a tribute to Dominique. He is waiting for Mr. Switzer. Maybe you could talk with him? Mr. Switzer is unexpectedly tied up." She smiled sweetly at me, mirth mirrored in her eyes. "Roger Frasier is the vice president of operations and second in command behind Mr. Switzer."

Roger's eyes narrowed at the second in command comment. He was thinking how to get out of talking with me, but I didn't want to let that happen. A good reporter always gets his interview even if the subject doesn't want to be interviewed.

"It would only take a minute." I gave him my best Boy Scout look.

"Okay, but I am very busy." He led the way to another door and opened it.

I was right about rooms on this side of the hallway. This office had a beautiful view of airplanes taking off and landing. I couldn't help but be drawn in.

"Wow. This is a great view." I infused excitement into my voice like a boy on his way to his first baseball game. His shoulders dropped as some of the anger left his posture.

"What do you do for Herman Steel? It must be pretty important for a great office like this." I was appealing to his vanity. He shut the door behind me, but didn't offer me a seat in the chrome and black office furniture.

"I run this company's day-to-day operations." A note of pompousness and a slight English accent tinged his voice.

"Really? That is quite an achievement. You look really young."

"Mr. Pewter recognized my gifts when I started at the company after receiving my MBA from Harvard. I moved through the ranks quickly under his tutelage." Roger turned his back to me and watched a plane just touching down.

"I understand Dominique was joining the company. I bet you were excited to work with another Pewter."

"Dominique was young and thought she knew the business world. The academic world is far different than the company's day-to-day operations. I would naturally have assisted her in whatever way I could. She needed to learn the business, but it would not have been as easy as she thought. That is just the naïveté of youth." He spoke as if we were discussing a pencil and not a human being.

"It must have been so hard for her to own a large part of a major company, a legacy her family started, but not have the knowledge to do it justice."

"Oh yes, but she hasn't been participating in the business. Her trustee, Seth Lynch, voted her shares during board meetings since her parents died."

"But wouldn't that have changed once she began working for the company?" This was finally getting good. Roger turned from the window, spearing me with a glance.

"I don't believe she had any plans to take an active part in being chairperson of the board until she learned more about the company. That is the more sensible choice and Dominique was nothing if not level-headed." I scribbled his quote in my notebook, but glanced up and caught a Cheshire cat look. This guy was greasy, I would bet on that. He would fire his own mother to run Herman Steel.

"Level-headed, huh? I would have thought she grew up with a silver spoon and been like those Hollywood kids. She did get killed running a stop sign, probably on drugs."

"Yes, that is the story of her tragic death. You media people take other's heartbreak and publicize all the details about their problems with drugs and alcohol. She did have a difficult life."

"She had a problem with drugs and alcohol?"

"I don't want to tell tales, but she had millions and was strong-willed.

I don't want to speak ill of the dead." I nodded giving him the permission he sought. "I'm surprised she hadn't had an accident before this. It was only a matter of time."

This was in direct contrast to what Mr. and Mrs. Albanese had said and his earlier comment about being level-headed. Could the Albaneses have not known what kind of girl their daughter was hanging around with? Also, there was no indication that any drugs or alcohol were involved, although it could take weeks to get the blood results back.

"The cops are keeping that quiet?" I allowed the question to hang unspoken.

"They would. She is a Pewter and that allows her all kinds of perks, even from the grave."

"She must have had some public relations machine to keep those exploits from not getting in the paper."

"With all of this—" He swung his arms around pointing at the building. "It was easy to keep things quiet. That was part of my job and I am very good."

The smugness was coming through loud and clear. Just a little more stroking of the ego.

"I'm sure you are. Who were her party partners? The lone survivor, Ashley Albanese?"

"Anyone she met. Ashley, Brittany, Caitlyn. She would flash a wad of bills and it was easy to pick up people to party with. They were her friends as long as the money was available."

I was surprised by the comment but wanted him to think I was taking it as the gospel truth. I leaned in. "Do you have any last names I could follow up on?"

Roger shook his head.

"Where was her favorite party place?" I tried to sound innocent, but I wanted more to go on. Maybe I could find some bartenders who would tell me who the real Dominique Pewter was.

Roger looked at me shrewdly. I needed to go into deflection mode. "I never seem to know where the good party action is. How do you find the party?"

"Pina Colada's Bar on Division is always fun. Jimmy Dean's on Bridge

Street is another one." I could see Roger's chest puffing up with his expertise.

I could only wonder if his recommendations were more personal experience than bailing out the debutante. In investigating any crime or accident there were always varying degrees of truth. Everyone had an axe to grind. The dead were easy targets. "Thanks, man. I want to check those places out. They got hot girls there?"

"They have babes and friendly, too."

"Speaking of babes, what did Dominique look like? I can't seem to find any file photos of her to run with the story."

He walked behind his desk and opened a drawer. He pulled out a five-by-seven studio portrait and handed it to me. The photo in the drawer unnerved me but I couldn't let it show. I needed to keep him talking and hoping something would slip. I made a show of looking at the photo, then giving a wolf whistle. "She's a beauty." And she was with long blonde hair and the most striking clear blue eyes.

"Yes, but ice ran in her veins." Roger abruptly looked down, shielding his face. He took his time shutting the desk drawer.

"Wasn't interested, huh?" I was trying to empathize with his comments, but immediately saw my mistake. He didn't like anyone to notice he had struck out. It offended his high ego. If this guy was in a gang, he would be bad news. He wouldn't hesitate to cut someone's throat who even hinted he wasn't the best at everything. How dangerous could he be in business? He would fire someone without a backward glance, but that would be it. The business world was so much more sophisticated.

"I've got an appointment I need to prepare for." His friendly tone was gone. I wondered about the quick change in personality. I wondered if the last comment was one he wished he could take back. No kissing up or cajoling would bring me any more information. I closed my notebook and headed out.

"Thanks. Maybe I'll see you at Pina Coladas or Jimmy Deans."

"You won't see me there. I have no need to rescue a dead girl. I was just there keeping Dominique out of the papers. You can keep the photo." His eyes were cold. Dead. The hawkish nose making him look even more predatory.

I shivered. Roger walked to the door and opened it. I didn't dally. I was ready to be gone and was hoping for more information from the pretty assistant. Luck was not on my side. Roger escorted me all the way to the elevator even punching the down button for me. When the doors opened, he waited for me to enter, then nodded slightly as the doors slid closed. I debated about returning to the executive level when I reached the bottom, but realized the guard was watching. Another day.

Not for the first time I wondered if I hadn't accidentally stumbled onto a much bigger story here. One dead heiress, no explanation for her crash and lots of company officials who would kill their mother to move up the corporate ladder. Maybe days wouldn't be such a bad thing until I uncovered what was happening in the corporate world, if I could just keep away from my buddy in the pink shirt.

■ CHAPTER 8

The phone vibrated on my hip. I pulled it out of its plastic belt clip and looked at the display. Inwardly sneering, I debated about whether to answer it or not. Resigned, I flipped it open and waited. "Malone, are you there?"

"Yes, but I can't hear you." I could hear just fine, but didn't want to talk to the newest editor at the *Grand River Journal.* I'd guessed the longer hair length was a throwback to his wilder days when having a beer would have been a major sin but he did it anyway. The wild man.

I wished Neil would let me do my job. Instead, every hour, the editor was calling me to ask about something he heard on the scanner in the newsroom, or sirens that went by. Was it a big story? He called to see if I was on it. Last week it had been flattering to be the subject of such intense interest. Now it was just annoying.

"Mitch, the sheriff's department has just dispatched its SWAT team to the Riverwood Mall just south of the city limits."

"The SWAT team?" I wouldn't have put it past Neil to have misheard a statement if it was over the scanner. I had been chasing ghosts of stories for days and not a word in print from anything Neil had sent me on.

"Yes, the SWAT team. We must really have a bad connection. Get right over there."

"Are you sure? I'm just about to meet with the heiress' guardian. I've been waiting thirty minutes while he finished a conference call." I wondered if Neil even knew what SWAT stood for or just heard it used so much on television shows, it had lost the meaning of Special Weapons and Tactical Team.

"That can wait. Get over there now."

I looked up to see the secretary holding the door to an inner office open. I'd get to the mall when this interview was over. Ten minutes tops. If they did need SWAT, it wouldn't be resolved quickly. Those guys were meticulous in their preparations and only fired if there was no other alternative.

I was ushered into Seth Lynch's office and his success was easy to see. The carpet was plush, the woodwork was dark and the view was prime. It wasn't my style, too showy, but the man behind the desk looked comfortable.

"Thanks for seeing me." My hand was enveloped in a strong grip that spoke of confidence, shaken briefly and then released. It was mid-afternoon and I was still searching for something to put a human face on Dominique for my follow-up in Tuesday's paper. I was hoping her guardian would be more forthcoming than the brass at Herman Steel.

"Dominique was like a daughter to me." Now this was finally someone who knew the girl. I'd been feeling sorry for her after my earlier trip to Herman Steel. That bunch of jackals was as self-centered as they came.

"Could you tell me what she was like, Mr. Lynch?"

"Please call me Seth." He motioned me to a chair and returned to his seat behind the large antique oval desk with spindle legs raising it off the floor.

I relaxed into its comfort and took a second look at the brown leather, wishing I had one of these to match my couch but it probably cost more than I made in a month. I opened my notebook and had my pen poised.

"I've known Dominique since she was born. I went to school with her father, Donald, and was there when he met her mother, Monique. Dominique's name was a natural if you put the two together." He got up, walked over to the wall and pointed to a photo of two people in graduation gear.

I let him drift a bit in his memory, glad to have found someone who spoke fondly of the girl. I pegged his age drifting toward sixty with a little bit of salt coloring his dark hair making him look distinguished instead of old. I rose and walked to the wall of photos, the only personal items in the office. I recognized Seth Lynch and a man with clear blue eyes that matched those in the photo from Roger.

Finally I could get this follow-up done and let this story rest. I wasn't the obsessive-compulsive type, but this accident had me working overtime. Why couldn't I just let it drop? It wasn't like me to do warm fuzzy follow-ups. That was for the interns after I wrote the compelling first story.

"We met at the University of Michigan. Donald and I were roommates. He met Monique in the library our senior year." He chuckled. "We spent every night for two weeks in the library watching and waiting for her to arrive. He finally got up the nerve to ask her out. The rest is, as they say, history." He pointed to a photo of a wedding with him standing beside the bride and groom. Dominique inherited her mother's high cheekbones and blonde hair.

"Sounds like love at first sight." I looked at the other photos, but didn't see any more of the Pewters. There was one with former President George W. Bush another with former president Gerald R. Ford.

"It was. Monique was a beautiful girl both inside and out. If it wasn't for the tragedy, she would be in your paper daily with the work she would have done on behalf of a dozen charities and organizations. She was devoted to helping people. Donald never worried about the large amounts she gave to charities. He just lived to make her happy."

Seth spoke with such warmth and caring. Dominique was lucky to have had him. "Tell me about Dominique. Was she like her mother?" I continued to glance at the who's who on the wall. A small photo near the bottom caught my eye. A young Seth was in a mechanic's blue jumpsuit, another man, who looked more like Seth today, had his arm around him and wore a matching jumpsuit. They were in front of a garage with a sign above it that said "Lynch & Sons."

"Oh, yes, sorry for being sidetracked. I don't often get a chance to talk about them." He brushed something off his cheek. Could it have been a tear? "Dominique was a unique blend of both. She had her father's drive to succeed coupled with her mother's generous heart. I kept telling her she was going to have to toughen up when she took over Herman Steel."

"When was she going to take over?" I sat up a little straighter. I didn't want to miss this answer. It would tell me who was lying at the pyramid.

"Today. She was taking the reins today if that horrible accident hadn't happened. Such a senseless waste. I can't believe how careless she was. She should have had that car checked before taking it out. She'd paid the dealership to do it. Instead she rushed them into letting her have it before they'd done a thorough check of its systems."

Seth was a goldmine. He had given me at least three or four reasons to continue on this story. Dying right before taking over. The dealership was negligent?

"Was there something wrong with the car?"

"I don't know. The officer who told me about the accident said there were no skid marks." He seemed upset at the memory. "I'd met her at the dealership to sign the paperwork. Major purchases required my signature from her trust fund until she was twenty-five."

"She was so happy." Seth wasn't talking to me anymore but he was giving me good copy. He was remembering the last time he saw her alive. It worked for me. "This was her first time picking out a car. She had researched it for months. Dominique had been to the dealership on every break making sure it would be here when she returned from graduation. The dealership could have gotten it earlier but she was adamant that she didn't want to take delivery until after she graduated." He walked back toward his desk. I followed.

"I didn't get a chance to have this one framed." He showed me an eight-by-ten of the same photo Roger Frasier had given me. "I'm sorry. You didn't want to hear all that."

"No, that's fine. I cover a lot of tragedies and it is important to talk about the people. It helps." We both took a few minutes to become comfortable on the chairs.

"Yes, it does help. She was just so happy, so alive. She got in the car and drove out of the dealership. Just before pulling out, she turned and waved. I will never forget how she looked."

Seth looked down at his hands and they were shaking. I didn't want to see the attorney cry. I needed to steer the interview back to less emotional topics. "What were her ideas for Herman Steel?"

After a pause and a deep breath, Seth answered: "She really had plans for that company. I have no doubt she would have taken the business her father put on the map into a larger Fortune 500 legacy. She had some great ideas that would have appealed to the next generation of office furniture buyers and made the profits soar."

I scribbled his quotes down but I was thinking about the lies I had gotten from Herman Steel.

"Dominique was so full of life and ready to take the world on. She was going to set heads turning, just like her mother. The company hadn't been doing well the last couple of years, earnings had been falling. There had been layoffs and such. She was committed to boosting the business and returning those employees to the full workforce when her father ran the business."

I was itching to ask why I'd received a different story at Herman Steel and if the accident had been no accident. I wanted to look again at Herman Steel and its officers at the top of the pyramid. Seth droned on.

"She had spent time at Herman Steel during her breaks for the last two years, but the suggestions she offered fell on deaf ears. She talked to me about it on several occasions. Dominique was frustrated with the company's direction. She was young, ambitious and ready to tackle the world."

I shuffled my 180-pound frame, hoping if I sat straighter and nearer the desk, Seth would pause in his ramblings.

"Dominique was beautiful, too, and generous just like her mother. Each year she donated too much to the Children's Christmas Program and Toys for Tots, the program the Marines do. She wanted every kid to get a present for Christmas. I tried to counsel her against such large donations but she was stubborn like her father. Once she made up her mind, you couldn't change it. I signed off on the checks."

Seth finally paused.

"What about arrangements for her funeral?"

"Mmm, yes. Guess we will have to look into that." He caught himself and looked up at me. "I still can't bring myself to believe she is gone. I keep hoping to see her walk through the door, blue eyes sparkling. We, of course, will begin working on the arrangements. The police haven't released the body. I can let you know when."

Her guardian, who loved her so much, who claimed she was like a daughter to him, hadn't thought about even a memorial service for the girl? Either he was too upset or something else was going on. Maybe his waxing quotes were not the end of the story. The more I turned and dug, the more questions and false information I got. What was the real story here? I decided against pursuing the more controversial questions and whether her death was an accident or not. Better to collect more details than suppositions. I had a feeling I would be back in this leather chair and I would be pitting myself against the lawyer who commanded a thousand dollars an hour in legal fees.

"Dominique will be missed." My lame reply brought at odd expression to Seth's face, but I stood. "Thank you for your time." We shook hands and I disappeared out the door.

■ ■ ■

I returned to the newspaper to write my follow-up to the accident. I'd called the sheriff's department to see about the SWAT team. As I figured, nothing was going on. I wished Neil had been right, because I hated writing these sappy tributes. They weren't my style. Interviews in the daylight weren't my style. I liked the nights, the edge, the danger. Crime was my beat and here I was trying to find something endearing to write about Dominique Pewter. The more I wrote, the more unsettled I became.

Dominique Pewter had lost her parents in a car accident and when she was going to take over the company, she lost her own life in a car accident. How ironic. The company VP called her a party girl, her guardian said she was ambitious, the Albaneses said she was a sweetheart. Who was Dominique Pewter and was it too late to find out now that she was dead?

I tried a couple of different lead paragraphs for my story but wasn't happy with any of them. If I didn't know who Dominique was, how could I write about her? I thought about the accident and how that was filled with questions too. It was nearing five o'clock and most of the day timers were packing up and shutting down their computers. My stomach growled. Officially, I was off the clock, my shift had ended, but my story wasn't finished. Maybe it was just the daylight that I couldn't work in and not my concerns about the heiress.

My hesitancy in writing the story had increased as well as the ache in my stomach. Maybe I would pop out, grab a bite, check some of the cop haunts to let them know I hadn't been fired. I was still on the beat but had to pacify the new guy for a couple of weeks and then back to business as usual. Maybe I would stop by the hospital to get an updated condition of Ashley Albanese or ask her about her friend and the dying apology. Maybe her family will be a little less anxious today and I could get more information on Dominique for the tribute article.

I grabbed my leather coat and stuffed my notebook in the back pocket of my khaki pants, hearing a couple of stitches rip. Another black mark against Neil. He said jeans were fine on nights but during the day a reporter needed to dress more formally, and then pointedly looked at my jeans. I got the message but I didn't have to like it. I needed to get back to my nights. My wardrobe couldn't handle it.

As I rose, I saw Neil just returning to his desk from an endless round of meetings I'm sure he'd called. My day was done according to the hours he wanted me to work and I didn't have to talk to him. I quickly headed in the opposite direction going out the front door of the paper. I heard him call my name but I ignored it. I knew Neil wouldn't yell and I could claim ignorance later if he asked why I hadn't stopped.

I hit the front door and felt a nip in the air, warning that while the calendar said May, winter may revisit just to show who is boss. I walked the blocks to the hospital and made my way to ICU without anyone noticing. I checked the family waiting room and was surprised to find it empty. Not a dark-haired, brown-eyed Albanese anywhere. I wondered if Ashley had been moved to a regular room or worse, had died.

Next, I headed for the nurse's station in the center of ICU, the rooms surrounding it like a bull's eye. The nurse was gone. I saw Ashley Albanese's name next to the door of the first room. At least she wasn't dead. It was dim but no one but Ashley was inside. I glanced around and didn't see any medical personnel and figured I would just pop in for a visit.

She looked better today. She was clean and dressed in a hospital gown, her left arm in a cast and the other laying beside her on the blanket, IV tubes attached. The monitors hummed softly but she wasn't attached to oxygen or other breathing apparatus. I figured that was a good sign.

Her head was still bandaged like a turban, but more wisps of blonde escaped from the back of her head where the bandage wasn't so heavy. The broken head was definitely the worst of her injuries.

"Ashley?" I whispered as I stepped closer to the bed. I wasn't sure if I kept my voice low to not raise suspicion or because the darkened room just lent itself to soft sounds.

"I'm Mitch Malone from the *Grand River Journal.* I was at your accident."

Her leg jerked. I jumped at the movement, then she was still again. I wasn't sure if she was coming awake or the movement was just a reflex.

"I wanted to see how you were doing. Are you still in a coma?" I stopped. What a stupid thing to say especially for a man who made his money by asking questions. Ashley didn't move.

"I'm trying to write a story about your friend, Dominique." Ashley's foot moved, but apparently was more like a reflex. "I wish you could tell me what she was like. Was she a good friend? I'm not getting a clear picture of her except she must have been lonely except for your family."

I stopped. I didn't know why I said that. My inner psychologist knew it was because I was so lonely after my parents died and I had buried myself in my studies and then my job. Was I having a hard time writing Dominique's story because I was afraid when it came time to write mine that no one would even know me or care? I didn't want to think about that now. I had a story to do, not psychoanalyze myself.

I didn't know where to go with the interview. This was one difficult subject to get a comment from. I doubted I could quote a leg jerk as a response. I took one last look at her and knew she would survive. I didn't want to guess how long it would take with the head injury but knew her family would be there for her. My five minutes of visitor time was up, per the ICU rules. I leaned in closer to better see her face, now that it was cleaned up. She had a large bruise that ran from her left chin up the cheek to her eye, and her head was swollen on the other side. You could tell she had clear skin where some of the bruising was beginning to fade to yellow. She was a pretty girl even with a drainage tube protruding from her head.

"Thank you for the interview, Ashley." I touched her hand because it seemed like the right thing to do. I looked at her face and saw a tear slip from her eye and roll down into the pillow.

I left the room, checking back over my shoulder a couple of times. I wondered if she heard my words and worse yet if she knew my thoughts. I knew she couldn't, but it seemed like the tear was for me.

As I was pushing the door open to leave the ICU unit, I heard laughter. Ahead of me, a mob of Albaneses came out of the elevators. They seemed in high spirits.

"Mr. Malone. Nice to see you." Mr. Albanese stuck his hand out and I shook it.

I was surprised he remembered me. "How's Ashley doing?"

"Better," he said.

"Good to hear." I started to walk around them when I felt something on my arm. Angie Albanese commanded my attention with only a light touch.

"They've put Ashley into a coma. It allows her brain to heal. The doctors won't make any promises but she's getting stronger. She's a fighter, our Ashley."

"I'm glad." I was surprised but I was. "Has she been conscious at all?"

"No." A bit of sorrow crept into Angela's eyes. "She's so still. The nurses suggested we not visit so often because her vitals spike up and they want her to remain calm. I just know she knows we're here."

Tony put his arm around his wife and they moved into the waiting room.

As I walked in the elevator, I realized I never had a chance to ask about Dominique but I wasn't going to return now. I hoped I didn't set back Ashley's healing by my visit, but I hadn't noticed a spike in heart rate or pulse on the monitors while I was there. Of course, I hadn't looked either.

■ CHAPTER 9

y head had only just hit the pillow. It was Tuesday morning and my tribute to the late Dominique Pewter would be running today. I had gone back to the paper and spent a couple hours late into the night trying to do the victim justice in her last newspaper appearance. I couldn't put a finger on why I was trying so hard. I had finally sent it to be edited, but the writing had taken an emotional toll.

When my head had hit the pillow, I was asleep but my dreams kept me active. I chased a tall girl with blonde hair and I could never catch her. I heard my time running out as the beeps continued its countdown. As I came to consciousness, I realized the repeated beeps were familiar and I rolled over, grabbing my cell phone from the bedside stand and saw that it was only four in the morning.

"Malone, this better be good." I rubbed my eyes in the hope I would be able to focus in on the clock.

"Mitch, this just came over the scanner."

Good god. I couldn't just work my twelve-hour shift, but had to be hounded by a news-junkie editor who couldn't remember a ten code on the scanner to save his soul.

"It's a DRT on the banks in River Bend Park…" I tuned back into Neil's words.

"Stop. A body has been found? Are you sure?"

"Yes and they are bringing it ashore at the park. I can see the lights from the newsroom window."

"Got it." I disconnected without waiting for more. I jumped in my clothes and headed out. Chances were, it was a drowning, someone having too much spring cheer and falling into the river at any number of bridges just down from the watering holes. The river water still moved melted snow to Lake Michigan and a person would have only moments to get out of the river before hypothermia set in.

But a body is a body and it leads at the *Grand River Journal*. This was the part of the job I loved, get the scoop first, working in the early hours of the morning, not the politics associated with days.

Less than fifteen minutes later, I pulled into a spot at the park near a trio of patrol cars with lights flashing and an ambulance and medical examiner vehicle. The sheriff's dive team boat pulled alongside a dock sitting on the shore that hadn't been put into the water yet. A large tarp covered a lump in the bottom of the boat.

Across the lot I saw a TV van pull in and before it could park, the bright lights were on and the film was rolling. Parasites all of them. I would get locked out of the information loop if I arrived with them. I meandered around the action at the shore, coming up on the back side of the group along the medical examiner's car. I smiled at Sheila Day who had the night shift at the M.E.'s office.

"How's that dog training going?" Sheila and I had waltzed around a relationship for the last couple of years but we just couldn't get past our jobs to find the time. I knew she just acquired a puppy from a litter found at a murder/suicide.

She looked up from her clipboard and smiled. "We are making progress but the slippages are hard to handle. She lifted up her leg and showed me her basic brown loafer. Half the chunky heel was missing.

"I don't make enough to replace all the shoes he thinks are his personal rawhides."

"Yes, but he sure is a cute bugger. What do we have here?" I pointed to the boat as the first deputy climbed onto the dock.

"Not sure. Wasn't much detail. Excuse me."

She walked over to the deputy, conferred for a few minutes and then climbed into the boat. As she lifted the tarp, I saw an officer step up to block the camera crew's view on the other side of the police cars and had to smile.

I pulled my camera from my pocket and snapped a couple of shots making sure there weren't any visible body parts showing, only the dark tarp and without the flash to alert the police. I slipped it back in my pocket before anyone noticed.

Sheila returned.

"Body's dead." She pulled her latex gloves off and slipped them in her pocket. "My work here is done."

"How long has it been in the river?"

"Not long, but you didn't hear it from me." She got in her car and started the engine.

The EMTs backed the ambulance toward the boat, positioning it to block the view of the body from the camera crew. The two-person crew pulled a stretcher toward the boat. The body and its black covering were loaded into the van. Sheila pulled in behind the ambulance as it left. The film crew packed it in as well after another unsuccessful try to get a video clip of the boat through the officer. I couldn't help the smile that crept across my whisker-stubbled chin. I loved the early morning hours.

"You enjoy death, Malone?"

I knew that voice. "No, Derrick, I don't, but I do enjoy watching the competition pack it in for the day." Because the body washed up here in the city, it was the city police's jurisdiction, not the county sheriff's department although it was their dive team. Derrick was only on crowd control.

"Why don't you follow suit and scram? No comment. You got it?"

"Got it, but since you don't have anything worthwhile to say, I'll just move along to someone who does."

I side-stepped around the moron in tan polyester and hailed a cop who was more friend than adversary.

"Dennis, how's that pretty wife of yours? Is she ready to throw you out so I have a chance?"

Dennis turned and took a step toward me. "Look what came in smelling like fish and don't even think about my wife." His small Irish eyes twinkled in jest rather than annoyance and that made him a friend, that and I had helped him solve a case or two in the past.

Dennis and I were friends as much as a police detective and a newspaper reporter could be. We respected each other's gifts and tried not to cross the line of professionalism. I had helped Dennis on several occasions wrap up cases and, in turn, I earned great exclusives for the *Grand River Journal*. Many suspected he was my source, but I never divulged where I got my information. He had been moving up the ranks quickly based on his reputation of closing cases with convictions.

"Whatcha got?" I pulled out my pad to take notes.

"I know this one." Dennis' voice was somber.

"Sorry man, someone close?"

"You ever meet Trace Richards?"

I shook my head.

"He's a private detective, retired cop, or at least he was. He was on the force when I started and then moved to his private practice. He was one of the best."

"I'm sorry. An accident or suicide?" A lot of suicides involved failing businesses.

"I don't think so. He had five, one-hundred dollar bills folded in his left shoe. He also had the back of his head smashed in. I want to get the bastard that did this."

"Murder? What or who was he investigating?"

"Don't know yet. As soon as they pulled him into the boat, he was recognized and a car was dispatched to his office and his home. His office was locked up tight and we haven't had a chance to go through it yet. The prosecutor is going to want a warrant before we touch it. So senseless. Probably some husband who didn't want his wife to know he was getting a piece on the side. I could use an easily solved case."

We discussed the lack of any evidence or clues for a few more minutes and then I headed out, avoiding Derrick and taking the direct route to my Jeep.

■ ■ ■

As I drove off, I pulled the telephone book from under my front seat. While I idled at a light, I looked up private eyes in the yellow pages. The sun was starting to crest the horizon and I could just make out the address from the light of the dashboard and the streetlight that wouldn't be on for too much longer.

The investigator, Trace Richards, was a one-man operation according to Dennis. His office was down river ten blocks from where he was fished out, in a building being redeveloped from a factory into hip office space. I parked in the lot and hit the front entrance not sure the building would be open yet. If I didn't stop now, I wouldn't get out of the newsroom until after lunch and that would be too late for the element of surprise. The door handle pulled easily and I checked the directory and saw Richards Investigations was on the second floor. I took the stairs and noticed the newer carpet on the floor and the freshly painted walls. Trace had to be making some good money to afford a newly-renovated office.

I knew the cops wouldn't be here to search it until the day shift detectives took over the case and went through the legal maneuvering to handle privacy issues on Trace's clients. Murder of one of their own — even if he wasn't still on the force — was something they wouldn't wait on. I figured it would be about an hour.

I wasn't sure what I hoped to find here, maybe a secretary who could talk about the man and his cases. This was a murder of a former cop and would get big play in the *Journal* but I didn't have any details except he was pulled out of the river. It was about seven a.m. and a bit early for office staff. I debated whether to find a large cup of Java and a doughnut to keep me company while I waited. The adrenaline from the dead body was wearing off leaving me less than ambitious.

I noticed lights going off and on further down the hall. Did the day shift start early? As I approached, I realized the activity was in the Richards Investigations' office. Was whoever had taken out Trace Richards looking for whatever the detective had found? I moved forward into the workplace. I had one hand on my cell with my finger on the 9-1-1 speed dial as I approached the door.

I reached to turn the knob when it opened on its own into the office, pushing my pulsing heart to even higher overdrive. In front of me was a twenty-something woman wearing something from a Star Trek movie on one ear and an ear bud with an unknown music leaking out the other making her prematurely deaf. She plowed forward. I could just make out the strains of the latest hip-hop tune. She pulled a vacuum cleaner and carried a carousel of cleaning products in a plastic bucket, looking like a housewife from the fifties.

"Ahhh," she screamed as her head lifted, pulling the ear bud from her ear. The other hand went to the device in her other ear. "I got a Bluetooth here and I'm calling 9-1-1." The vacuum handle clattered to the floor.

I jumped back bringing my hands up, palms forward in an automatic gesture of hold on here, I'm not going to hurt you. I showed her my cell in one hand. "I was going to call the cops on you."

"You scared the living shit out of me, man." She bent to pick up the handle. "Ain't no one here. Tracey don't come in any before ten. Try back later."

"Hi, I'm Mitch Malone from the *Grand River Journal.* You clean here often?"

"Once a week. Tracey's my uncle and I hope to join him in the business. He won't let me do anything until I finish my degree next spring. The only part of the business I get to do now is clean up after his sorry ass."

I did not want to be the one to tell her she would soon be unemployed and her uncle was dead.

"Shoot." I scratched my head. "I'm on deadline and thought your Uncle Trace could help me with some information. He was working on a case that had just wrapped up and was going to give me a lead on my next investigative piece."

"Wow, Mr. Malone. I read your stuff all the time. That was a great story about those terrorists who were training right here in Grand River. Who would have thought? I pay attention to people around me a lot more now." She wiped her hands on her denim overalls and then reached out with her right to shake my hand. "Stacey, Stacey Richards."

"Nice to meet you. Thanks for that great review. You never know when some small detail will help crack a case. That's why I wanted to see your uncle."

"He wasn't working on much. Was just complaining the other day about how boring detective work can be. Said he was sick and tired of following a college student like myself around. Even let me help him. He said he would stick out like a sore thumb at the younger hangouts."

"That was his latest case?"

"Yeah, but it didn't work out so well. After he quit following her and gave his report, the girl was killed in an accident."

"What kind of accident?" My interest was piqued.

"Just a traffic accident, pulled in front of a cement truck or something."

My mouth went instantly dry and I couldn't speak. Could this be related? Grand River wasn't big enough to have two cement truck fatalities. When coincidences cropped up, a good reporter paid attention to the detail.

"Who hired him?" I tried for a conversational tone. I didn't want to alert her.

"He wouldn't say. Some suit. Wouldn't even come in to his office. He was in early one morning complaining the guy wanted him to meet at five at some bar downtown right before closing." She reached down and picked up her supplies.

"Did you ever see the suit?"

"Nope. Hey, is this important? My uncle wouldn't like me talking about his business. He trusts me to keep his affairs private." She reached back to shut the door.

I backpedaled because she was starting to give me the cold shoulder and I didn't want to alert her or be forced to tell her that her uncle was dead. "I'm just looking for background material for a story. I thought your uncle could help me. I'll check with him later today. I didn't realize he wouldn't be working." I reached in my pocket and pulled out a business card.

"Hey, maybe he's meeting that suit to settle up and I could meet him afterward. I really wanted to get some information for my story today." I handed her the card.

"I don't think so, but if you want to go into that sleazy gay bar, Temptations, go ahead." She inserted a key from a lanyard around her neck into the door's lock and turned it.

I had a twinge of conscience for not telling her my story on deadline was her uncle's death, but that wasn't my job. Mine was to write the stories. My instincts told me his death was linked to the accident earlier this week. That was just too much of a coincidence. I felt my blood pumping and realized I didn't need coffee to keep me awake anymore.

This was big. I just had to figure out the connection. Was Bertram Switzer or Roger Frasier the "suit" Trace was meeting? I was being ridiculous. CEOs and VPs didn't throw private detectives in the river.

They may investigate rivals or the stealing of trade secrets or upstarts who wanted to replace them. Murder was more of a plot for a B-rated movie. But the newspaper was filled with stupid deaths every day. Maybe I could check out the bar and see what crawled in. It was the little things that broke open big stories. I was a detail man.

I turned and walked down the hall to the entrance where more people entered the building. Tracey wouldn't be working ever again, but, thanks to his niece, maybe he wouldn't have died in vain.

■ CHAPTER 10

It was just after five and I was in the grocery store stocking up on essentials on my way home. My cupboards were bare. I wheeled my cart up and down the nearly empty aisles, not knowing what I was looking for. Only occasionally, I grabbed something off the shelf to put it in my cart. No rhyme or reason or meal planning involved.

My cell phone buzzed on my hip. I'd avoided the newsroom all afternoon. Neil wanted to suck me into lunch then a meeting during the afternoon, but I'd told him I needed to track down some more sources for the gang piece that weekend. My main objective was to track down Bob Johansen, but couldn't find him.

I'd ignored every phone call and assumed this was one too. I dutifully looked at the readout and stopped. This wasn't a call but a text message. Didn't know my phone had that feature. Welcome to the new millennium.

"231-555-1234 Ken Clark."

I stared at the readout. Ken Clark had been my direct editor before Neil made it to the scene. Ken worked nights and we worked well together. He understood my need for freedom and I always took his calls because I knew they were important. I'd only talked to him briefly when I'd updated Ashley Albanese's condition the night of the accident. I missed our camaraderie. We were literally on opposite schedules. I checked my watch and realized it wasn't Ken's shift time yet. My curiosity got the better of me. I dialed the number.

"Ken Clark."

"Talk to me."

"It's good of you to call, Mom, but I'm in an important meeting right now. How about we meet for lunch, say noon tomorrow at your favorite pizza place? My treat."

"Sure, but no brass."

"Sure, Mom, no problem. See you then."

I closed my phone and replaced it, and continued down the last few aisles. Why had he texted me if he couldn't talk? I didn't get any answers and found myself at the checkout. I loaded my meager items on the belt, paid the woman and walked out with a single bag and twenty-five dollars lighter. No answers to the mystery of Ken's call either.

After returning to my apartment, I stowed the few things I had purchased, surprised to see the makings for spaghetti, maybe for dinner.

■ ■ ■

My goal for Wednesday was to pin down Bob Johansen and do a follow-up on the accident victim from the weekend. I was used to working weekends but now I was strictly days, nine to five under Neil's thumb and then doing the real job at night. It was killing me. Even with a good night's sleep last night, I was more tired today. I wanted only nights and my days to sleep. I wanted freedom to work the way I wanted.

I made a few calls after deadline during the midmorning. I called Bob Johansen again and left a voice mail, again leaving my cell number. I called the hospital and talked to the public relations person and got a new condition for Ashley Albanese. Still critical in ICU. I'd checked on her condition yesterday even though I wasn't doing an update.

I also made a few more calls to the city police department, looking to talk to a couple of officers on the gang task force. The gang piece wasn't my choice, but I wanted the most the department had and my new schedule didn't help me track guys who worked the nightshift. My stomach rumbled and I remembered I had a lunch date. I glanced around the newsroom and saw no sign of Neil. Time to make my get away. I would be early, but getting away clean was the most important thing.

Lou's Bar and Pizza was only a couple of blocks from my apartment in the direction of the seedier part of town. It was on Division Avenue and had some black filtering paint covering the store front window of a previous, more prosperous life. Now, it had a long dark bar and a kitchen at the back that turned out the best pizzas.

The crusts were crisp on the bottom then soft like bread. The sauce had a vague sweet taste and Lou loaded up on the toppings. These pizzas accounted for much of my vegetable intake with the supreme featuring green peppers, onions, mushrooms and olives.

As I entered the dark interior from a day that promised afternoon sun to chase away the overcast clouds of the morning, I knew instinctively how to maneuver to the bar without falling over any tables or chairs while my eyes to adjusted to the low light.

By the time I reached my normal stool, I was able to read the beer placard on the tables. The bar was L-shaped. I liked my back against the wall at the end so with only a half a turn, I could see everything that happened here. Lou's pizza was a favorite with the cops, too, and many a story had details filled out over a good pizza and beer.

The day bartender, a reed thin man of indeterminate middle age, sauntered over.

"A beer and loaded pizza, make it a large, I'm expecting company."

The man nodded and slid over to the tap to draw the amber liquid. He slid it the two spaces to my seat.

A shaft of light streamed into the place announcing a new arrival. I turned and watched my favorite night editor stop and survey the crowd. It took him a minute to find me in the dim light; then he nodded and negotiated his way to the stool beside me.

The bartender looked over from the other end of the bar and Ken pointed to my draft. "I'll have what he's having."

Ken turned to me. "Did you order?"

"Supreme with all the trimmings, super sized so there would be a slice left for you." Ken didn't smile at my joke and I wasn't sure if it was the lighting in the place creating larger shadows on his face or if the lines had deepened and furrowed in the last week since I'd been on the day shift.

I took a long drag on my beer and then licked the foam residue from my upper lip. Waiting. Ken took a long drink, too, and swiped his hand over his mouth before turning to me.

"Thanks for the meet."

"No problem. I was hungry and it isn't often you offer to buy."

Ken half chuckled at that, then his face went gray again. I was becoming concerned. My friend and I had been through a lot on the night shift and I always admired his sense of humor in the face of adversity. This had to be bad.

The bartender returned and slid a couple of paper plates in front of us and a wire stand to hold the pizza right under our noses. "You want refills?" He pointed to the mugs. I nodded, knowing the beer might help soften whatever was to come.

The beers were slid into place as the empties were removed with what seemed like a slip of the hand. He left again only to return moments later setting the pizza on the rack, steam rolling off, carrying smells that were making my mouth water. We each took a slice and bit into it, enjoying the melted cheese dripping down our chins mixing with the grease from the pepperoni.

After the first slice disappeared and we each had a second, Ken turned to me.

"I'm getting out of the newspaper business."

"What? You love your job." It would have been easy to knock me off my barstool with that announcement. I thought he was coming to tell me I was fired if I didn't get my ass back into the newsroom.

"Not any more. I can't work nights and attend god awful meetings during the day. The ideas Neil has, if he is allowed to continue, would turn our well-respected newspaper into a tabloid." Ken took a huge bite from his fresh slice as if he was biting off Neil's head. Can't say as I blame him there.

"Do you think the brass is going to buy into it?"

"Looks like it, from what I saw at the meeting today. He rolled out his redesign and, I kid you not, the masthead will have pink."

"Pink. You mean the *Grand River Journal* will be in pink on the top of page 1A?"

"The name will be in black but the pink will be the new swooshes he is adding under the name that roll up on each side like bookends. The only people that will appeal to are the housewives in bunny slippers and we know those are a dying breed when you need two incomes to survive." Another large bite of pizza disappeared. I hadn't touched my second slice yet. I better get a move on it, but I still couldn't believe what he was telling me. My hard-hitting newspaper was going wussy.

"What about the publisher? He's a man who doesn't love change. He will put a stop to it. They don't come more conservative than old Ed McBane." I took a bite and chewed slowly, the pizza going to cardboard.

"It's like Neil has them drugged and anything he says is a great idea. I've never seen anything like it. I know I don't want to be there. I'm looking at my options."

"Don't be rash. Hang in there. Neil has only been at the *Journal* for a few weeks. He can't change everything overnight." I took another bite.

"Look at you. It only took him a couple of weeks to pull you off nights and onto days." Ken took another long draw on his beer like he was in a desert looking for water.

"I'm not going easily. I'm working from home and I ain't sitting in any more meetings. I've had my fill. What we have to do is put our heads together and plan a way to get him out of Grand River for good." Crap. I had a meeting that afternoon. Neil had pinned me before deadline making it mandatory. Well, after that I was done with meetings.

"How we going to do that?" Ken finished his beer and signaled the bartender for another. This would be his third. I'd never seen him have more than two. I've never seen him roll over especially not for a journalistic principal. I had to do something, but what? I took another bite and chewed, running through possibilities.

Murder was first on my list but I discarded that. What about an accident? Too hard to stage and I thought about Dominique Pewter. Nothing seemed appropriate or fitting. Then I hit on a plan.

"I've got it. We are going to investigate our friend Neil. We are going to find some skeletons in his closet. Then we are going to get him a job in another city and let him wreak havoc there."

Ken looked up, his eyes trying to focus on me and finally succeeded.

"Do you think he has something to hide?" Hope filled his voice.

"Sure. We all have secrets. We can exploit his like he wants us to do in our stories. Let's threaten to put him on 1A and see how he likes it."

"Yes, let's do it. How we going to do it?" Ken helped himself to his third piece of pizza and I hoped it would sober him up.

"Let's just see what Neil does for fun, who he sees and take it from there. I'm talking about staking him out."

"Great. Let's get some incriminating photos that will go with that lovely pink masthead." Ken's voice was stronger now. The editor I knew to be a major hard ass was returning.

"Sounds good." I wanted him to get his mojo back. This wimpy Ken was scary.

"I'll get a camera set for low light from the picture men and you can tail him tonight."

"Wait a minute. I have to tail him? Why me?" I was already exhausted from a lack of sleep.

"Because this is right up your alley. If Mitch Malone, bad ass cop reporter can't find some dirt, we're toast."

"Oh. Okay. That makes sense."

"That's the spirit." Ken pounded me on the back.

Yeah. What else did I have to do? I was working days. Might as well spend my nights following the man who was making my days a living hell.

■ CHAPTER 11

I was stuck in an editorial meeting and sleepy from the beers at lunch. I hated these meetings. About once a year Publisher Ed McBane, the guy in the dark paneled office, who rarely came out from hiding behind his secretary, thought I should be more involved in the newsroom. I would be required and receive overtime pay to attend two-hour meetings in the afternoons once a week to participate in the current topic of self-improvement.

One year it was team-building activities. That worked well. As soon as the mandatory meetings were done, I went back to my solitary existence. Most of my "team" have since moved on to other newspapers. I stayed, and am an easy team of one to work with. That was money well spent.

When I was green, I tried to fight the meetings, now I knew better. I tolerated the intrusion for about six weeks and then quit coming as does everyone else. Now that I was on days, it was even harder not to be drawn into them. Neil called them at least three times a week. I returned from my lunch with the promise of the camera being ready by three. I thought I could claim to be on a hot story. I would make a few calls and see if I could connect with Bob Johansen. He couldn't duck me forever. Unfortunately, the minute I walked in I was pulled into the meeting. Neil was deaf to my excuses.

This time the topic was increasing our approval rating in the Grand River community. To that end, the Journal had hired a public relations firm to suggest activities, commercials and advertisements that would improve our image. I was dutifully sitting in our conference room with a beautiful view of the Grand River and high rise condos, offices and hotels that grew and flanked the river's banks in the last decade. Neil was at the head of the table making sure everyone was listening and agreeing.

A smart looking female with a dark sophisticated bob and suit that didn't leave enough leg to look at, was popping another videotape into the mouth below a thirteen-inch TV, mounted from the ceiling. This was the third tape and the whole project was a waste of time in my estimation.

"Now, this one looks at the economic impact the *Journal* has on the community," blah, blah, blah, I thought as her perky voice encouraged our attention. I looked up and my interest was caught.

It was the corner of Lake Drive and Vista Point. The camera panned down the road which wasn't under construction. "This segment shows how we provide employment for three hundred carriers including the boy next door." The voice droned on, but I froze, staring at the Vista Point intersection. It was the accident scene that haunted my dreams, but from a different angle.

The camera was positioned four or five houses behind the stop sign where witnesses said Dominique stopped prior to pulling out in front of the cement truck. The kid peddled his bike up from the stop sign, winging newspapers that landed perfectly on everyone's front step. Like that happened in real life.

What caught my attention was a clear view of the curve from between a couple of houses. As the camera continued to pan on the kid, a car came around the curve in the background. If someone had been parked in one of the driveways farther back from the stop sign, they could wait for a certain vehicle to go by, pull behind it and then force the car into the intersection.

I was being absurd. Why would anyone lay in wait? Who would have known they would come this way? I was being way too sinister. This was a simple accident, nothing more, but I couldn't leave it. I wasn't sure why it kept drawing me in. It had to be more than feeling sorry for the dead little rich girl.

I felt like I was missing something. I kept running scenarios. Why would somebody lay in wait? How would they know that the pair of girls would spend so much time at the stop sign? Was it a crime of opportunity? Maybe they had been followed and the man was just waiting for an opportunity to create a traffic accident, an insurance scam. Maybe the construction company wanted to retire Mabel. That possibility seemed so wild, I immediately began to discard it as too fantastic, too full of the exact timing to have worked, but there was an accident. It had taken the life of a beautiful girl in the prime of her life, a rich one. That wasn't right no matter how it happened. And no one missed her except for maybe the girl fighting for her life in ICU.

"Now here the customer is waiting anxiously for his paper," the perky voice continued, right behind my shoulder, but I was itching to get out. Everyone stared in a trance at the screen. I wanted to grab the tape, track down Bob and test my theory. It still seemed way too fantastic and full of too many ifs to work. My phone that I had dutifully switched to vibrate at the beginning of the session buzzed on my hip. Just the excuse I needed. I made a show of looking at the number and shrugged my shoulders at Neil, my friendly editor, indicating I needed to take the call. I got a dirty look as I quickly exited the conference room.

"Mitch Malone." I walked to my cubicle.

"It's Bob. I got your message. What's up?"

"I think I may have something that might make sense of your computer model of the accident. Can we try it out?"

■ ■ ■

I arranged to meet Bob at the scene of the accident. I wanted to show him how someone could lay in wait and then barrel into the intersection. I didn't have a handle on the why at the moment but I think I was narrowing down the how.

Bob was already parked on the shoulder about 500 feet from the intersection on Lake Drive. I pulled in behind him and was just at the edge of Mrs. Dobson's property. I wondered if she'd recovered from the ordeal and if I dared bring Bob over to talk about the accident.

"You gonna dance for me again?" Bob snickered as he waved his arms a bit to simulate my fast feet on the oil patch.

"You get that lubricant analyzed yet?"

"You know our labs aren't that fast. It was an oil-based lubricant but don't know what specifically yet. What did you want to show me?"

I motioned with my head in the direction behind the stop sign and started walking.

"Watch out for oil slicks." Bob chuckled again.

I said nothing and just kept going.

"How far you going to take me?"

I could hear Bob breathing heavy as we walked up the slight incline. I could have made a joke about cops staying in shape but I decided I wanted him open to my idea and not defensive. I could stay the butt of his joke in the search of a story.

I had reached the point not far from where the camera had videotaped the paperboy. I turned and looked back toward the accident. I surveyed the area. This point was higher and dropped to a lower elevation toward the stop sign. I noticed a little pocket park—a neighborhood play area. It had a couple of parking spaces, some playground equipment and a small square restroom building.

"What did I need to see?" Bob puffed out the words as he reached my side and looked around.

I turned and pointed to the far side of the house on the corner. "From here you have a perfect view of the traffic coming. If you wanted somebody to die, you could wait here and when you saw the next construction vehicle coming, you make your move and strike the car, forcing it into the intersection."

"You're talking murder?" Bob looked hesitant and unconvinced.

"What if you were two girls out for fun and stopped at the sign. You were in no hurry to pull out or someone had walked up to you on the corner and had asked for directions or something. They were already stopped at the corner, maybe only had a little pressure on the brake. Someone waited in this lot here for the opportunity, then barreled down the hill, pushing them into the intersection. That would have given them the momentum needed for your computer program, wouldn't it?"

"Mitch, that's a lot of assumptions with little fact."

"There was someone who caught the girl's attention while they were stopped at the corner. We have a witness testimony for that. Have you talked to the passenger yet?"

"No. She's still in a coma. And I didn't see a witness report that said that."

"You did not have an investigator extraordinaire interview her." This was where I could pay Derrick back for his callousness. Bob wouldn't tolerate shoddy interviews on any of his cases. The best part was Derrick would never know how it had happened.

"How about the driver screaming after the accident, saying she was sorry?"

"You serious?"

"According to Elsie Dobson, who was washing her dishes from that window right over there." I pointed to the small house with the gingham curtains. "She saw the truck hit the car. She left her house immediately and heard, 'I'm so sorry, Ashley.'"

"Is she credible? Are you confident that's what she heard? That wasn't in any of the reports from the officers at the scene."

I wanted to smile to myself and complain about Derrick's interview techniques, but I didn't. "The officer didn't think the witness was credible. She kept adding more detail into her original story. Her details didn't make sense to the officer, only the ramblings of an old woman. You could read the *Grand River Journal* and get the rest of the story," I teased, knowing he wouldn't take offense.

"You published what the victim screamed while trapped in the wreckage?" He chuckled at the thought. "I know you have more class than that, not much more for a reporter, but enough."

"The woman, while old, did have her faculties together. The accident shook her up, but I trust her observations. She couldn't have made up the screams."

I watched Bob pace and knew he was concerned about something, but not sure what. After a couple a minutes he made up his mind and pulled his cell from his hip.

"Chet, Bob here. Have you completed the autopsy on the fatality on Lake Drive Saturday?"

"You have? What did you find?"

I wanted to step closer to hear the other side of the conversation, but knew Bob would walk away to keep his suspicious to himself until he had proof.

"Who made the ID?" I heard while looking around the scene trying not to be obvious I was listening.

"What about dental records?"

"Call me when you get the records." Bob disconnected the call and turned from me.

"Anything interesting?" I walked toward him, but he wouldn't face me.

"Nothing I'm willing to comment on." Bob's reply was terse.

I walked around him so we were face to face. "Off the record?"

"No." He pushed around me and headed back to his car parked down the hill beyond mine. His chin was on his chest, his shoulders slumped. He was troubled, deeply troubled.

I took another look around and added more photos from each angle especially the easy view from behind the house. I was heading back to my car. I had other things I wanted to follow up on. Bob had removed a clipboard and measuring device from his car. He was taking measurements and writing them on his clipboard.

"Yoo hoo. Mr. Malone." It was Mrs. Dobson with a bright red apron around her waist.

"Good afternoon." I walked across her grass to where she was standing on her front porch. "How are you today?"

"Much better. I don't mind telling you that was one of the worst things I've ever seen. How's that Ashley girl?"

"She's still in critical condition, but they are hoping she'll pull through." I wanted to get on my way and not share trivialities. I had gotten all the information I needed the day of the accident. I opened my mouth to say I had to get going, but before I could, she started again.

"I read what you wrote, Mr. Malone, and you did a good job, but I didn't tell you all of it. I was too upset. I've been thinking about it ever since." Elsie broke eye contact and stared at the ground.

"What do you mean? You did see the accident, didn't you?" I was sweating. Was she a scatterbrained old woman as Derrick had figured?

"Yes I did, but I don't think it was."

What was she getting at? I didn't want to take the time to decipher the ramblings of a senior citizen, no matter how credible a witness. Elsie's gaze met mine, and I saw the cloudiness of cataracts around the edges but her eyes were sharp and intelligent. I decided if I humored her and listened to her ideas, I could get away faster.

"Elsie, what are you talking about?"

"Elmer always said you had to tell the truth, the whole truth. I need to tell you the whole truth, Mr. Malone."

Great, we were back to the late, sainted Elmer Dobson.

"I kept replaying what I saw and I don't think I did a good job telling you how it happened. Your story in the paper was accurate enough. I'm sure I said what you printed, but I didn't tell you the most important part and I didn't tell that nice young officer who ran off just as fast as you did. I need to tell someone what I saw."

"Bob Johansen at the sheriff's department. I'm sure he would be interested in what you saw." I pointed in Bob's direction. "Let me call him over."

"Bob," I yelled and motioned with my arm.

I saw Elsie's eyes narrow into speculation. "Why did you come back today, Mr. Malone?"

"I…" I stopped. Why had I come back? The accident had haunted my dreams. "I had questions."

"I thought so. I may have the answers you're looking for, but if you need to go…" she trailed off and turned her back on me to enter her house.

I hated it when people made me beg for information. If Bob had witnessed this exchange, he wouldn't have any doubt that Elsie was in control of her faculties. I wanted to walk away and leave it to the professionals, but that was not how I worked. I had to ask.

"Elsie, would you tell me what you saw?" I thought I sounded contrite.

"Why don't you come in for a cup of coffee, Mr. Malone?" Her voice was sweet and a small smile broke out.

"Why don't we invite the traffic accident specialist? He needs to hear what you have to say as well."

She did have good coffee. I only hoped she had something important to say that was as good as the coffee. Bob was nearly to us by now. I made the introductions and we made a parade into her kitchen. Elsie Dobson was the perfect host as Bob and I took a seat at her kitchen table. Elsie set about getting extra cups and I thought I heard her humming.

"Do you need cream or sugar for your coffee, Mr. Malone, Deputy

Johansen?"

"No thank you, and call me Mitch."

"Sugar, please. Thank you," Bob responded.

I was back at the gray Formica top table with the ruby red vinyl seats and chrome frame chairs. Elsie set the percolator back on the stove after filling our cups.

I wasn't happy she was using her good china. Elsie was not the type to have it ready to use unless she was expecting visitors. The handles were hard for my large fingers to use but I vowed to manage, get her information and get out as fast as possible. Bob could stay and probably would until the coffee ran out.

She returned to her chair closest to the stove, sat and sipped at the coffee laced with cream.

I waited, my index finger tapping on the rim of the cup, just above the pink flower I thought might be a rose.

"You make a great cup of coffee, Mrs. Dobson." I took another sip, hoping the compliment would get her warmed up to spill the rest.

"Thank you. Mr. Dobson always liked my coffee too."

Crap, now she was going to wax on about Mr. Dobson and I never would get out of here. I nodded my head and sipped again.

"But you don't want to hear about that." I nodded again, this time hoping she would continue.

"What I don't believe I made myself clear about Saturday was there was another car."

I set down my cup, pulled my notebook out from my back pocket and sat poised to take some notes. I noted that Bob leaned in closer, straightening his clipboard to jot notes.

"The reason I saw the accident was I couldn't help but notice the fancy red car at the stop sign. Those girls looked like they were having a great time and I was a bit sad. I was feeling bad because Mr. Dobson is gone and I get lonely here on my own. I watched their blonde locks tousled by the wind. I envied their carefree spirits while they sat at the stop sign for several moments. I could see them talking and laughing and no one was behind them. They even got out of the car for a minute, doing one of those things kids do running around the car."

"Chinese fire drill," Bob supplied.

Elsie nodded and continued. "Made me want to be young and carefree again." She smiled to herself as she remembered. I touched her hand and brought her back to the present.

"Like I said, they sat there for several minutes and a black car was up by the park. It was a sleek shiny thing. I remember it because it was unusual for two new cars, black and red to be just sitting there."

"What kind of car?" Bob asked.

"I don't know except it was expensive and had four doors. It was long and sleek. Anyway, it was up the hill, a good two or three car lengths behind them, no cars between them, just sitting there. I could tell the minute the girls noticed. The driver of the red car glanced in the rearview mirror and sat up straighter and looked both ways getting ready to pull out." Her voice trailed off and I thought I would have to drag her back to the present again.

"The black car pulled up and I think it hit them. I still can't believe it. I've played it back in my mind several times and I still can't believe it. The black car pushed them into the path of the cement truck that was just coming into view. Made a U-turn and drove away, the way it had come. It didn't wait or anything."

Elsie got up and I thought she was going to refill our coffee cups. Instead she went to the sink and pulled back the curtains. "I had these open that day and now I can't stand to look out without remembering. Come look."

Bob got up and went to the window and Elsie moved off to the side. He took care to position himself as Elsie had shown him before raising his eyes. He rubbed his chin in thought, then looked at Elsie and nodded.

I wanted to see, too, and hurried to the window. Bob retook his seat. I saw the corner and up the street clearly visible in the window. She did have the best seat in the house for the accident. I pulled out my camera and took a couple of shots making sure the window frame was visible on each side. Elsie and I returned to the table and sat. No one said anything for a minute while we sipped our coffee.

"Did you get a license number?" Bob leaned forward intently, scratching notes.

"Goodness gracious, no. I was so shocked, I couldn't move for a minute, then I rushed out." Elsie looked down at her cup but I didn't think she saw the rich brown color of the coffee.

Bob piloted her deftly through the rest of the story that matched what she had told me Saturday.

Our coffee cups empty, Elsie was looking tired. I connected with Bob and we both rose in unison.

"Thank you for that wonderful cup of coffee." Bob did a little formal half bow.

I swear Elsie blushed. Bob was a good investigator. I'd never seen him with witnesses before, just with his sketch pad and computer program. I saw now how he got to his position. He had deftly dragged every detail from Elsie.

"I may need you to come to the sheriff's department and make a formal statement. Would you be willing?"

"Yes, I would. Mr. Dobson always said we must perform our civic duty."

Bob gave her his card and made arrangements for her to come in the next day. I was nearly out the door and could have left, but I wanted to talk to Bob about my theory again.

I walked back and dug a ragged card from my jacket pocket and set it on the table. "Thanks, Elsie. Call me if you ever need anything." That was my standard line to useful sources in stories. I figured they tossed the cards within days since I never heard from them again.

"Come back again, anytime, you two." I nodded and walked back to the road. Bob followed a few steps behind me. Glancing over my shoulder, I could see he was looking at the scene from Elsie's viewpoint, imagining it from her details. Her mind was still sharp. There was no doubt about that.

I looked back at the house and Elsie was still at the door. I quickly turned away before she could call us back. I was sure we hadn't heard all the Elmer Dobson stories yet.

I hung back a step and let Bob catch up. "What do you think of my theory now?"

I saw anger in his eyes. "Why wasn't this in a report?"

I was silent. I'd never seen Bob mad before. I would not have wanted to be on the end of his anger.

"This is the worst police work I've seen. What else wasn't in his reports?" Bob turned to me. "This was Derrick Smother's work, wasn't it?"

I'd wanted to get the power-hungry cop in trouble, but now I worried this could cost him his job. It seemed a bit more serious than the dressing down I had intended. "I read his reports and they are scanty at best. He's been filling in on investigations with the budget cuts, but this…"

I knew that Derrick would be an all-out enemy now. And he could be mean, underhanded and dirty. This wasn't a harmless prank to get even. Had I gone too far?

I realized I still had my notebook in my hand. I was a reporter. It was my job to get the news. Investigative reporters looked into things. I was looking into this and there was nothing wrong with floating my theory to Bob and pointing him to a witness. Derrick could do what he will. I had only done my job.

"Mitch?"

I turned to Bob.

"I'd like to ask a favor. Could you hold off printing that this would be anything but an accident for a couple of days?"

"Bob, this is big news. Heiress murder made to look like traffic accident."

"Yes, but I'm worried about the survivor. We need her statement. If the driver of the black car suspects we are on to him, he'll cover his tracks. I need to do more work on this. I'm only asking for a couple of days."

I hesitated. I had held stories in the past, but this was big. Then I remembered the CEO in the hospital. Maybe Ashley was in danger.

"I will give you all my findings, an exclusive, isn't that what they call it?" Bob was still trying to bribe me.

His report would lend more to my story than just Elsie's quotes.

"Okay, but I need it by the weekend." We shook hands on the deal. While I had agreed not to print Elsie's comments yet, I hadn't agreed to quit searching on my own.

My phone vibrated on my hip.

■ CHAPTER 12

I rolled my eyes when I saw Neil's number come up on the caller ID. My stomach rumbled and I realized my last meal had been with Ken. Might as well get my surveillance started.

"Malone." I tried not to snarl but it was really difficult.

"Neil, here. Want to get some dinner? We can go over what you missed at the meeting."

I rolled my eyes. "Sorry, can't. Following a big story."

"Really? What is it?"

"I don't want to go into details over a cell. Those news crews wouldn't be above listing in on a cell transmission. I'll let you know tomorrow."

Neil liked details, but I promised not to print this one yet. As soon as I told Neil anything, he would put it in print with or without my byline. Wouldn't matter if I burned a source. Neil didn't know how it worked on the cop beat. By holding a story for a day, you ended up with a better one the next day and a favor you could cash in for another story. It was a win-win.

I watched Bob taking more measurements but this time from the park's drive down to the stop sign.

"Mitch, you there?"

I returned my attention to the phone call. I needed to find out where Neil was going if I was going to follow him.

"Where you going? If I can break free, I'll try to meet you there." That was a whopper of a lie.

"Was thinking about that new restaurant in the Marriott. Chez Jean, but I could meet you anywhere." I heard the excitement in his voice and had to remind myself that he was making my life miserable and had put me on days.

"No. That's okay. No guarantees. Don't wait to order." I only wanted his location to begin the tailing.

"Try and make it." I heard disappointment. I'm not sure why I had a conscience. Maybe it was the daylight hours I was working. It was hard to be underhanded under the cold light of day. At night, the lines of good and evil were murkier.

It looked like Bob was wrapping up his latest measurements. I headed in his direction.

"Whatcha think?"

"I think I have lots more work to do on this accident before I sign off on the report." Bob's anger had cooled. "I'm not letting go of this one until I'm satisfied. I don't care who puts the pressure on."

Bob was being a bit cryptic. "What do you think of my theory?"

"No comment."

I thought he was kidding until I looked in his eyes.

"Mitch, this could become a high profile case. I need to keep a lid on it. How about, 'the investigation continues'?"

"How about just a small quote? How about looking for a witness in a dark car?"

"No. I want them to think they got away with this. The best I can do is promise to call you when I am ready to release my findings."

I knew that was the best I was going to get. I nodded, then turned to head to my car.

"Mitch?"

"Yea?" I turned and pulled out my notebook.

"I'd steer clear of Derrick for a while. He is not going to be happy when I get through with him."

I nodded and continued to my Jeep.

■ ■ ■

I'd been following Neil for the last two hours and it had been pretty boring. He went to an overpriced French restaurant attached to the tallest hotel on the river. I almost felt sorry for him. He ate dinner alone. I expected him to go home wherever that was, but I had been wrong.

Neil hailed a cab and I followed it into a west side neighborhood of modest homes. I couldn't figure out where he was going. The cab pulled over in front of a two-story home with tan speckled asbestos shingles for siding. I pulled into a driveway a half-dozen homes down, trying not to be too obvious. I didn't pick well and couldn't get a clear view. Was this where he lived? Somehow I didn't think this was Neil's style. There was no flash, no fashion, no chrome, no views. I did note the address.

I figured that was what a private investigator did. That made me think of Trace Richards and his bruised and battered body washing up in the Grand River. Trace wouldn't be sharing his tricks with anyone. I wondered if Bob had a report from Trace's niece and his last investigation. Then realized he didn't. That would be a homicide investigated by the Grand River city police department, not the sheriff's department. I doubt they would make the connection. I made a note to mention it to Bob and to Dennis.

The taxi's horn sounded and a reed-thin boy who couldn't have been old enough to drink came out of the house and jumped in the taxi. I had been so absorbed in watching, I had forgotten to take a photo. Stupid, stupid, stupid. I needed to get something and fast. This following people was bullshit. I was feeling like a tabloid reporter making up scenarios to fit photos and I didn't like it.

I backed out of the drive and continued to follow my quarry. I grabbed the camera off the passenger seat and nestled it between my legs for easy retrieval and to remind me to use it. The cab headed back toward the downtown as the streetlights were beginning to pop on. I ran scenarios of who this mystery man could be. Maybe he was the new graphic designer who was helping Neil create the overhaul of the paper. They were going to get some work done.

The cab crossed the river and turned south, the opposite direction from the paper. Taking a right on Division Avenue, it passed Lou's Bar and Pizza which was where I had gotten conned into doing this job because I was the good one at investigation. Ha. Ken Clark just didn't want to feel as ridiculous as I did, following a middle-aged man on a school night. The cabbie slowed down to cruising speed.

"Great. They'll be picking up hookers." I slammed my hand against the wheel in frustration. The action jostled the camera and it reminded me why I was here. "Go ahead, pick up a hooker and then I can be done with this charade."

I leaned in closer over the wheel. I was only going twenty miles per hour. I was garnering some attention from the ladies on the corner. One pushed herself off the lamppost and strutted over to my car. I lowered the passenger side window.

"Hi Grace. How's tricks?"

"Mitch, what are you doing down here? It isn't even dark yet. Working on a story?"

Grace was an average-height black woman who had bleached her hair blonde. She wore a short black leather skirt, leopard print v-necked shirt and knee-high boots.

"Yes, I'm following a lead in a story. He's in the cab at the next light. You ever do business with him?"

"How am I supposed to tell from here? I left my x-ray glasses in my pad." She straightened and looked toward the cab. "That's Harold's cab. I can get anything you want after he gets rid of the fare."

"No, that's okay. I'll let you know if I lose them. Gotta go."

Grace stepped back and I continued. Grace had been a source for a series I had done on prostitution. I'd hoped she would have gotten off the streets but not yet. She had two kids to feed at home and this was all she was trained for. Her mother would only watch the kids at night when they were sleeping. She'd said turning tricks had the best hours and best pay she could find.

After a couple more blocks, the cab turned right. I followed and almost blew my cover. The cab had pulled over at Temptations – a seedy little bar that was also rumored to have a strong gay clientele. It also where Trace Richard's niece said he'd met a client. I couldn't see Trace following Neil. Then again, I never thought I would be following Neil.

I quickly pulled over and grabbed the camera. I got photos of the young man exiting and then Neil. I zoomed back and got one of them entering the bar with the name of the establishment clearly visible. I zoomed in again just as they reached the door. Neil turned and said something to his companion and I got a great side view of his face.

Would this be enough? I doubted it. I needed more.

I was double parked so I moved down the street, turned around and found a place to sit just down from the bar with a clear view of the entrance. I debated about what to do. Who knew how long I would be sitting here? I didn't want to go in. Just didn't. Not my kind of place.

How could I find out what was going on? I watched a hooker try to drum up some business from a car stopped at the light at Division. The car drove off and the woman headed toward Temptations. She took one last look around and pulled the door open, disappearing inside. Maybe Grace would be interested in helping me after all.

I put the car into gear and headed left onto Division and down three blocks. Grace was still in her position. I turned left and stopped midway into the turn, pulling over in the crosswalk adjacent to the curb.

"Grace. I have a proposition for you." She again strutted toward my car, giving me a show of her many talents.

"I thought you'd never ask, lover," she said in a rich seductive drawl that had kept her kids in food and clothing for several years.

"Get in."

She climbed in rather gracefully and I wondered if that was how she got her name. It wasn't easy to climb up in that short, tight skirt and remain modest. But then, modesty was probably not part of her job description.

I put the Jeep in gear and continued down the street for a block, I turned left and headed south, turning three blocks later on Barclay. I pulled into a parking spot I had only vacated moments ago in front of Temptations. I pulled a fifty out of my pocket and held it up. She reached for it but I pulled it back.

"What do you know about this place?"

"General information or attributing it to a source?"

"General information."

"It's not a bad place. Bartenders don't mind a working girl stopping in to get warmed up or having a drink."

"What persuasion?"

"Anything goes in there, gay, straight, bi. You name it, they stroll through."

"The pair I was following went in there. How about you go in and see what they are up to? You get anything good, I will add another Grant." I handed her the fifty-dollar bill and it disappeared in her cleavage.

"Deal." She started to open the door.

I pulled out a paper from the stack on my back seat. It was the day Neil was announced as the new editor. His mug shot was there with his smiling face. I thought I saw recognition in her eye, but it was quickly gone. Recognition was not a good trait in her career.

She slipped out the door and strolled across the street before I could put the newspaper back.

I turned the car off and slouched down in the seat, glad the street light wasn't operable. It was a great view to observe the secret life that came out as full darkness set upon the strip. This was my time. This was when I was on the cop beat, not pushing up daisies during the nine to five bullshit.

I pulled out my notebook and started taking notes. I clocked my time in following Neil and the address where he picked up his date for the evening, describing the house and neighborhood. I didn't plan to use this information, but you never knew when an observation would make or break a story. Some little detail turned an okay story into something that grabbed the reader and never let them go. The details would prove to Neil I knew my stuff and he had to back off.

When cars came down the street I absently noted the make and model. I surmised the dark Mercedes was looking for a working girl, the rattletrap pickup was looking to buy a nickel bag for a little fun before heading to farm country. Every car had a purpose in this neighborhood during the evening hours. The pink Cadillac was obviously making sure his working girls were filling his pockets.

That brought my thoughts to Grace. Did she have a pimp? Would he be happy with the work I'd given her? It was money. What was the going rate for hookers? I thought the fifty was right for an hour. I hoped it wouldn't be more than that. I didn't have much more cash beyond the other fifty I had promised her.

As if she had read my thoughts, she materialized along the sidewalk and popped open the passenger door, closing it quickly.

"So what's this cloak and dagger all about?" Her voice was jazzed, the whites of her eyes shining.

I wondered briefly if she'd taken my cash and scored some drugs using them instead of doing the job.

"Why do you care?" My voice was sharp. I hadn't seen her come out the front entrance and was a bit unnerved by her quick appearance.

"I can only hang out at the bar for so long and I'm going to find me some business. What do you need? I got work to do, clients willing."

Her voice wasn't accusing, it was flat, stating an obvious fact in her life.

"I'm looking for some dirt on him. I need to discredit him somehow. I'm stuck working days until I can get him out and get back to my nights. I'm not a day trooper, Grace."

"That you aren't. Tell you what. You got that little camera you took that shadowy photo of me for your story?"

I nodded, not sure where this was going. I still had the larger camera I had borrowed between my legs. Obviously Grace hadn't seen it.

"Put it in your pocket and follow me."

We exited my Jeep after I stashed the larger camera under the seat. I followed her along the side of Temptations, hugging the wall. I felt like a second story man. I again had to give Grace credit. For walking in three-inch heels, she moved like a cat and just as silent. The only presence was her blonde hair catching the light out of the darkened window.

We took a turn at the back of the building and she held a dark, steel door open for me. "The bartender understands a working woman's life. She may need to slip in or out in a hurry. This door is always unlocked."

That explained how she had materialized without my noticing. She paused in the entry, letting our eyes adjust to the single bulb illumination before she continued.

"This here is the stock room and that door there leads to a hallway. Take it to the left and it enters the open bar area, to the right and it's bathrooms."

I nodded and she moved forward away from that door. "This is an entrance from behind the bar." She pointed off to our left and then pointed up. "That camera has announced our arrival in his storeroom." She gave it a wave. "Bill knew I was bringing you in. He don't care what you take photos of as long as it don't come back on the bar. Get your camera out and you can stand in the alcove and shoot your photos."

I nodded and she opened the door slowly and quietly hitting the lights as she did. I blinked and adjusted back to complete darkness before I started noticing dim lights in the direction of the bar. I inched forward and peered around. The bar was totally grungy. Scarred tables and mismatched chairs were flung without a care around the room. Only a half dozen had occupants, none of which I recognized or was interested in. Booths lined the far corner and back wall making an L shape. In the half-circle corner booth was Neil and what looked like his boy toy. They had their heads together, sipping on some drinks that looked like they came out of a cruise ship with pink umbrellas and orange-colored liquid inside. The pair looked cozy.

A sharp rap hit me in the rib and I looked at Grace. She signaled with her arms moving forward which meant get on with it.

I pulled my camera out and leaned against the door frame as I adjusted the settings for the dark light. The shutter would need to stay open longer than normal and if I wasn't braced properly, the photo would only show a blur. Any use of a flash would be a dead giveaway. I focused and rattled off three shots, two of which should be in focus and clear.

Grace pulled on my jacket to get me to move back but they were leaning in close and I wanted that photo. Blackmail wasn't too good for the man who wanted to create a pink masthead in my paper and put me on days.

I just stepped back in the shadows as I realized the door to the front was opening and I would have been in view from the lights of the bar's sign.

"I gotta get out of here," Grace whispered.

I nodded and fished another fifty out of my pocket and slipped it to her. "I'm going to hang here a few more minutes and get a couple more shots."

"Don't get caught. The bartender will hang you out to dry. He don't mind helping but he won't stick his neck out." I heard the click of the door and knew she was gone.

I peeked back out into the bar and the new arrivals had taken a table front and center. I recognized two of the girls as Grace's compatriots. They worked for a pimp who was trying to take over the strip, which explained her hasty departure. This was not Grace's turf and getting caught here could be dangerous for her.

I owed Grace more than a hundred bucks. I needed to see if I could get her off the streets. I didn't have time to dwell on that subject. My attention was pulled back to the latest arrivals.

Something about one of the guys with the new group caught my attention. His back was to me. He had a small build and wore a large five-gallon cowboy hat. It looked ridiculous on his smaller frame but it did add to his height in a sad way.

He stood and I stepped back into the shadows, photos of Neil forgotten. I knew this man and wanted to know from where.

He turned and recognition jolted my synapses. I saw the mean set of his eyes and the hawk shape of his nose. It was Roger Frasier, vice president of operations for Herman Steel. The man who recommended Pina Coladas and bragged about his prowess with the ladies—ladies of the evening that is. He was with two street workers. I guessed he had the money to pay. Maybe he was too insecure to get them for free. Poor guy.

Out of habit, I snapped a couple of photos as he approached the bar and again when he took drinks backs to his ladies making sure I got the hookers in the shot. Never hurts to have a little material if I ever wanted to do a Herman Steel story.

I turned my attention back to Neil. Their drinks were gone and it looked like they were getting ready to leave. Neil was leafing through his wallet. I took another photo and exited.

I ran out the back of the bar and retraced my steps at a gallop. If I was going to follow, I needed to be in my car or I could be spotted. I pulled up short at the front corner. My car was just across the street. I looked at the entrance. No sign of them. I ran across the street and jumped into my Jeep, just as Neil and his friend walked out.

I was pretty sure I had made it before they appeared, glad I had disabled the interior light years ago, leaving the interior dark. I sank into the seat and watched them walk toward Division Avenue. They weren't touching but walking close enough to hold hands if they wanted. When they hit the street, Neil's hand shot up, hailing a cab.

I started my engine and pulled out to the stop sign as the cab pulled from the curb. I turned and followed allowing the taxi to get several car lengths ahead. It headed south out of the strip, through an industrial area and toward a major destination for those looking to eat or shop. The cab pulled into what had once been a Howard Johnson's Motel complete with the orange-tiled roof over the office area. I pulled into an empty parking lot adjacent to the hotel. As I recall, it had been a twenty-four-hour diner, but was now boarded over. I hoped I wasn't obvious, being the only car in the lot.

Neil didn't even look around. The pair climbed the steps to the second floor. I pulled out the long-lens camera from under the seat taking some shots of them entering room 219 together.

I debated about seeing how long they stayed but a yawn slipped out. I needed a little shut eye to be able to function in the morning at my new start time. I wondered if Neil would be chipper after his late night escapade.

I guess my work for tonight, err, this morning, was done.

■ CHAPTER 13

I was only a block from my bed and the sleep I so desperately needed when my phone vibrated on my hip. If this was Neil and he'd heard the scanner, I was going to have to kill him. Then I remembered he was locked up in a hotel room. I pulled the phone off my hip and didn't recognize the number. You never knew when a big story was just a phone call away, so I answered.

"Malone, speak." I was tired and wanted to go to bed.

"Mr. Malone, is that you?" The voice was shaky, old and female. "It's Elsie Dobson."

Mrs. Dobson? What was she doing up at two in the morning? Maybe her cat was up in a tree and the fire department refused to get it down, but I didn't remember her having a cat.

"I need to talk to you." Her voice wavered at the request.

"I can stop by tomorrow." I really wanted some shut-eye before arriving at the newspaper in only a few hours. Why did I have to leave my business card?

"Could you come now?" Again, the voice was shaky but there was de-termination, too. This was one tough, smart old bird. Mr. Dobson must have had his hands full. No wonder he was pushing up daisies now.

"Alright. Let me grab a cup of coffee and I'll be there in about fifteen minutes."

"I already have the percolator going."

"Fine, but I want a big mug, no fancy china." I disconnected before she could respond. I did a U-turn in the middle of the empty street. All the sane people were in their beds sleeping. I headed across town, making good time without traffic and few stoplights working their red-green-yellow rotation.

The clouds were moving out and the moon was sinking in the sky. I could feel the temperature dropping and kicked the heat up. Dew lined the grass making the moonlight magnify the lawns to shiny beacons in the residential section of the city.

I chuckled to myself that this was my third visit to see Elsie but the only time I had ever driven in her drive. Every light in her house was on and tire tracks marked the dew on the grass adjacent to her drive. Something wasn't right here. Elsie never would waste electricity without a good reason. Not if it was Elmer's money. That made me smile, but it didn't last long.

Before I got to the door, Elsie had it open. She was dressed in a velour sweat suit with a zippered jacket, elderly ladies' wear for walking the mall. As my eyes traveled to her face, I saw the whiteness in her cheeks, the shallowness of her eyes deep in her face, and anger.

"Thank you for coming, Mr. Malone." She placed a mug of coffee on the table. Her hand shook but she didn't spill the liquid caffeine. I eagerly sat and sipped at the brew hoping for a jolt.

"Please call me Mitch. When a man visits a lady in the middle of the night, they should be a on a first name basis." I was trying for levity, but Elsie wasn't interested.

"Somebody tried to break into my house tonight and that, that…" she trailed off trying to come up with some word to do justice to her anger. "…that nincompoop deputy that was here before didn't believe me." She paused and then went on with her tirade.

"He tried to tell me I was just looking for attention and calling 9-1-1 was not the way to go about it. I should visit senior centers, meet others my own age. Like I would call the police because I was lonely."

"Why don't you tell me what happened from the beginning?" Elsie wasn't making much sense but she had called 9-1-1 and I was sure she had a reason.

"I was watching a movie in my bedroom. *Casablanca*. I love that movie and Elmer had been stationed in Morocco during the war. It started after the news at ten and I was only going to watch it for a few minutes. I had already turned out the light and the TV was the only illumination. The film is in black and white, you know."

I nodded and hoped she would get on with the tale.

"I heard something. It sounded like my back door rattling. I never use that door and keep the storm door locked as well as the entry door. Then it sounded like someone kicked the door. I called 9-1-1. Someone was out there. That nasty Deputy Derrick Smothers arrived. I showed him the door and he started in how I needed to get out more."

Her hands balled into fists, red infused her cheeks. I moved her cup toward her hoping to get her to take a sip and calm down although I wasn't sure caffeine was what she needed.

"Show me the door." We walked out the kitchen into her mudroom. On the left was the door I'd entered and beside the door, a window. On the right side was the same matching door and window. Ahead was a door to the garage. I looked out the window to the back yard, but I didn't see anything. I didn't want to open the door.

"Wait here."

I went out the door to the front and around the garage to the back door. I didn't see anything at first. The dew in the back yard hadn't been marked. I had walked under the three-foot overhang where there wasn't any dew. Sunlight was only a small hope on the horizon, but it was clearly glowing red. I couldn't help but think of what my mother used to say: *Red Sky at Night, Sailors' Delight; Red Sky in the Morning, Sailors Take Warning.*

I shook off the eerie feeling and looked closer at the door. There were a couple of muddy marks. It looked like someone had kicked it. I pulled out my camera and took a couple of shots, this time with the flash to show the shoe prints.

I returned to the mudroom and found Elsie waiting for me. I was worried.

"You already have done more than that so-called officer of the law." I steered her back to the table and felt her elbow shaking.

"Elsie, I believe you, and there was someone here. But you have to calm down. This can't be good for you."

She dropped into the chair, and looked worn out. She hadn't had any more sleep than I had. "Who do you think did it? Some neighborhood kid?"

"I don't know. Ever since that accident, I haven't been the same. I haven't been able to get a good night's sleep." She sipped on the coffee.

I wondered if her visitor had anything to do with the accident that wasn't. I printed Elsie's name and address in my story as a witness with her great quotes. Had I been responsible for bringing the night visitor to her home? I was being fanciful.

Then I remembered Trace Richards washing up along the river after following a co-ed. Maybe I was onto something. I needed to update that story and see if there were any suspects. I finished the last of my coffee that was only warm.

Now I needed some sleep. "You going to be alright?" I asked as I stood.

She nodded and pushed her chair back to walk me to the door. As she started to rise, she crumbled back into the chair.

"Elsie, Mrs. Dobson." I grabbed her just before she slid out of the chair. I kicked it out of the way and laid her out on the floor. Her eyes fluttered open.

"Elmer? Don't leave."

"Elsie, wake up." I felt for a pulse in her neck. It was racing. At least she was alive. I didn't know what was wrong, but I needed to do something.

I glanced around and saw a multi-colored afghan on the back of the sofa. I grabbed it and draped if over the white and still form.

"Elsie, don't do this to me." I tapped her cheek but didn't want to hurt the fragile face. She wasn't coming out of it so I scooped her up in my arms and headed for the door.

I placed her in my Jeep and seat belted her in.

I ran round and jumped in the driver's seat, and gunned the engine in reverse. On the way downtown, I pulled my cell out and hit 9-1-1. "Mitch Malone here. I need you to notify Our Lady of Mercy Hospital that I will be bringing in an old lady that I think is dying."

"What are her symptoms?" the dispatcher said.

"Unresponsive. Racing heart, talking to her dead husband."

I dropped the phone as I was nearing the downtown and the traffic picked up. I weaved in and out of vehicles in my path and saw the large letters of the Emergency Room ahead. I hit the horn and saw Elsie jerk. I squealed up to the double doors I had snuck in and out of, and hit the horn again before running around to Elsie's door. Medical professionals and a gurney appeared at my side and I stepped back to let them do their job.

Elsie disappeared into the emergency room and I ran a hand through my hair.

"Sir?"

A hospital worker in print scrubs was at my side. "You need to move your car and then fill out some paperwork."

"But I don't really know her."

"Sir, an ambulance is on its way in, move your car and then we will sort out the rest."

I did as she asked and entered the bright lights of the ER. The woman was behind a desk and I headed in her direction.

"How's she doing?" I asked.

"The doctor is with her and they are running some tests. Does she have a history of a heart condition?"

I shrugged my shoulders then realized I needed to say something. "I don't know her that well. I only met her this weekend. She never said."

The woman handed me a clipboard and told me to fill out what I could.

I found a seat and went to work. I knew her name and address I found in my notebook with the notes from the accident. That was about it for the form. I struggled out of the chair and handed it in.

The woman entered her name and address and then clicked some keys. "Here she is. This will help the doctors. Someone will be with you shortly."

I just stood there staring at the double doors that lead to the treatment rooms. After a few minutes, a man in a white coat and stethoscope around his neck came in. "Did you bring in Elsie Dobson?"

I nodded.

"Can you tell me what happened?"

"She thought someone had broken into her house and wasn't happy with the way the police had handled it. She called me and I took a look. I was getting ready to leave when she collapsed on the floor and started talking to her dead husband."

"Did she hit her head?"

"No, I grabbed her and laid her out. When I couldn't get her to wake up, I carried her to my Jeep and brought her here. How is she?"

"She's resting."

"Can I see her?" It felt like déjà vu and I was taking Mrs. Albanese's role. I hated hospitals. No one I ever knew walked out alive.

"Not at the moment. We are taking her for some tests. Do you know who her next of kin is?"

I shook my head. "I don't think she had children and her husband is dead."

The doctor looked thoughtful.

"What?"

"We won't be able to keep her at the hospital if we can get her heart rate regulated but we can't send her to an empty house. She will have to go to a nursing home until we're sure she is okay."

I could just picture Elsie's face when they told her that. She would have that same look she'd had when she'd pinned my ears back in the front yard on my second visit.

"She isn't going to like that." Elsie was as independent as they come. "She just needs to be with somebody?"

The doctor nodded and I couldn't believe the words were coming out of my mouth. "Could she stay with me?"

■ CHAPTER 14

looked at my watch and realized it was nearly time for me to get to work. "How long will she be here?"

"At least a couple of hours until her test results are back and the medication works to moderate her heart rate into a normal range."

"Great. I'm going to go to work and finish up a couple of things and then I'll return."

I left, kicking myself for volunteering to nurse Elsie Dobson. What was I thinking?

Before I left the hospital, I wanted to run up to ICU and check on the condition of Ashley Albanese. If nothing else popped up on my rounds, I could do another follow up. I skipped the waiting room, not wanting more drama than I'd already had bringing in Elsie.

My focus shifted to my next story as I rode the elevator to the fourth floor. I wanted to look at Ashley and see for myself if she was getting better or not. I saw a nurse come out of Ashley's room and another nurse coming toward her. I pushed open the door and caught the exchange.

"I don't understand it. She is alert and responding to us. We get a member of her family in there and she dozes off. Do you think her family hurts her?"

"I don't know. It's strange. It's like she doesn't want them in the room with her."

"Do you think she doesn't remember them?"

"Brain surgery of any kind can cause personality changes. Maybe that's it."

I had my own idea. I thought it was survivor's guilt. The nurses moved away from each other to their own duties and other patients.

I wanted to slip into her room, but my phone vibrated on my hip. I looked at the readout and it was Neil. I put it back but knew I needed to get to the paper.

When I entered the newsroom, by some miracle, I was able to slip in unnoticed. Luckily, Neil was taking a leak or something. I quickly penned an updated condition on Ashley Albanese calling it a tragic accident and attributing it to Bob. I'm sure he was going to love that, but I had to write something new. I added a lot of detail from my walk the day before but never mentioned or attributed the descriptions. I had a good twelve inches of copy, and then went back and laced in the background of the accident and then background on Dominique from the previous story. When I was done, I had a good twenty-five inches of copy. That would be good enough. I sent it to the editing queue and the minute it arrived, I saw Neil rise up and peer over the cubicles.

"Mitch, I need to speak to you."

"I was just on my way to grab something to eat." I tried lamely to get out of a tête-à-tête, but my good Karma was gone. I was exhausted, had to pick up an old lady at the hospital, and now I needed to talk to Neil. Wasn't he tired from his late night? I was.

"Let's go in the conference room." He ignored my excuse. I was in bigger trouble than I thought if he needed privacy. The newsroom was all about everyone knowing everyone's business because the editors screamed at people in the open about misplaced commas or lack of attribution. Their theory was if they yelled, no one would make the same boneheaded mistake. It was a working system but not one that was good for the ego when you were the subject of the abuse.

Neil held open the door for me. After I crossed the threshold and took a seat on the far side, he closed the door and took the end seat nearest me. There were two seats between us. Those seats would give me time to get myself under control if I felt the need to hit him at any point.

"Mitch, I'm concerned about your habits." His opening line set my teeth on edge. I hadn't slept and was wearing the same clothes as yesterday. Not exactly up to the *Grand River Journal's* dress code.

"You don't understand the team concept. We're all working together here to improve the newspaper. When I don't know where you are or what you're working on, I can't plan properly. Do you see what I mean?"

He paused and looked at me. I felt like I was in second grade and was hording Crayolas. I didn't say anything or move. He continued.

"Mitch you are one of the *Journal's* most recognized assets in the community. We need to use your talent and knowledge to beef up subscriptions. I need more stories with your byline to draw readers in. Remember the marketing expert?"

I remembered her but only for the great lead she had given on the accident story. I desperately wanted to get back to that or at least some shut eye. Not this heart-to-heart. My response wasn't needed.

"We need to be a well-oiled team. I need to know what you are working on so I can promo it the day before. I would like to do some billboards and signs on the side of buses using your photo with a catchy phrase like: 'Scoop the cops on crime, read Mitch Malone in the *Journal.*'"

I wanted to laugh in his face. How effective did he think I would be with that on buses traveling past beat cops? I would be a piranha with dentures, unable to take a bite of anything. My access to crime scenes would dry up as would my ability to get into the bowels of the police station. Neil, the observant newspaperman he was, didn't realize my distress and continued.

"I don't have the phrasing finalized, but think how that would boost our circulation. I also want you to give interviews with the local media. I want you to become the go-to man for crime in Grand River. Picture it." He stopped and lifted his arms, spreading his hands wide like he was holding up a giant marquee. "Mitch Malone, *Grand River Journal* Crime Expert, Answers All."

"I'm thinking we could do a weekly column where people write in with mysteries and you could solve them. Then we could syndicate it. Mitch this is going to be big. You could be famous."

How did you tell the man who is responsible for giving you a paycheck that he is off his fricking rocker? He was making me sound like a freak of nature, a man with a crystal ball. Do I stay and fight or resign now? My instinct was to jump the two chairs separating us, grab him around the neck and shake some sense into him. I decided on a rational explanation. I wasn't holding out much hope that it would work, though.

"Neil, the cops aren't going to like that much."

"We don't need the cops. We have you." His smugness was maniacal. How could someone be so stupid and so sure of himself?

"I am only good when I have access to information. You do this campaign and my access is going to dry up. We'll get nothing."

"Mitch, don't sell yourself short. You don't need the cops; you've solved plenty of crimes on your own. Look at your last national story. The one about terrorist training in Grand River and the FBI agents shot execution style. That was all you. That story caused a five percent spike in newspaper sales that week. We did extra print runs, our advertising inches increased. Think what our newspaper circulation rates would be if we had more of that."

"That was a once in a lifetime story. You can't duplicate that."

"Don't be so sure. Your biggest weakness, Mitch, is you lack confidence in yourself. With my guidance, you will be a household name, not only in West Michigan, but across the United States. The FBI will be calling you to consult on crimes."

The FBI comment had my mind drifting back to my favorite FBI agent and reason for my national success on the terrorists story—Special Agent Patrenka Peterson—at least I think that was her real name. I had kicked myself on several lonely nights when I thought about my refusal to take her up on the offer of a one night stand. At least I would have the memories.

"Neil, the FBI will never consult with me. You don't understand how the cops work. This plan is only going to ruin my career. I'm not interested. End of story. Think of something else to boost circulation, because I am not your man." I rose and walked along the long end of the table the farthest from him to get to the door. I had an uncontrollable urge to strangle him and didn't want to get close enough to test my self-restraint. My face on the side of buses? Get out of here and that was just want I wanted to do.

"Mitch, I don't think you understand. This is a business decision. It has been made." I looked at Neil and didn't see the idiot in the pink paisley shirt. I saw determination. If he was holding a gun, I knew he would shoot. It was something mean and a touch crazy in his eye. It made me want to stop and reconsider my anger, but I couldn't. I was not going to be the *Grand River Journal's* pin-up face. I was tired and this was the last straw.

"Like hell it has. I don't get any say in where you're planning on putting my picture? Think again." My blood was boiling. This was not just a laughable matter, he was serious.

"Think about this. Think about your future. I can make you a household name." Neil was calm, sure of himself.

"I don't want to be a household name." I reached for the door and opened it, then turned back around. Neil had a funny half smile on his face. It pushed me over the edge.

"If you continue with this plan, I'm going to kill you." I walked out of the conference room, slamming the door on my way out and ignoring the looks from a half dozen people within earshot. I grabbed my coat out of my cubicle and was gone.

■ CHAPTER 15

My adrenaline drove me for four blocks. I was outraged. I was pissed. I was livid. Before I had figured out how to handle my problem of Mrs. Dobson, I found myself at the hospital and parked. I entered via the main entrance and asked at the front desk about Mrs. Dobson. She was still in the emergency room and the woman at the front let me go in to see her.

As I approached the right door, the doctor I had talked to earlier stopped me.

"You still plan on looking out for her?"

I nodded. "Anything I should know about her test results?"

"No. Her heart rate is down and all the tests came back in the normal range. She was simply overwrought, too much excitement."

I figured Mrs. Dobson hadn't been so pissed since before Mr. Dobson made his demise, but I didn't tell the doctor that.

"She needs to take it easy and unless she complains of any other symptoms, she should be okay in the morning to return to her normal activities."

I nodded again.

"I'll sign the paperwork and she can leave whenever she's ready."

"Thanks." I pushed the door open.

Elsie sat in bed, wearing a faded hospital gown. Her face was pale but the sparkle was back in her eyes.

"You're going to take me home, right?"

"You are being discharged." I stopped. How do I tell an independent senior that she has to have a nursemaid and I'm it?

"And…" Her jaw clinched. I saw the green line on the monitor start to rise.

"Elsie, please. They want someone to stay with you to make sure you rest." I stepped toward the bed and tried to pat her hand.

"Horse feathers. I'm fine. Now get me out of here."

Fine. I would get her out of here and take her to my place. She could rest there and if all went well, I could take her home to sleep and maybe I would stay on her couch.

Before I could explain any of it to Elsie, a nurse came in.

"I see your son is here to take you home." She smiled at me. I was too stunned with the pronouncement to say anything.

"Yes he is. When can I go?" Elsie confirmed the nurse's assessment. What was I missing here?

"We need to unhook all the monitors, remove the IV and get you dressed. Shouldn't be too much longer."

The nurse efficiently started unhooking the equipment.

"Do you have any clothes?" the nurse asked.

I looked around and didn't see any.

"They took my sweatshirt off when I arrived. It has to be here."

There was a taller cabinet behind the door that looked like a small pantry. I opened it and there was the sweatshirt, T-shirt and some strappy white thing hanging on a hook that was too much material for a bra. On the bottom of the cupboard was the afghan.

"Here they are." I stepped back so they could be seen. I was not going to witness the dressing. "I'll just go get my car and make sure it is all warmed up and pull up to the front."

I bolted. I walked to the parking lot and had to think for a minute where I parked my Jeep. I'd been angry, not observant. I started the car and sat in the front seat and thought how I'd gotten into such a mess. I'd probably be fired from my job and was stuck taking care of an old woman.

I remembered my evening's investigation and the camera under my seat with my photos of Neil and his male date. Could I blackmail Neil to change his plans for me? Or maybe I could get even more dirt on Neil, an exclusive. I could get Neil fired before he could fire me. I rationalized that he had to go. He was ruining the newspaper. I was saving jobs.

I could follow him tonight. I could take more incriminating photos of him in a romantic tryst with his boy toy. That should kill the deal with our super-conservative publisher. With my plan in place, I backed out of the spot and pulled up to the entrance and waved to the guard.

"I'm just picking up a patient."

"Fifteen minutes max," the guard said.

I nodded and headed around the registration desk to the emergency room treatment area to pick up Elsie. I'd hope she had used her time wisely to get dressed.

I knocked and then pushed open the door. Elsie was sitting on the bed fully clothed and I breathed a sigh of relief. "Ready to go?"

"Definitely." She struggled to get off the bed and I stepped closer and helped her down.

She sagged a bit when her feet hit the floor. My adrenaline, which was sadly lacking in my tired state, kicked into high gear. I thought she was going to pass out again.

"Guess I should take it slow."

I was glad to see her wit return and she became steadier on her feet. She grabbed my arm and we took a step toward the door. It opened and a perky candy-striped volunteer pushed a wheelchair in. "Hospital rules. One taxi ride to the entrance."

Elsie stepped over to the chair and sank into its depths. The fact she wasn't arguing told me she wasn't that strong. I walked alongside the chair, carrying the afghan and opening doors until we reached the Jeep. I reached for Elsie's arm to help her out of the chair. I could see the small woman wouldn't be able to make the high step-up. I released her arm and grabbed her under her armpits, lifting her onto the seat. She scooted her legs around so they pointed forward. I settled the afghan over her legs then got in myself.

I pulled out of the lot and drove the four blocks to my condo and pulled into the underground garage.

"Where are we?" Elsie asked.

"My place. I haven't been home in two days. I'm beat. I need a shower and a change of clothes. I thought maybe you could rest here as much as home. I'll take you home later."

"I'm sorry to be a burden."

I held up my hand to stop her while I pulled into the parking spaces reserved for visitors next to the elevator. "Let's just get you up there."

Elsie seemed to get stronger just from getting out of the hospital. She still held my arm as we got into the elevator. My stomach rumbled and I realized I hadn't eaten and it was the middle of the afternoon. I wondered if Elsie was hungry. I realized I didn't have much in my cupboards for breakfast even after my meager shopping trip. I should have made a doughnut run but it was too late now. We had made our way to my apartment door and I saw my neighbor's closing.

I smiled to myself. Let my nosey neighbor think what she will of this. She never liked it when I brought women home. I wondered what she thought about really old women. I got my door open and knew the neighbor was burning up the peephole. I guided Elsie to the couch, gave her the remote and showed her how to work it. She was pale again and I wondered if I shouldn't have put her in the bedroom.

As if sensing my thoughts she said: "I'll be fine here. I just need to rest." I grabbed a pillow and blanket from the closet and got her settled. I went into the kitchen and opened the cupboard. I saw a loaf of bread and put two slices in the toaster. I grabbed grape jelly and butter. The toast popped and I buttered it. I took a piece out to Elsie and she waved it away. She was nearly asleep.

I returned and ate both pieces slathered in jelly. I left everything out, too tired to take care of it and crawled into my bed.

■ ■ ■

I awoke to the smell of something wonderful. Italian, if I didn't miss my guess. Something was amiss and I came out of my bedroom. The blanket was neatly folded on the end of the couch and the pillow on top of it. The afghan lay on the chair. Elsie. Some nursemaid I had turned out to be.

I followed the smell to the kitchen and Elsie was stirring something at the stove. She turned and saw me. I noticed the color was back in her cheeks.

"Mitch, I thought the smell of food would wake you. Sit. It's ready."

"Aren't I supposed to be taking care of you?"

"I'm fine. Cooking for someone does my heart good."

I couldn't argue with that. We ate the spaghetti in silence. You couldn't talk with your mouth full.

"This is wonderful. Thank you." She'd even made garlic toast from my loaf of bread I'd never put away.

"Your neighbor across the hall is a lovely woman. She lent me some spices to add to your jar of sauce to spice it up and the garlic for the bread."

"You didn't tell her anything, did you?" I panicked. The old bat had been trying to get me booted from the condo association since I moved in. She didn't like my late night hours.

"About you dear? No."

I suddenly felt like I was the invalid and Elsie the caregiver. I needed to get her back home. She was obviously feeling well enough. I thought about other things I had to do and realized following Neil was next on the list.

The huge mound of spaghetti had disappeared and I felt ready for another nap with the weight of the meal, but that wasn't on my schedule. I had dirty work to do.

Elsie rose and started clearing the table.

"Leave it and rest. I'll get it later."

"Don't be ridiculous. I enjoy doing dishes." Her comment hung in the air as I remembered what she had seen while doing dishes.

I left to shower. When I returned to the living room, Elsie was sitting on the couch with her eyes closed and her head tilted back. I hoped she wasn't dead.

She stirred and opened her eyes.

"Ready to go home?" I asked.

"Yes." I could see the fear in her eyes.

"No one is going to hurt you. The longer you wait, the harder it will be. You can't stay here forever."

"I know. I just miss Mr. Dobson and cooking for him."

I thought she was going to cry. I felt helpless and didn't know what to do but she couldn't stay with me. Lucky for me she got herself under control.

"I'm ready to go now."

She didn't have a purse or a coat because of her hurried departure. I grabbed my jacket and draped the afghan around her shoulders.

■ CHAPTER 16

"Mitch?"

"Yes."

"Mitch Malone from the *Grand River Journal?*"

"Yes. Who is this?"

"Stacey, Stacey Richards."

Silence. I was trying to process who Stacey was. I wasn't coming up with anything.

"I'm Trace Richard's assistant. You came looking for him after he died. That was a low blow by the way. You could have told me."

The smart-aleck college student. Yes, I remembered her now. "Right. What's up?"

"Are you still interested in what happened to my uncle?"

"Yes." I remembered I'd never told Dennis the connection between the accident and the investigator. I couldn't let Elsie's loneliness and medical problems distract me from my story.

"I've been poking around and I think I came up with something."

"Stacey, you have to be careful. Look what happened to your uncle."

"I told you I was good." Her voice sounded miffed but I knew whoever was behind this was a murderer who would kill again without thought.

"What did you find?"

"I found a billing statement that never got mailed. It was in the outbox and the mailman returned it because it didn't have postage on it."

"Who was billed?"

"Some company with offices in that big building by the river."

"Stacey, the name of the firm?"

"Are you going to use me as a source in your story? It would really help me keep Trace's operation going. I'll need some cases because I won't be getting paid to clean the office anymore."

"Stacey, the name?"

"You have to admit, I'm a good private investigator." Her emphasis on investigator almost made me laugh but I held it in.

"Stacey, this is serious. You could be killed if anyone suspects. Who else have you told?"

"No one."

"What did you do with the bill, turn it over to the police?"

"Not exactly."

"What does not exactly mean?" My intuition told me this could be bad.

"Well…"

Silence. I'd thought I'd lost her. My heart sank. I knew she had done something stupid.

"Where are you?" A pause, no response. "Tell me you are not at Trace's office making this call?"

"Maybe."

"Get out. Get out now. Whoever is behind this has deep pockets and lots of resources."

My warnings didn't seem to faze her. I had to try for something else to get her out of there.

"Stacey, I will use you as a source in my story. Now get out of there before I have to write a story on your body being found."

"You're not just jacking me around, Mitch, trying to steal my glory? I've heard about reporters doing anything to get a story."

"No. This is serious. Take that bill and get out of there."

"I can't."

"Can't what?"

"I can't take the bill."

"Why not?"

"I didn't get my last week's pay from Trace and there aren't any bank accounts or nothing. I need my money."

"Yes?"

"I mailed the bill."

My heart sank. If the murderer had anything to do with the case, then she'd mailed them an invitation to do it again.

"Stacey, get out of there now and don't come back to the office. Wait for all this to settle. You are in danger."

"No one is going to come after me for mailing a bill. That's just crazy."

"Is it any crazier than someone killing your uncle and dumping his body in the river just because he did some work for him?"

I heard a sob quickly inhaled. Mentioning her uncle's murder had struck a chord and maybe she would listen to me now.

"Killing you won't even require a moment's hesitation. This person is getting desperate, the case is dropping around him and he doesn't want to get caught. You would be an easy loose end to clean up. Are you getting out of there?"

"You're scaring me." A little hysteria was creeping into her voice.

"Good, I'm trying. This is serious. I don't want to see you get hurt. Now go and don't mention to anyone that you worked for your uncle, please."

"Okay, but how am I going to get paid if I don't come back and check the mail?"

"Stacey, the killer is not going to pay that bill. Trust me. How much does your uncle owe you?"

"A hundred bucks, but the bill was for a couple of thousand. That would let me keep the office open until I had my own clients and your story ran."

"Fine, meet me at the *Grand River Journal* and I'll give you a hundred bucks. Just get out of there. Are you gone?"

"Just locking the door."

"Great. That's great. How soon can you meet me? I'm at the paper right now." I had a bad feeling building. I got up from my chair with the cell phone still to my ear. Neil gave me a strange look. I just shrugged my shoulders. I hadn't said a word to him since I returned after dropping Elsie off. I had hoped to get in to see the publisher, but he had been tied up in meetings.

"I've got my bike. It will only take a few minutes."

"Keep talking to me. What do you see?" I walked out of my cubicle and started pacing in front of the windows as I looked for her.

"I'm just waiting for the light and I'm crossing Division Avenue."

"Is there much traffic?"

"Nothing but a dark sedan parked down the street."

Too many dark sedans lately. I had to get her off the road. Something told me that car was the same one that had pushed another into an intersection.

"Is there any damage to the front of the car?"

"It looks like it has some kind of scratch across the grill. It could be red or maybe that is something from the engine. I can ride closer and see.

"No." My tone was sharp, loud. Neil gave me another look. I turned my back to him and walked the opposite direction, down the bank of windows.

"Keep an eye on that car. Look around for possible escape routes. If that car starts moving in your direction, don't take any chances. Get something between you and the car."

"Mr. Malone, you are just a bit paranoid. I'm not sure I want to meet with you."

"I may be paranoid but at least I'm walking around. I want you to get your butt here and not smeared down the road from a hit-and-run driver." I let that sink in for a moment.

"Everyone in the case your uncle was working on is either dead or in the hospital. I don't want your name added to that list."

"That car is moving," Her voice was a higher pitch. "It did a U-turn right after I went by and is coming up behind me."

I looked down Michigan Avenue and I saw her. "I see you. Jump the curb and get on the sidewalk."

She was on the curb but the car was still coming. There weren't any parking meters or benches in front of the building to impede the car. She was only a hundred feet from the paper but had to cross an intersection.

"Get close to the building." With that, I left the window and ran out of the newsroom and down the steps to the lobby, the phone still in my ear. I pushed on the front door just in time to see Stacy swerve as the car jumped the curb.

Stacy jumped off the bike and bumped it up the steps toward me at the front entrance. The car swerved back onto the road, executed another U-turn and was gone. I tried to get the license plate, but it was covered by something.

Stacy made it to my side and was panting, her eyes dilated in fear.

"Let's go." I guided her around the side of the building to the back parking lot.

"Where we going?" She lifted her bike over a curb.

"To the police station."

"No way, nope, not me."

I grabbed her coat as she started back toward the front.

"Somebody just tried to kill you. Your best protection is to have the police know all the information." We made it to the back of the newspaper building and my Jeep was parked by the loading dock.

"I'm not leaving my bike."

"Fine. We can stow it in the back of my Jeep. Come on. I need to hit a money machine to pay you. We'll do that after the police station." I opened the back of my vehicle and pushed the bike in.

"You better not be jacking me around. I want my money."

"You'll get your money. We've got to report this. You've got to tell them where you sent that bill."

She was sullen as she flopped into the passenger seat. I hoped my friend Dennis was working. That would make it easier. He wouldn't hassle her or write it off as a drunk driver. As we drove, I craned my neck in all directions but whoever was driving the car had disappeared. I didn't think that would be the last I saw of it, though.

◼ CHAPTER 17

Dennis wouldn't allow me to be there while he took Stacey's statement. While I waited, I walked across the street and down to the middle of the next block and hit a money machine in the bank building to replenish my cash. I didn't want to be responsible for getting her home, but I did want the name of the attorney firm that had hired her uncle. I hoped Stacey would tell Dennis about her uncle's last case.

It was nearing ten o'clock and I wanted to get on Neil patrol. I had to get him out of my hair. The only good thing about spending a couple of hours at the newspaper is Neil didn't talk to me once. When I came in, he turned and snubbed me. It was wonderful.

I knew that wouldn't last so I needed to follow the plan I worked with Ken to get him out. There must be another newspaper he could ruin. Speaking of Ken, I placed a call to his desk. He answered on the first ring.

"Hey, honey, thanks for calling," Ken replied when I told him who I was.

"Is Neil right there?"

"Yes, honey. I can pick up some milk on my way home, anything else?"

"Do you know where Neil is going to dinner so I can pick up his tail again?"

"That's a toughie. I'm not sure I know any. Just a minute."

I could hear his voice but his words were hard to decipher.

"I asked Neil about a good place, and he suggested an Italian place out by the mall. Said they had good lasagna. He was going to be leaving in a few minutes to meet some people."

"Great. Thanks."

I disconnected and decided to follow him from the paper. If he was going to the mall, I could wait by the police station and if I parked in the back part, I could see the newspaper's parking lot down the hill. Would Neil drive tonight or take a taxi? Did he drive?

I collected my Jeep and realized I still had Stacey's bike. I couldn't take it with me because she'd accuse me of stealing it and I couldn't leave it here, or it would be stolen. I continued watching the parking lot but didn't see anyone leave. The lot only had a handful of vehicles.

The side door I just exited opened and Dennis walked out with Stacey. I opened the back of my Jeep to get the bike out. I couldn't take her home. She walked over and held her hand out. I stared at it for a minute then remembered the hundred I owed her. I took it out of my pocket.

"You gonna see she gets home?" I asked Dennis as I set the bike down and opened its kickstand.

"Sure. What's up?"

"Just a little information I need to get." I saw car lights go on in the newspaper parking lot. That could be Neil leaving. Dennis followed my gaze and had questions in his eyes.

I wasn't proud of my blackmail scheme but I had no choice. My face on the sides of buses? Never.

"Gotta go. Be careful, Stacey!" I jumped in my Jeep, starting it as I pulled on my seatbelt.

My phone vibrated and I looked at the readout. It was one of the lines from the editor's desks. It could be Ken or Neil. I decided to ignore it. If it was something important, they'd leave a voice mail.

As I was pulling out of the police lot, I saw Neil on the sidewalk by the front entrance not far from where the car had tried to hit Stacey. I had a wild urge to jump the curb, but saner thoughts prevailed.

The only reason I spotted him was he was wearing a large brimmed hat which looked like it had an ostrich feather on one side. In the dark he looked like a fruity pirate in the opera *The Pirates of Penzance*. He walked down Monroe Street toward the hotels and the Civic Center. Halfway down the block he hailed a cab. I had just turned onto Monroe after making a left turn, and was afraid I would have to drive past him, possibly giving away my pursuit. Instead, the cab was just pulling away from the curb and I settled in a couple cars behind.

I thought he would head out to the west side and pick up his young date but I was wrong. He went straight to Temptations.

I parked and debated about whether I could use the back door again. I wanted to see who he was meeting. I pulled the borrowed camera from under the seat and turned it on, focusing on the door. I decided to chance it, but wanted to wait a few more minutes to see if anyone looked familiar and could be meeting Neil.

A black sedan turned down the street. The brights hit me square in the face, blinding me. Jerk, I thought. No one needs brights for city driving, even if the street lights rarely worked in this area. The sedan drove down the street and executed a U-turn , then pulled in behind me, the entrance to an alley being the only separation. I slouched lower in my seat.

A man got out. He wore a long, dark trench coat with the collar turned up, hiding most of his face. I hoped he wasn't trying to hide from his sexuality because he screamed feminine. I thought he would look good in Neil's hat.

I pulled the camera up and snapped a couple of shots of the trench coat just because it was so funny. I followed him through the viewfinder and as he got to the door I realized I knew that nose. It had a little hawk end and it was Roger from Herman Steel. I snapped three photos in quick succession as he went in. What happened to the cowboy hat?

I didn't recognize him at first because he didn't have any hookers. Maybe he was meeting them inside. I thought about the dark sedan behind me. It looked familiar. I wish I'd thought to take photos of the car chasing Stacey from my window. I was too worried about her to think about the news implication. Was I losing my edge? Was it time for me to retire my pen and pad?

What were the odds this was the same car that had tried to run down Stacey? How many dark sedans were in the city of a half million people? I tried to think about that, but also remembered a dark sedan had been described by Elsie at the accident. Was that just a strange coincidence?

I discounted the theory. Who would be stupid enough to use the same car to run down a girl by the newspaper and then drive it to the bar only a dozen blocks away? No one, but I didn't like coincidences.

I got out of the car, taking the long-lens camera with me. I took several shots of the sedan's front. I didn't see any damage, but it was dark. I then went to the rear and snapped a couple shots of the clearly-visible license plate and the back of the car.

Never hurts to have the license number. Maybe Dennis or Bob would run it for me and see if it was a company car or Roger's personal transportation. Thinking about Bob, I still hadn't crossed paths with him. I still needed his okay to run the story and let him know about the connection to Trace's death. Typically the police and sheriff departments didn't share information especially about ongoing investigations.

I crossed the street and went down the side of the bar and in the back way. I waved to the video camera and made my way to the back side of the bar. I let my eyes adjust. Both of my quarries were in the same back booth Neil had been in before. I was surprised they were arguing back and forth. I couldn't hear what they were saying but I snapped some shots. It looked pretty heated on Roger's end. Neil would smile in a way I knew well. It was the smile I saw just before he told me my face was going on the side of busses.

Neil said something and I thought Roger was going to have a coronary right there. The red rose in his face. He picked up his drink and threw it in Neil's face, some of it rising up over the hat and then dripping back down like a double play. I wanted to cheer because I felt like that when I was trying to explain something to Neil and he just wouldn't listen.

The bar didn't have napkins under their drinks, so Neil had to pull his monogrammed handkerchief out to wipe off the fluid. He was still smiling but his eyes grew dark and nearly disappeared, like a viper ready to strike, as he cleaned his glasses. I wanted to hear what they were saying, but the noise in the place prevented it as another song started on the jukebox and it was the Who's "Mama's Got a Squeeze Box."

Roger got up and left the building. I watched Neil. A cold smile played across his face. He finished his drink and signaled to the waitress. He was getting ready to leave.

I hustled out the back door, ran to my car and hopped in. The sedan behind me was gone. Neil came out. His hat was on, covering most of his face. I wondered if that was why he was wearing it. I would have a hard time recognizing him with it on. He walked to the corner of Division and after a few minutes, he hailed a cab.

I started my car and made the turn keeping him in sight easily in the late hour traffic. The cab wound its way south. He was headed in the direction of the hotel he had gone to the night before. Was this where Neil was living? Why? Or did he have two places, one for show for the newspaper and another for his other interests?

I watched Neil make it to the same second floor room that had lights on. I wondered if his guest was already there. I watched for a few minutes and the boy came out carrying an ice bucket, filled it from a machine under the stairs and returned. I snapped some grainy shots of him just to keep me awake. I needed a good night's sleep.

I saw the lights dim and wanted to go up and interrupt. I wanted to tell him to back off or his midnight rendezvous would be frontpage news. I yawned again. Tonight was not the night. I needed to be on my best game and I was too tired.

I watched for a few more minutes then put my idling car into gear and headed home.

As I pulled in to the visitor lot at my building, my phone rang. It was the newsroom. I was too tired for a story but it was only Ken wanting an update and asking if Neil was any closer to leaving.

■ CHAPTER 18

My rise to consciousness was slow. I was being pulled and I didn't want to comply. The buzzing wouldn't stop. It would bleat, pause and then start again. I tried to stop the sound but it was out of my reach. As I broke the surface of my dream into reality, I realized the bleating was my cell phone on my dresser across the room vibrating for attention.

I'd come home from my night's escapade tired but feeling like my old self that had been lost in the nine to five grind that Neil had been putting me through. That was going to stop and today was going to be a good one, if I could only get the person calling me continuously to stop.

I slipped out from the sheets and walked two steps and retrieved the phone and it buzzed again. I had only been asleep for a couple of hours. Who died that couldn't wait until my morning shift? I looked at the readout. It was a *Grand River Journal* number but not one I was familiar with. It was not an exchange at the news desk and it was not Neil. That was good news. Who else would call me continuously? I scrolled through the other numbers. They were the same. Unless Neil had taken up residence at another location, it had to be someone else.

The phone buzzed again and more out of curiosity, than anything, I answered.

"Mitch, you are never going to believe what happened." The voice was vaguely familiar but I couldn't place it.

"Who is this?"

"Joe, Joe Mason, *Journal* photographer. You borrowed my camera the other night."

"Yes, yes. What's so important that you're calling me so early?"

"I wanted to know if my camera was okay. That it didn't get hurt in the fight."

"What fight?" I was still groggy from sleep and this was not making any sense.

"When you beat the crap out of Neil. Not that I wouldn't have done it, but you shouldn't have just left him in the parking lot to die."

"Wait. Neil is dead? We are talking about news editor Neil Speilman?"

"Yes. And Mitch? The cops are probably on their way to pick you up for questioning. Before they get you, can I get my camera back? I can't have it locked up as evidence."

The part about getting questioned by the police propelled me into action. As he talked, I stuffed my long legs into jeans and hauled a T-shirt over my head. I was heading to the door. "Joe, I'll have to get back to you on that."

I closed the phone and headed through my apartment grabbing my laptop, the phone charger, the camera, my notebook and car keys. Lucky for me, my car was parked in the visitor's slot because I was too tired to walk from the police station last night. I loaded all my gear inside. I wasn't sure if I was coming back anytime soon. I just needed to sort out this mess.

My phone rattled and I looked at the readout. I knew this number and I wasn't ready to talk. I turned my phone off until I could think. I needed to go somewhere where my car wouldn't be found and give me away. I also needed to get to the internet.

I realized as I pulled out of my building that I never stopped yesterday to check on the condition of the accident victim. The cops would never be able to find me there. I could set up shop in the ICU waiting room. It was a perfect arrangement in theory, but it also meant a prolonged stay and that made my stomach queasy. I gave myself a mental pep talk that this was like any other place I worked and just because it had sick people in it, I shouldn't be such a ninny.

I drove six blocks to the hospital and circled in a trail of one-way streets until I got to the parking garage. I drove up to the fourth of sixth floors and backed into a spot close to a cement abutment where no one would be able to read my license plate. I packed all my gear into my laptop briefcase and sauntered casually down to the second floor walkway into the hospital. A white-coated, tired-looking professional exited a combination lock that offered a direct entrance into the hospital's bowels bypassing the lobby and cameras. I wedged my foot into the door just as it was closing, opened it slightly and slipped through. No one paid any attention as I went the length of the corridor to another bank of elevators usually reserved for transporting patients. No one entered the elevator and I exited into the ICU behind the double doors between the nurses' station and Ashley's room.

It was quiet and no one was looking for visitors that were in the wrong place. I slipped into Ashley's room. She looked a little better today. Her cheeks were not the color of chalk and her breathing more even as if sleeping. She sported a new bandage on her head that seemed smaller. The swelling was leaving—a good sign.

I left her room and made it to the waiting room without anyone being the wiser. The only family member present was her sixteen-year-old brother, Anthony Junior. He looked up when I entered. I nodded and he went back to his electronic toy, playing furiously.

"How's your sister doing?"

"They say she's getting better, but she hasn't woken up yet." He never looked up from his game. No conversation worked for me. I plugged my laptop into an outlet by a round coffee table along the bank of windows. My new office was in business. From my perch next to the window, I could just get a signal from a free internet source. I wasn't sure whose it was, but I was going to use it.

I went to the local news station's website and read the story about the editor's death. It didn't say anything about a suspect, just that there were people of interest that they were questioning. Not a lot of details except he was found two hours after I'd left the parking lot and it was just after six now.

Joe said he had been beaten to death. I would have liked to get in a couple of good punches. I looked at my hands. No scratches or nicks. Time to return the last call.

"Where are you?" asked the professional-sounding voice of Police Detective Dennis Flaherty, not the voice of my friend and source.

"What do you know about Neil Speilman's murder?"

"I know you're a person of interest. We need to talk. Where are you?"

"Am I a serious suspect?" I couldn't figure out how they knew I had been there.

"You're the last person to see him alive." They knew I'd been tailing him? This was serious. Dennis would testify against me at trial, saying he observed me at the police station, waiting for Neil to leave.

"No I wasn't, the murderer was." I was indignant that Dennis would even consider me for murder.

"That wasn't you?" Dennis' voice was serious, too.

"No. How could you think that?" I was annoyed that he had considered it.

"I didn't want to but if you will remember our last conversation you were mad enough. You even said you were gonna kill him in front of several witnesses."

"It was a figure of speech."

"I know, but your car was seen leaving the parking lot during the window when he was getting pushed and shoved which lead to his death."

"Did anyone ask the boy he was sleeping with?" I paced in front of the window looking out, but only seeing the scene from the last night.

"The boy? Who's that?"

"The young thing Neil was shacked up with in room 219."

"Neil was in 219?"

"Yes. Or at least he had a key. The night before he took the boy toy with him from Temptations. Last night he met the kid at the hotel."

"How do you know this and who is the boy toy?"

"Don't know. Neil picked him up on Olive on the west side. Hang on. Let me check my notes, I have a house number here somewhere."

"What were you doing, following him?"

"Yes."

"Why?"

"It sounded like a good idea at the time to get something on him so he would leave me alone. But that didn't include murder. I just wanted him to back off the pink masthead and let me go back to nights instead of days." I didn't tell him about my face on the busses. No sense in giving him more ammunition for a murder charge.

"The man of mystery doesn't do so well in the daylight, huh?" Dennis chuckled, which was a good sign he believed me.

I yawned. I couldn't help it. The adrenaline was wearing off. The hospital was starting to come alive as the sun began cresting. I didn't want Dennis to figure out my location by overhearing a page for a doctor.

"Tell you what, Dennis. I will send you a photo of the boy toy so you know who you are looking for, then forget about looking for me for a while. I didn't have anything to do with his death. I give you my word."

"Will you do it right away? We need to get moving on this. The morning news shows are having a field day with the *Grand River Journal* editor getting killed in a seedy hotel parking lot."

"Right away. Gotta go." I slapped the phone together to break the connection just as the PA system started its announcement for Dr. Ricardo wanted in ICU.

I went back to my computer and moved all the photos from the camera to my laptop. A couple in the bar from two nights before weren't bad. I pulled them into Photoshop and cropped them down tight to a photo of just Neil and the boy toy without much background to see where they'd been taken.

I sent them to Dennis and then turned my attention to the TV screen Ashley's brother had turned on and saw the parking lot and hotel where Neil was found.

The nurse came and got Anthony Jr. and allowed him to see Ashley. He came back and slumped in the chair.

"How's she doing?"

"Don't know. The nurses say she is awake and you go in and she is asleep. I don't get it." His voice was sullen, concerned, anxious.

"She probably is just tired and only having her eyes open for a few minutes really wears her out. It will get better. You wait."

"Yeah, sure." He picked up his electronic game and started to play.

"Hey, I'm going to run down to the cafeteria. Do you want me to bring you back something?"

His eyes lit up. "A Mountain Dew would be great." He paused as if remembering his mother's admonitions. "If you're sure it's no trouble."

"No trouble, just keep an eye on my equipment." I nodded toward my laptop and bag. While heading to the elevator. I reached into my pocket and pulled out a ten. Good thing I had hit the cash machine. I needed to use only cash until my name was cleared. If Derrick found me, I might not be in any shape to talk by the time I got to the police station.

■ CHAPTER 19

I found my way up to the ICU carrying the Mountain Dew. I glanced at the surgery unit remembering my unease from the first dark night. I wondered if I had imagined it all. Nothing sinister with the sun streaming through the windows. I looked back to the elevator and the surgical unit was lit and alive with activity. Disinfectant filled my senses.

The professionals donned different colored scrubs denoting their station from lab technicians, to registered nurses, to licensed practical nurses and then the nursing assistants. All bustling, doing their job in efficiencies the rest of the world could only hope to achieve. I slowed my pace as I reached the double doors to the ICU. I walked back into the waiting room and set the drink down next to the kid who was still intent on his game.

After eating, I was awake and aware what I was facing. The cops could build a case against me for murder. I had motive, means and opportunity. I'd written about people who were arrested for less and had been convicted. The only way to get my life back was to solve it. The key to that was Ashley who was lying in a bed.

I turned back toward the elevator. Before I took three steps I was berating myself for allowing my discomfort at being in a hospital, all the sick and needy people that made my skin crawl, dictate my actions.

I turned back around and marched determinedly to the ICU doors.

I didn't need to be here, but then I thought about the police wanting to question me. I could leave. I was a reporter for the *Grand River Journal* and could hide behind my press credentials, but that wouldn't get me far, if the police wanted to question me. There would always be the Derricks in the department who would enjoy putting the cuffs on too tight and hauling me to the station in front of the media's cameras.

I had to wait until the police looked elsewhere for Neil's killer. I knew Dennis would be on it and I just had to give him some time. While I was here, I could at least do an update on Ashley's condition. Maybe even do more of a human interest piece about waiting in ICU. I could see the headlines with my byline: *By Mitch Malone, Journal staff writer.*

I pushed the double doors open with more force than was necessary, one door popped loudly against the doorstop. The nurse looked up from the desk where she had been scribbling in a chart. I nodded and shrugged my shoulders in apology and continued forward. Her eyes dropped back to the chart.

Just after the ICU was a rest room and drinking fountain. My unease made my mouth dry and I leaned over, pushing the silver square to get a drink. I knew it was a delaying tactic but I took it. After finishing I was straightening when I heard a nurse say:

"I don't understand it. She is out of the coma but won't talk with her family. It's like she can't stand the sight of them." I knew they were talking about Ashley. Maybe she wouldn't talk to her family but maybe she would talk to me. I was at the accident.

I glanced around and while there was a hum of activity overall, there was nothing in the immediate vicinity. The wall opposite the drinking fountain had windows along the hall for the nurses to see in. I peeked in and connected with a lovely pair of blue eyes that quickly turned from me.

I glanced at the plaque beside the door. A. Albanese. Shouldn't Ashley's eyes have been brown like her family? Her head was wrapped in a turban of bandages. Her left arm in a sling.

The eyes compelled me back. I couldn't see them. The face was turned. In that brief second, they assessed me, filled with intelligence. The nurse at the desk started my way. I turned around and entered the men's restroom. After taking care of business taking extra time washing my hands, I left the restroom. I looked in the room and knew she was still awake and wary.

I looked around for the nurse, but didn't see her. Farther down the corridor a light protruded from the wall flashing red rapidly. A nurse and doctor entered the corridor from the opposite end of the hall and bustled into the room.

I took the opportunity to slip into A. Albanese's room.

The eyes confronted me, but mirrored fear and strength. Even with the head bandaged, no sickness or pain dulled her expression. Seconds stretched as we appraised each other. I saw the right hand that wasn't bandaged moving along the side of the bed as if searching for something, but subtly. I figured she was searching for the call button. I needed to allay her fears. I wasn't trying to kill her after all, but maybe someone else was.

"I'm Mitch Malone from the *Grand River Journal*. I was at your accident. Do you remember any of it?"

The eyes dropped down to her hand in the cast. I waited. I didn't want to push. I wasn't totally heartless. Many accident victims can't remember anything from an auto crash and this victim had a brain injury. I went to pull out my notebook but it wasn't there. It was in the briefcase in the waiting room.

"Can you tell me your name?"

"Why?" Her voice was soft. "You're the reporter. My name's on the door."

"Can you tell me what happened?"

She shook her head. Tears started coming. I didn't want the tears. I needed to switch tactics. "Your family is mighty worried about you."

More tears. I had said the wrong thing again. "Do you have any pain? Do you need a nurse?"

I searched around, looking for someone to rescue me from the crying fountain.

I heard a giggle.

Tears were still wet on her face but a light was shining in her eyes and her lips in a half smile. She was beautiful. She looked familiar but it wasn't like the family that had been staking out the waiting room. Suddenly, it all fell into place! This wasn't Ashley, it was Dominique! She looked like the photo Roger had given me. This was my scoop, and without thinking I blurted out: "You're Dominique, aren't you?"

I saw panic and quick turns of her head looking for escape and all she found was pain from the movement.

"Don't tell anyone," she whispered. "I'm safe as long as they think I'm Ashley." She was starting to get agitated, and I didn't want to make her condition worse.

"Okay, but why?"

"I was supposed to die. Ashley wasn't." Tears started coming down her cheeks. I glanced around, looking to escape. Never a nurse when you needed one.

"Don't get upset. It's not good for you. Who was trying to kill you?" Good questioning technique, Malone, I berated myself. Tell her not to get upset and ask about who is trying to put her lights out.

"I can't tell you."

I wanted to say that was a dumb reason because if they succeeded no one will know where to look, but then I remembered the shadow lurking on the edge of ICU the night before.

"It's Bertram Switzer isn't it?"

Her eyes enlarged to look like saucers. It would have been comical had it not been so serious.

"Why do you say that?"

"Bertram was eavesdropping outside the waiting room after your surgery. I couldn't figure out why he didn't just come in."

Her pale face dropped a few shades of color to translucent, almost disappearing behind the whiter bandages.

Crap. I was going to kill her with my revelations. Why couldn't I just stay in the hall and write a tell-nothing follow-up like the rest of the fourth estate?

"I need to get out of here." Ashley, err, Dominique looked around and swung her legs toward the edge of a bed.

"No you don't. You need to get better." Was her paranoia from drugs, the head injury or the truth? Why would the CEO want her dead? His behavior was curious, but not murderous.

"This is the safest place for you. The Albaneses are guarding the door. No one will get by them." I needed to keep her in her bed.

"You did." Her tone was accusatory.

"Yes, but I'm a master at getting information and around obstacles. I'm the best at the *Grand River Journal*." I realized I sounded a bit pompous, but it was true. It also made a murder charge seem like a weak reason to avoid a great story.

Dominique raised an eyebrow that disappeared under a bandage and then squinted in pain.

"You are safe here. Just keep being Ashley. Give me some time to investigate." I thought of Dennis. "I could have the police come and take your statement?"

"No. Once the police know, I won't be safe. I can't trust anyone."

"Mr. and Mrs. Albanese are trustworthy."

"Yes, but I can't tell them their daughter is dead and I killed her. They won't want to protect me then."

"But you didn't kill her. It was an accident."

"No, it wasn't." The voice only a whisper and I wasn't even sure I'd heard her correctly.

"Just stay here for a little longer. You need to get stronger."

"I can't just lay here. I need to do something."

I saw a nurse go by the window and I moved back into the shadows of the room. I needed to get out of here and fast.

"Let me look into some things. It's daylight. No one can get in here during the day with the Albaneses in the waiting room. Just fake sleeping and no one will know unless they see your eyes."

I reached in my jacket and pulled out my business card. "If something happens, call my cell. I'll try and be back before nightfall."

As soon as the last five words were out I wanted to pull them back. What was I doing? I was getting a story, not babysitting. It was Elsie all over again, and I hadn't even called her to see how she was doing. I couldn't have people depending on me. That wasn't how it worked. I was never there for the people that needed me. I was a loner.

Now I was committed to coming back later today. I was trapped here because the cops were looking for me.

"Thanks." I looked into those sapphire orbs and saw trust and gratitude.

Ouch. I was committed.

I turned and left before I promised something else I didn't want to deliver. If I could prove that the CEO was trying to kill her, I would have another national headline. I could see it.

"CEO charged with murder scheme of company heiress."

■ CHAPTER 20

I went to the door and the coast was clear. I slipped back to the waiting room. Tony Jr. pushed buttons on his electronic game. I needed some help. Whether Dominique trusted the cops or not, I knew there were some above reproach.

I opened my cell and called Bob Johansen. After three rings, his voice mail kicked in.

"Mitch Malone, Bob. I need to speak to you as soon as possible." I left my cell number and disconnected.

What to do now. I couldn't stay at the hospital all day. That wouldn't accomplish anything. Time to see where the investigation was leading. I hit a speed dial number.

"Dennis, how's it looking?"

"Honey, I'm in the middle of things here," Dennis replied.

Crap. He couldn't talk. "Okay. Call me when you can."

"Sure, honey. I'll have a talk with him when I get home."

I disconnected.

What should I do? Before I had time to think, Mrs. Albanese came into the waiting room.

"TJ, how's Ashley?"

"No change. She's sleeping. Every time I go to see her, she's sleeping."

I felt guilty. Mrs. A gave him a quick hug and a kiss on his check.

"Where's Dad?" he asked, turning off his game.

"He's talking to that nice sheriff's deputy that came to the emergency room. He wants to know if he can question Ashley yet."

Shit. I couldn't get caught here and not by Derrick Smothers of all deputies. I would be cuffed and dragged from the hospital in front of everyone.

I could hear Mr. Albanese's voice coming closer. I had to get out of here but there was no way. I packed up my laptop and went into the corner of the room closest to the windows and behind the door. In order to see me, Derrick would have to walk past the waiting room and then look back into it. If he came in the room, there was nowhere I could hide.

"I'm sorry, but we haven't talked to Ashley yet. The doctors say she is out of the coma but is sleeping." The voice belonged to Mr. Albanese.

"I'll check at the nurses' station," Derrick responded. "I need to get this interview done and finish my report."

I bet he was a little under the gun to get this interview after screwing up the witness. I couldn't gloat about that now. When he went to the nurses' station, I would slip out the door and disappear. In the glare of the window, I could see the pair. They shook hands, and Derrick headed out of view. Mr. Albanese entered the waiting room.

I nodded at him and slipped out the door before it had time to shut. I opted not to wait for the elevator and took the stairs down. I wanted to put as much distance between Derrick and me as I could.

As I hit the last flight, my phone vibrated.

"Mitch Malone," I said as I exhaled and then sucked in a lungful of breath.

"Running from the cops," Dennis said laughing.

That was closer than I wanted to admit. "Very funny. What's up with my status? Am a wanted man?"

"Yes and no. You are wanted for questioning but have been pretty much been ruled out as a suspect."

"How?"

"Your neighbor across the hall saw you come home and the timing was just too tight."

"Who is suspected?" I asked.

"Is this for personal use or print?"

"Dennis, what's going on?" I was getting tired of this cat and mouse game.

"We found the guy in the photo you sent. He admits to being with

Neil but about an hour later, Neil received a call and left. He didn't see him again. When the police lights lit up the parking lot, he left."

"Who called Neil?"

"A Tracfone. Don't know the owner but when we find it we can match the number. It wasn't your phone."

I wanted to point out that I could have a Tracfone phone but then I would be in hot water again.

"The night editor," Dennis paused and I knew he was looking at his notes. "Ken Clark said he was talking to you about a story at the time the other call was placed."

Ken gave me an alibi. Interesting because he was the one who I thought might have done it. "Any other leads?"

"No, other than there were a lot of people who didn't like him and he had only been here a few months."

"Tell me something I don't know. He knew how to get your attention." I wondered how long it would be before I could go back to nights. I only felt a tinge of regret thinking of what was best for me when he wasn't even cold yet.

"So when do you want to make your statement? It shouldn't take too long."

"Now's good." I could go back to investigating. My mistaken identity story was big. "Furniture heiress not dead in mistaken identity." Time for Mitch Malone to follow the trail.

■ CHAPTER 21

I was still jazzed about my exclusive. I needed more information. I couldn't let the cat out of the bag about Dominique being alive, but I needed more detail for my story. I tried Bob again and left another message. Where was he?

Then I remembered Elsie. I checked my call log and hit send.

"How are you feeling, Elsie?"

"Fine, Mr. Malone and you?"

I was getting the cold shoulder and I didn't know why. It shouldn't have bothered me, but it did.

"Sorry I haven't called sooner. I'm working on a big story and my boss got killed last night."

"I understand you're busy." Her tone was crisp, controlled.

"I'm on my way over. Do you need anything? Milk, medicine?"

"I don't need anything, but I will look forward to your visit." She disconnected the call.

"Damn that woman." Now I had to visit. I tried Bob another time and got voicemail and hung up without leaving a message.

I knew I couldn't go to Elsie's empty handed but didn't think she was a big candy person. I thought about a pizza because I was hungry but she didn't strike me as a takeout girl.

Flowers. That would get me out of Elsie's doghouse. Drop in, make nice and get out. I had a big investigative journalism piece to write.

My plan chosen, I made my stop and hustled over to Elsie's. It had been nearly a week since the accident and I couldn't look at the spot without remembering the carnage. I don't think I ever would. The accident continued to haunt me.

I pulled into Elsie's driveway, and carried my bouquet of yellow daffodils in my left hand. I knocked on her front door with my right, thinking she might approve of using the more formal entrance. No one answered. I knocked again, thinking she may be hard of hearing, although I'd never noticed it before.

I listened intently for any noise or movement or a "come on in." Nothing but silence. I tried to look in through the door's three small windows at various levels. Nothing. Had she passed out again from the anger in our telephone call? I walked back and looked in the kitchen window. The percolator was going on the stove but no sign of Elsie sitting at the table, laying on the floor or elsewhere. Good and bad.

I walked to the mudroom door that I had entered on previous occasions. I tried the door. It was locked, even the screen door. I walked around the garage and tried the door of the break-in. Its screen opened in my hand but the main door was locked. Elsie told me she never unlocked the screen. I was really worried now. Something wasn't right. It wasn't just an old lady who was lonely. Something was wrong here.

I opened my phone and dialed 9-1-1. I quickly advised the dispatcher what I had found. The dispatcher asked that I stay connected and I could hear her dispatch a car. I thought of Derrick. How unlucky was I? If Derrick was the deputy dispatched, Elsie was history and it would be all my fault.

"Sir, I have dispatched a car to the scene, ETA two minutes."

"Thank you."

"Please stay on the line until the deputy arrives."

I dutifully held the phone to my ear. This was wrong. How did I get hooked into reporting a crime? How did I get hooked into caring for Elsie? I had only met her last Saturday and I would be heartbroken if something happened to her. Dear old Elsie would break my heart if she didn't come out of this and I didn't even know what this was yet. The unlocked door is what bothered me the most. Elsie wasn't forgetful and would have had no reason to unlock the door she never used.

I looked up and down Lake Drive for the patrol car. Nothing. There wasn't much traffic either. I realized I had the phone in my hand. "Excuse me, ma'am?"

"Yes."

"When will the car be arriving? Can I break in?"

"Sir, please wait for the deputy. We don't want something to happen to you, too."

I heard noise in the background and the dispatcher's voice in the background.

"Sir, the officer will be there any second."

"Thank you." I looked up and down the road and heard the noise of a car coming. I walked back to my Jeep and the patrol car pulled in and I speed walked back to it. I looked in the driver's seat and felt relief to see Hank Baldwin, the deputy who interviewed the cement truck driver.

"Mitch? You call this in?"

"Yes. I just talked to Elsie less than an hour ago and she knew I was coming." I realized I still held the daffodils, many of which had broken stems. I laid them on the hood of the patrol car.

"You knock on the door?"

"Yes, and she didn't answer. I didn't hear any noise but the percolator is going." I ran my free hand through my hair.

"The thing that bothers me the most is that someone tried to break in the other night. She told me she never uses the back door since Mr. Dobson died. She always keeps both the screen door and heavy door locked. The outside screen door is unlocked. The big door is locked. She wouldn't have forgotten to lock it."

I was out of breath after having all that information spew out in a rush. I wanted the deputy to tell me she was fine, just napping. He didn't. He looked worried.

"Stay here." He pulled his gun and disappeared around the garage. I heard the creak of the screen door. Then silence.

The deputy's window was open and I heard the static reply of radio traffic. I half listened out of habit.

"This is one-Adam-twenty requesting back up at this location."

"Ten four, one-Adam-twenty. One-Adam-eleven, proceed to 1122 Lake Drive. One-Adam-twenty is requesting backup."

"Enroute. ETA two minutes."

The address of the dispatch caught my attention. I thought 1122 Lake Drive was somewhere close to Elsie's. It was Elsie's address. I looked at the green reflective sign at the end of the driveway. It read

1122 and confirmed my anxiety.

What had the deputy found? The other patrol car drove in and my luck ran out.

Derrick got out of the car. "Looky what we have here. Didn't realize he needed help with an arrest. I would be happy to help him."

"It's not me, you moron. Something's happened to Elsie Dobson. Deputy Baldwin went behind the house and then called for help. I haven't seen him." Of all the deputies on duty, he had to be the closest to respond. We were in trouble. Derrick just wouldn't move fast enough and I was afraid Elsie was running out of time.

"You planning on giving those daffodils to your sweetie in there?" Derrick just stood by his car, leaning on the door.

The static started again, this time louder and in stereo from the two cars.

"One-Adam-twenty requesting status of that back up."

Derrick looked at the radio and realized they were talking about him. He leaned his chin into his microphone attached to his collar. "One-Adam-eleven. On scene."

"Ask him what's wrong?" I said.

"No exclusive for you, Mr. Hotshot Newspaper Reporter."

I wanted to lay him flat, but Elsie needed him and he better get going. "Do your job, Derrick. There will be time for me later."

I could see the indecision in his eyes, but he finally walked around the garage and disappeared. I paced, watching the house for any signs of movement. Any sign of life. I was worried there wouldn't be. If they had simply found her, the officer would have asked for an ambulance, not back up. What had he seen? It was times like this that I wished I carried a badge instead of a notebook.

Had the intruder come back to finish off the job? I had a sickly picture of Elsie lying on the floor, blood pooling behind her head.

A shot rang out. I saw movement at a curtain on the far corner of the house in what I assumed was some type of bedroom. Two more shots were fired. I wanted to run and see what was happening. I saw the window in the front start to rise.

"Officer shot. Officer down." The voice was high, filled with emotion.

Do I run around the back and risk getting shot? Do I go by the window? Then I thought I was the perfect target standing between the cop cars. I started to make my way around them, to at least put the cars between me and anyone shooting from the house. I heard sirens in the distance. The cavalry was coming.

The curtains were pushed again and I saw hands on the sill. No light emanated from the room and I couldn't see who was looking out. Friend or foe? The hands were on the window and I couldn't believe my eyes.

A gray head of hair popped into the window and then disappeared. I started in toward the window at a run. I was halfway there and the top of her head appeared again. I wanted to yell but didn't want to alert whoever had fired the shots. Then my stomach sank. I hoped Elsie hadn't fired the shots, thinking they were breaking in.

Time to sort that out later. I needed to get Elsie out. I reached the window just as the head appeared again.

"Damnation."

"Elsie? You alright?"

"Get me out of here."

I saw her squat low and then jump. She'd been trying to hoist herself out of the window but not succeeding. I reached in and grabbed her under the arms. As I pulled, she jumped again, the momentum flung me backward, my feet going out from underneath me. Elsie cleared the window and we both landed on the ground. I was flat on my back and Elsie on top of me.

Elsie pushed herself up, and I awkwardly rose to my feet, embarrassed to have Elsie on top of me. I saw Elsie wobble a bit and I scooped her up. The sirens were deafening and I realized I still didn't know if someone could shoot at us.

I carried her back behind Derrick's police car just as three more police cars parked like dice out of a Yahtzee cup. Five deputies came running toward us, guns drawn.

"Behind the house." I pointed around the garage. "Three shots." All but one of the officers circled the house and disappeared.

I turned to the woman struggling to stand.

"Damn fool."

"Who?" I propped Elsie on her feet but kept my arm around her shoulders tight to me.

"Some crack head sent to kill me. Fired that gun by accident. Hit that officer looking in the window."

"Where is he in the house?" I reached around Elsie and opened Derrick's door.

"Lying on the floor in the hall, last I saw."

"Lying?" Why would he be lying down? I turned, moving Elsie and let her drop onto the seat, her feet still outside the car.

"I hope Elmer can forgive me."

Now I was worried. The last time she talked to Elmer was when she was unconscious. I checked her color and her face was flushed but not bad.

"Elsie. Tell me what happened." I squatted down so I was eye level. Her face went beet red. "I hit the danged fool with Elmer's urn."

■ CHAPTER 22

The deputy with us suppressed a chuckle and relayed the information to the other officers. One officer reappeared around the far corner and disappeared through the window Elsie exited.

An ambulance arrived and then a second. Three of the EMTs disappeared behind the house and one listened to Elsie's heart and pronounced her fine.

The stretcher returned with two EMTs who were ignoring the victim. It was Derrick with a bandage on his head that gave him the appearance of a pirate with a white eyepatch.

"Don't tell him anything. This isn't for print. No comment. You hear that, Malone? No comment!" Derrick was screaming. It was a relief when the EMTs shut the back doors of the ambulance and with a bit more force than was necessary. He was still bellowing, but it was muffled. For once, I was happy to hear the beeping that signaled reverse and the ambulance would soon be gone.

Until Derrick had mentioned it, I hadn't thought about getting any information. Now he had reminded me and Elsie was safe, I pulled my notebook out.

"Ready to get your name in print again?" I asked Elsie. "I think you were quite the hero here, you and Mr. Dobson, that is."

Elsie smiled. "Mr. Dobson always did take care of me."

Another car arrived and it contained a plainclothes detective sergeant. He immediately commandeered the scene and ordered everyone into action. He spotted me and was about to order me to leave when the first deputy on the scene called him over. The detective looked at me and scowled as he heard I was the one who called it in. He didn't like it, but allowed me to stay but had Elsie sit in the front of a patrol car.

She wanted to return to her house but the detective said they needed to do a thorough search and collect evidence.

"You're not going to take Elmer." Elsie started to charge him and I was just able to intercept her before she took a swing at him.

"Elsie, calm down. We'll work something out."

The detective looked confused.

An officer called him into the home. A Michigan State police trooper walked up.

"We are overseeing the investigation on account of the officer-involved shooting."

I nodded and walked over to the first officer on the scene.

"You okay?" Not my usual first question to an officer of the law, but in this case I thought it appropriate since I was the one who put Hank Baldwin in danger. The trooper had followed me.

"You just never know." Hank shook his head trying to puzzle it out.

"Can you tell me what happened?" the trooper asked.

"I was in the back. When I peered in the living room, I saw the suspect with the gun pushing the older woman in front of him down a hall. That's when I called for backup. I tried to see where they went, but couldn't. I didn't want to see her get hurt. I was checking each window as I went by, then Derrick came blundering around the house to me. I heard something in the room on the other side of the window and was trying to motion him to be careful. "Said some lonely old lady lived here and was only seeking attention. That's when the shot came through the window. I think it only grazed him, but it started bleeding and he passed out. I called it in. The pair disappeared from the window while I helped Derrick. I didn't see where they went." He paused and looked at me. I shrugged and he continued.

"I didn't know what to do. I went around the end of the house to see if I could see them in another window. I heard a horrible ding. It was like a thud that rang a couple of times. I know that doesn't make sense."

I smiled and the deputy looked at me.

"What was it?"

"The lonely old lady hitting the bad guy with the urn containing her dead husband's ashes."

The hardened trooper whose eyes were barely visible under the bill of his hat started laughing. It was contagious. The stress, fear and adrenaline melted away as our belly laughs became uncontrollable.

We'd walked around the house as he told the tale and we were back at the front.

The front door opened and two deputies brought out a suspect who also had a white bandage around his head and his arms were cuffed behind him. A gun was in a plastic bag and carried by one of the deputies.

I pulled my camera and snapped a shot. It would be perfect for the top of page one. The suspect seen from behind and in the background, the police cars and ambulance.

I saw the newly-arrived TV crews shout questions and more officers had arrived while we had been behind the house.

As I headed toward the car I saw a pile of yellow, the daffodils on the ground where they had slid off the hood. There was one that still had a stem and wasn't crushed. I picked it up and carried it to the police car.

I handed it to Elsie. "I'm sorry I didn't stop by sooner."

"I know, dear. You had a job to do. Sorry I was so hard on you, but I knew that boy had gotten in the house and was trying to convince himself to hurt me. He was talking to himself in my hall closet. I didn't want him to know I knew. You got the message."

"Why was he here?" Elsie didn't live a lifestyle with cash stuffed in her mattress.

"Said he lost his sugar daddy and didn't want to return to the streets. Was promised a lot of money if he hurt me and made it look like an accident. He kept saying he was sorry, but he had to do it."

Her voice softened. "I felt sorry for him. He was starting to relent when that deputy started talking. He started shaking so bad I think the gun went off by accident. After that he knew he was done. He pushed me in the bedroom and I grabbed Elmer off the dresser and turned, swinging it at his head. He crumpled back into the hall and there were more gunshots. I didn't know who was shooting so I just got out but couldn't pull myself out the window."

"Mitch, here," she stopped and bestowed on me a beautiful smile. "Mitch pulled me to safety." She reached up and cupped my chin.

Other officers converged just off the front porch and the cop joined the others. They were in a football huddle to get all the info everyone had collected before deciding on the next play.

The state police trooper returned. "We'll need statements from both of you but we would like Elsie to get checked by either her physician or at the hospital. Then we'll take her statement."

I agreed to take her and we were allowed to leave. I glanced at the car with the punk locked in the back seat cage. He turned his face away from me. He looked familiar but I figured it was the attitude I recognized and not the face.

I would get more information on him later when I checked in for my story. First was making sure Elsie was not having any heart problems. She directed me to her doctor's office and after explaining the problem, the doctor saw her right away. She was given a clean bill of health and we headed to the sheriff's department to give our statements. The traffic was heavy as I realized it was the nine-to-fivers trying to get out of town for the weekend. Luckily we were headed in the wrong direction to get tangled in their snarls.

My statement didn't take long and I was free to go. I knew Elsie was going to be a while and I had a story to write. I left my number with the desk sergeant to call me when Elsie was ready to go home.

I entered the *Journal* feeling wrung out and went to work getting my story out for the early morning Saturday edition. The story didn't have much attribution except for generic witness accounts and nameless police sources. I felt a little sad as I sent the draft to the editing queue. This was one story Neil would have loved. It would have a huge headline and three column photo of the guy in cuffs. I could almost forgive him for his pink masthead but not for my face on busses. I called up the photo of the suspect from behind again to look at it.

Something was familiar about the guy. What was it? Tall, thin, gawky. Didn't look too old. The boy toy! The kid in the police car looked like the kid I had seen Neil with. That couldn't be. Why?

Was this a random assault or was this part of a bigger spree? Elsie's troubles all started when she'd seen the accident. My phone buzzed on my hip. Elsie was done with her statement. I sent the photo and the story through the electronic lines to the appropriate editors. I shut off my computer. It was still daylight, but I knew Elsie would be exhausted.

As I came into the sheriff's department lobby, I nodded to the desk sergeant. I thought about the last time I talked to Bob Johansen. I needed to talk to him but that could wait. Elsie needed to get home.

Elsie was sitting in a chair beside a desk in the detective bureau. She looked frail. That scared me. She brightened when she saw me.

"Ready to go?"

She nodded.

"Where to?" I asked as we negotiated out of the office and to the lobby.

"Home." She looked down at her hands which shook a bit and she tried to clamp them together.

"You sure?"

Elsie nodded but didn't look at me.

"How about we go to my place?" If she was scared to go home, she could stay with me. She did know how to cook.

"No. I belong at home. It will just be empty without Mr. Dobson there." A tear escaped down her cheek.

We had reached my Jeep and I helped her up into the seat.

"Elsie, look at me." She lifted her head. "Elmer is there."

"No, he's not. They wouldn't let me take him home. He's evidence." She sniffed.

"Elsie, Elmer isn't in the urn. He's here." I pointed to her heart. I was worried about spewing this emotional drivel, but she seemed to be buying it. I kept going.

"He's never left the woman he loved. I think he is just telling you it's time to open your heart to others."

I walked around and got in. Elsie twirled her wedding ring and seemed to make a decision. "Take me home, Mitch." Her voice was strong. She'd made her decision.

I started the car and her hand touched mine as I started to put the car into gear.

"It's good advice, Mitch. Wouldn't hurt you to take it, too."

■ CHAPTER 23

"Hello." My voice was groggy, unrecognizable even to myself.

"Mr. Malone?" The whisper was soft.

"Yes?" I was trying to wake but the pull of sleep was strong. I sat up.

"You have to help me."

"Who is this?" Anger started to creep into my voice. I was waking up, but I wasn't happy.

"Dominique."

The heiress was calling me for help. She had millions and was ensconced in ICU with doctors and nurses waiting on her. Now she was waking me up.

"What's wrong?"

"It's Bertram. I saw him. He's here. I've got to go."

"He can't hurt you there. Hit your call button. Your room is in full view of the nurses' station."

"You got in to see me in full view of the nurses' station and that was during the daylight. At night there is only one nurse."

Good point, but I wasn't going to hold her hand in ICU. "Dominique you've had a head injury. You need to be where there are medical personnel. I don't have any medical training or police training."

"I'm leaving. You help me and I'll give you an exclusive story." Anger tinged her voice. "'Heiress accuses CEO of murder.' How do you like that headline?"

This chick was tough. She knew my weaknesses and was willing to exploit them. I was a professional. It was my job to get the story any way I could.

"If it isn't true, it's libel. I'll need collaboration."

"I'll get you collaboration. Just get me out of here."

"Okay, but it will take me a few minutes. Don't leave your room."

She'd seen Bertram. Was he working with Roger? I wanted to get my hands on either one and wring the truth out of them.

■ ■ ■

I pulled up and parked outside the emergency room entrance, just out of the glow of the main entrance lights. It was a warm evening for a change, but the air was heavy with rain that I'd hope would hold off until my mission here was done. I wasn't happy about picking up an heiress, but it would be a great story.

I slipped in the door as an ambulance pulled up and the doctor and nurses went to meet it. I was in the elevator heading to ICU before I could talk myself out of it. I'd grabbed a pair of old sweats and stuck them in a plastic grocery bag as I left my condo. Anyone in a hospital gown was bound to attract attention.

The doors opened and I glanced each way before stepping out. I took a longer look toward the surgical unit after my last late night visit. It was dark and looked deserted. I hoped Dominique's call was an overactive imagination aggravated by pain killers and antibiotics.

I was tiptoeing down the hall and past the waiting room. It was empty and dark. Had the Albaneses given up the vigil? Had Dominique's odd behavior driven them away for a night of peace and quiet without the noises of doctors' and nurses' rubber-soled shoes? I didn't want to think beyond that. They were home, safe in their beds. I felt my neck begin to cramp from the endless turns to look over my shoulder. I was looking for Bertram or Roger or both around every curve. As I reach the double doors, I looked into the unit and was surprised to see it unnaturally quiet and the nurses' station empty. I pushed through and looked into A. Albanese's room. Dominique's bed was empty.

I pushed to open her door.

"Dominique," I whispered. Where could she have gone? My throat was tight. Was she right and I didn't act fast enough? I heard a creak behind me and my muscles tensed even more. The bathroom door opened slowly, no light escaped from behind.

"Mitch?" Her voice soft, not domineering like the phone call.

"Yes. You scared me to death." I returned her whisper.

"Something squeaked and I got scared and hid in the bathroom."

"Are you okay to stand? Dizzy? Nauseous?" She looked terrible but maybe it was just the muted lights from her equipment that cast a greenish glow.

"No. Just a little headache. Doctors are amazed by my recovery but can't figure out my amnesia." A small smile had her teeth catching the light.

If she was making a joke, she had to be improving. I was looking for anything that could justify my reason for removing her from medical care. "They are moving me to a regular room in the morning. I won't be safe there."

"Here, put these on. Can you manage?" I pushed the plastic grocery bag in her direction.

"Yes, just fine." I moved back into the room into the shadows while she returned to the bathroom to change.

The unit was way too quiet. I understood her paranoia. Where was the staff? No one had returned to the nurses' station. At this rate, getting her out would be a piece of cake.

"Everything alright?" I asked softly.

Silence. The woman was in intensive care and I sent her into the rest room to dress by herself. What was I thinking?

I knocked lightly on the door. Again, nothing. What should I do? I didn't want to be accused of being a peeping Tom, but what if she'd fallen and hit her head? She'd had a brain injury. I was the biggest fool. I was only thinking of the headlines and not the ramifications of my stunt.

I wanted to pull the emergency cord and hightail it out of the room and never return. This was stupid. I was about to bolt when the bathroom door opened.

"Could you help me?" Her face was gaunt in the bright light from the bathroom. That would cast a beacon to a passing nurse.

The sweat pants hung low, barely on her hips the drawstring limp down the front. The gown was still on but the T-shirt was underneath, at least over her head and with her good arm in it. I wasn't sure how much it covered of her torso.

She did have a nice figure, flat stomach and a nice sized chest or maybe that was just the roll made by the T-shirt.

I hesitated, not sure what to do.

"What do I do with the arm in the sling?" Frustration tinged her voice. She was not a girl who was used to asking for help.

I stepped closer. examining her problem as much as I could see with the hospitable gown casting a tent over the situation but providing some modesty.

"How about we leave it under the T-shirt and just let the arm hang empty."

"Can you untie the gown? I couldn't reach the tie in the middle of my back." Again, her voice was tinged with frustration at being unable to perform simple tasks.

I twirled my finger in the universal symbol to turn around. She did have wonderful curves but I had to remember she was only twenty-three—more than a decade younger than me. I pulled the string and with her good hand she pulled the gown forward and she smoothed the T-shirt down over the cast hugged to her stomach. Good thing the T-shirt was large over her slim frame.

The problem was going to be the turban around her head. That was sure to attract some stares and I didn't want to be the object of concern when they started looking for her.

I pulled at the sweatshirt around my own neck thinking. My hoodie. It was perfect. We could pull it up over her bandages. She would look like an ill-shaped gangster. No one would look twice. They would avoid us.

I reached down, crossing my arms and pulled it up. Luckily I'd left my T-shirt on in the rush to get dressed. I rolled up the gown and put it in the bag the clothes came in. I took out the regular sweatshirt I brought for her and slipped it on.

"How about we put the hoodie on to cover your bandages?"

"Great idea." She smiled. Her face was classic beauty with high cheek bones and perfect teeth even in the dim light that masked the fading bruises.

I motioned her to sit on the bed so I could stretch the neck hole and hood as far as possible. I didn't want to bang any incisions or bruises.

Again the left arm was hanging empty. Overall, not bad. The oversized garments hid a wealth of curves. Dominique was tall and could easily pass for a reed-thin thug. I grabbed the empty sleeve and tucked it into the center front pocket.

Dominique moved her other hand into the pocket. It wouldn't pass a close inspection but I was hoping we wouldn't have any.

"Ready?"

She nodded. I glanced at the nurses' station and it was still empty. I opened the door and looked the other way toward the double doors. All was quiet. Too quiet. I couldn't shake the concern that created.

I looked back and spotted the empty bed. That wouldn't do. I motioned her to stop. I went back and glanced around. On a chair tucked in the corner of the room lay another pillow and a blanket as well as additional bandages on a wheeled cart labeled ICU 1.

I grabbed my supplies and placed the second pillow perpendicular to the pillow in the bed. I rolled the blanket and placed it at the end of the pillow. I pulled up the covers. I unfurled the bandages next and loosely wrapped them around each other and placed them on the pillow. I pulled the sheet up a bit farther and bunched it over most of the bandages. It, too, wouldn't pass a close inspection, but might buy us some time if the nurse returned any time soon.

I turned back, ready to leave.

"Nice."

I liked her soft voice and appreciation.

We slipped out the door and through the double doors of ICU. Nothing stirred. I debated about using the stairs but wasn't sure how much energy she would have. I opted for the elevator. I motioned her to the dark alcove by the stairs where I had watched the CEO a week ago.

I punched the elevator down button and waited.

It seemed like an eternity. The bell signaling the elevator's arrival sounded like an alarm in the quiet. When the doors parted, I held them open and signaled to Dominique to slip in.

I hit one.

While waiting for the elevator to close, I heard the whoosh from the surgical wing doors open, a whisper on the silent floor. Then another that caused a shiver to run down my spine.

Squeak.

■ CHAPTER 24

The doors closed. I didn't see who made the noise but only an idiot would wear the same squeaky shoes if they were intent on murder or mayhem. The elevator quickly stopped at the first floor and slid open. I stepped, out looking in both directions and motioned Dominique to follow me.

We walked side by side, her head bent, hiding her facial features behind the hood. The hall was brightly lit but empty. We approached the doors to the emergency room and the hall to the front entrance and waiting room.

I heard a siren in the distance and couldn't believe our luck. We could sneak out the emergency room exit without much notice just after the ambulance arrived. It sounded serious with the siren blaring so close to the hospital in the late hour.

I slowed and Dominique matched my pace without pause. I pushed the door open and saw the bright red flash from the brake lights of the backing ambulance. The siren and lights had been stopped.

I pushed the door open farther and we moved through it. We kept to the left around the nurses' desk toward the waiting ambulance. A doctor and nurse waited and when the backup beep signal stopped, they had the doors open.

Dominique and I moved as one as we slipped through the open sliders while the medical professionals saw to their new patient.

As we got closer to my Jeep, Dominique's step faltered. He face was pasty and I realized that the exertion was too much for the frame battered by the accident.

I slowed and wrapped my arm around her torso. She looked up.

"You okay?"

"Yes, just tired."

"We're almost to my car." I dug the keys out with my free hand and hit the unlock button as I negotiated our way to the passenger door. I opened it and helped her step up and inside, then shut the door.

After I got in and started the car, I let out a long breath. I was tired too from the early morning hour and the adrenaline seeping from my system. I started the car and backed out of the parking spot.

"Where to?"

I glanced over at my companion. Her head was against the back of the seat and her eyes were closed. Her face was still white in the on and off flood of light from the parking lot lamps.

"Any suggestions?" Her voice was barely audible.

"What about home or a friend's house?"

"Home would be the first place they would look and my only friend is now dead."

I wanted to dump her at the nearest hotel but was worried about her. Could she die if left unattended? I didn't know and I didn't want to risk it. I made a quick turn, went a few blocks and pulled into the underground parking ramp of my condo.

Dominique turned her head slowly and looked at me.

"My place."

She nodded and her eyes closed again. I didn't want her to fall asleep so I told her about my pad.

"It used to be the local YMCA that was converted to condos when a new one was needed. My place used to be a racquet ball court with the original wood floors."

I pulled into the visitor spot closest to the elevator. Killing the engine, I turned to my passenger. "Can you make it to the elevator? We'll be there in just a few minutes and then you can rest."

■ ■ ■

In an instant, I knew something was wrong. I didn't know what. I glanced around at my living room. It was my own joke that there was nothing great about my living room, but it was mine. I couldn't stop to dwell on my lack of decorating sense now. I needed to do something. I needed to find something. I was groggy from sleep and as I sat up, I stretched feeling a sharp ache in my neck and dull pains in the small of my back from the hours spent sleeping on my couch.

It came to me slowly. The late night rescue of the heiress princess. I stumbled over my shoes next to the couch in my haste to reach the bedroom. She was gone. I stared at the bedcovers thrown back against the other side of the California king bed. The only trace I saw was a slight indention where she had laid.

Not only was I stupid for giving up my bedroom for the chick who had nearly died only days earlier, but she had ditched me at the first opportunity. I slowed my thoughts, trying to bring logic and my observation skills together.

Daylight began to seep around the edges of the room-darkening shades I had drawn to allow my guest to sleep through the morning. Fat lot of good that had done. I walked over and felt the bed. It was still slightly warm. She hadn't been gone a long time but probably long enough.

I walked to the window and pulled the covering toward me to peep outside. It was later than I thought with the gray skies. The city was still quiet and traffic was light. I glanced up and down the street and saw nothing moving on the sidewalk. The street, glazed with moisture from some evening showers, was empty. Nothing moved, not even a rat.

My rat. Had she feigned exhaustion the night before to lull me into a false sense of security? How could she go from barely escaping the ICU to escaping from me—all within six hours? Had she played me and conned the hospital staff into thinking she was injured more than she was? I replayed the escape in my mind.

I would bet that her stiffening, frequent position changes and discomfort were real. Could she have been forcibly taken? I left the bedroom and walked to my front door. The deadbolt wasn't locked. I opened the door and didn't see any sign of forced entry. I damned my attention to detail in keeping the door well oiled and silent to keep the old lady across the hall from knowing of my comings and goings. The old bat made it perfectly clear I was unacceptable when we met in the elevator during my mid-afternoon grocery runs when I had only just crawled out of bed or when I was wearing my Homer Simpson lounging pants to carry my trash to the dumpster. I didn't operate on a nine-to-five schedule and she didn't approve.

I couldn't think about that old busy body and her hobbies. I had an heiress to find. Where would I go if somebody wanted to kill me? Damn, Dominique hadn't talked. I thought I would have plenty of time to get the details for my story. I still hadn't even printed that she wasn't Ashley.

What had she talked about the night before? Did she give me any clues? What was it about women, particularly damsels in distress that had me forgetting my skills? Think, Man. You have to find her.

But did I? I could print my story. I knew who she was. What was the worst thing that could happen?

Her killers would know she was alive instead of just suspecting and had the resources to mount an all out search. Then she would be dead. I had a responsibility to my paper but I also had a responsibility not to put someone in danger. I couldn't blow the whistle until Dominique was safe.

While I tormented myself for my heavy sleep and stupidity, I quickly threw on jeans and a navy hooded sweatshirt with Michigan emblazed in maize across the front. It wasn't my school but they did have a football team.

I grabbed my jacket, keys, notebook with pen and wallet and headed out. I didn't know where to begin to look. Dominique's only close friend had been killed in the accident meant for her. The gray sky was lightening, but still overcast.

I marveled as I drove the streets that there weren't more people around. Then it dawned on me. It was Sunday. Most people were enjoying the warmth of their beds a little longer today. Others were getting ready for church.

Church. Dominique never mentioned it but it oozed from the Albanese family. Their Catholic faith was a way of life and I would bet money that Mrs. Albanese went to church every day. Where did they say they went? It would be a neighborhood church, one Mrs. Albanese could walk to. What church was near them? I tried to think and knew it was useless. I had given up on churches a long time ago and ignored their existence. I pulled over to the side of the road and grabbed the phone book I kept in my car. I flipped to the yellow pages under C and looked at the hundreds of entries. What did I expect? Grand River had a church on nearly every corner from Buddhist temples to Islamic mosques, Jehovah's Witnesses to Baptists. For Christ's sake, the Christian Reformed Church was based here for the large Dutch population. Luckily, the phonebook also listed the churches by denomination and I scanned the list of Catholic churches. St. Bonaventure. That had to be it. It was only three blocks from the Albanese house. Would Dominique seek refuge in a church?

I saw a lone taxi cruise down the street and knew how she had gotten wherever she was going. My street was part of an easy loop that made it past every major downtown hotel and event venue.

I didn't have any answers and I didn't have anywhere else to look. I steered in that direction. It was about a half hour before the ten o'clock mass listed in the yellow pages ad, but several older ladies where making their way in to say their prayers before church. I parked my Jeep. I hadn't been to church in more years than I could remember. I kind of half thought that maybe God would strike me down but I rationalized I was here for a story, not for myself. This was strictly business.

As I crossed through the entrance headed for the sanctuary, I automatically dipped my finger in the holy water and crossed myself. Some habits die hard. I slid into the last bench and scanned the surroundings. There were about twenty women scattered around the cavernous sanctuary. St. Bonaventure's was an old church with large grey stone walls and arches holding up the ceiling at least two stories high. It could comfortably seat five hundred people. I guessed that it rarely was filled to capacity these days.

No one even looked remotely like Dominique or even within several decades of her age. This had been a long shot. I would wait a few more minutes but I was not staying for church. I scanned people for Dominique sightings as they walked in but was out of luck.

The church was beginning to look half full and the music was starting. I needed to leave. I stood and took one last look around. I spotted an alcove built under an arch on the right side of the church just before the altar area. The statue of the Virgin Mary with her arms outstretched caught my attention. Underneath the statute was a rack of red votive candles with a half dozen of them lit. Below that was a small figure with a hooded sweatshirt up over her head that was bowed in prayer, kneeling on a small stand for just that purpose.

It was Dominique. I recognized my sweatshirt. I moved down the aisle in her direction and kneeled beside her. She didn't acknowledge my presence. Her head stayed bowed. As the last of the prelude echoed and faded, she crossed herself and rose pushing hard on the railing to raise herself with her good arm. I could see the color fade from her face even with the red cast from the flickering candles.

I rose and grabbed her elbow, startling her. She looked up with such fear, my anger at her disappearance vaporized. She was deeply into her prayers and, luckily, I had found her. She moved toward a side door that I hadn't noticed and we slipped through it just as the congregation rose for the opening hymn.

"How did you find me?" Dominique whispered, still holding the sanctity of the church even though no one could hear us now.

"A good reporter can find anyone." I leaned in close to her ear. "Why did you leave?"

"I needed to pray for Ashley. I killed her and the least I could do is see that her soul gets out of purgatory and into heaven." Tears started to stream down her face, the guilt, exhaustion and fear since the accident were coming to a head.

"Let's get out of here." I grabbed her arm and steered her toward the Jeep.

As I crossed around the front to get inside I quickly scanned the parking lot. If I could find her, maybe others could, too. I didn't see any black sedans with tinted windows so I hoped we would be safe. I wasn't taking any chances though. I took the long way back to my apartment and doubled back a couple of times making sure we weren't followed.

Dominique never noticed. She blotted her tears with the sleeve, my sleeve of the white sweatshirt she had nicked from my drawer before leaving. She also was wearing a pair of my navy sweats. Damn, they looked good on her young frame.

Breakfast. We needed sustenance. I pulled into the drive-thru of a Dunkin' Donuts as we neared the downtown close to my apartment. I would have liked to have gone to my favorite haunt, Donna's

Doughnuts, but was afraid Dominique would take off when I went in. I also didn't want anyone to see Dominique. Someone might recognize her and the jig would be up.

I pulled to the drive-thru window and Dominique wasn't paying any attention so I ordered a dozen mixed doughnuts and a couple of chocolate milks.

Within minutes, we had the doughnuts and were pulling into my underground garage. I assisted Dominique out and she leaned heavily on my arm as she awkwardly got out. Her caper around the city of Grand River hadn't done much for her injuries. I told myself to keep a grip on things, I had information to get for a story. As we approached the elevator, it dinged, signaling the car was at our floor. I pulled the hood up over more of Dominique's face to hide her identity and stood blocking the entrance.

What rotten luck. My nosy neighbor was inside when the doors slid open. On her way to church, if I hadn't missed my guess. It was the only time that the garish pink hue of lipstick covered her lips.

I nodded in her direction and watched her try to see around me. I shielded her view of Dominique with the Dunkin' Donuts bag and just smiled and nodded like nothing was out of the ordinary. Courtesy said she had to get out of the elevator, which she did. I turned to guide Dominique continuing to block the disapproving old lady's view.

"Well, I never. What kind of people do we have living here, can't even make a simple introduction." My neighbor's tirade was cut off as the doors slid blessedly shut.

"Nice lady. Approves of you, I see." The blue eyes sparkled with humor and what I thought was an apology.

"You can't win them all." I punched the button for the third floor and waited impatiently to arrive at my condo so I could start grilling Dominique.

As we stepped from the elevator, she shook off my arm and straightened her back. She was getting a little of her spirit back, I was glad to see. I unlocked my door and retreated, allowing her to enter first. She went right to the couch and gingerly fell into its soft depths, closing her eyes.

"Here, let's get something into you." I opened the bag and held it out so she could have first choice. She picked a cake doughnut with chocolate frosting and took a bite.

I went to the kitchen and returned with two glasses and poured the chocolate milk into each.

"Here, you need to get some protein in your system along with the sugar. We don't want you to get dehydrated."

She drank half the glass and set it down with a small brown mustache above her lip.

I handed her a napkin and pointed to her lip. The mustache disappeared and she continued eating the doughnut and chased it with the rest of the milk sans mustache. I held the bag out to her again but she shook her head.

She looked whipped, but I wanted answers and couldn't take the chance she would bolt again.

"Why did you leave?"

"I realized it was Sunday and no one had prayed for Ashley's soul. There hasn't been a funeral or anything. She needs to be able to rest in peace with a decent burial with her own name."

It made sense. "Why didn't you ask? I would have taken you."

"It was something I had to do. Ashley deserved more."

The silence hung in the air. It was time to get everything out in the open. I pulled my notebook and pen out.

"I think it's time you gave me that interview, Ms. Pewter."

She dropped her head to her chest letting her blonde hair not shaved for her bandages cover her features for a moment. She raised it and I could see the resignation in her eyes. She looked defeated again, but I couldn't let that stop me. I had a story to get, a responsibility to the newspaper and I needed to figure out what was going on.

"I wanted to go into the family business. That was my first mistake. The furniture company is all that I have left of my parents. My objective was to get my education and take over." She looked at me to see if I understood. Dominique was apparently satisfied that I did when our eyes connected, while I scribbled down her words to be used as a quote later. This was going to be a good interview. I could feel it.

I looked up at her. I wanted to remember her expression to add to the story. "What do you remember from the accident?"

I could see the pain in her eyes. She took a deep breath, then winced at the pain from her bruised ribs that hadn't healed.

"I had just bought the car. We were celebrating. I remember the flowers, the tulips. They're my favorite. They were so pretty, bright reds, pure whites. That was the first thing I noticed when I left this morning. The tulips were all stems, the petals lying on the ground, knocked off by the rain."

I didn't want pithy quotes about flowers. I wanted facts about the carnage.

"Do you remember the accident?" I knew some people block out any details of a traumatic experience. They can remember the rest of the day but nothing surrounding the accident.

"I wanted to share the fun. I finally convinced Ashley to drive. I never should have done that. If I had been behind the wheel, then an innocent wouldn't have been killed."

"You don't know that. You can't beat yourself up over a decision like that. Save your recriminations for the people who caused the accident. What did cause the accident?" I certainly hoped she wasn't going to say Ashley's bad driving. The interview would be in the toilet then.

"The bastard did it." The hate, anger and betrayal dripped from her voice belying her fragile exterior and bandaged head.

"Who?" I was sounding like an owl. I was expecting her to say the CEO, who I had seen sneaking around at the hospital.

"Roger, that rat."

"Roger Frasier?" The man I had seen with Neil.

"Yes, Roger. Mr. Yes Man. 'I'll take care of it.' Well this time he didn't take care of it, he failed. And he is going to pay."

"What about Bertram? Was Roger doing it on his orders?" I was losing this interview fast. She wasn't even answering my questions.

"Roger Frasier, the former vice president." Dominique placed heavy emphasis on the word former.

Roger had met with Neil and argued. If he could have set up the accident, how hard would it be to have killed Neil? What about Trace, too? "What did Roger do?"

"He pushed us into the intersection. Ashley certainly didn't pull out in front of that truck. She was the most conservative driver ever. She always looked both ways a half dozen times before she even considered pulling out."

At least that confirmed one of my suspicions. "You were pushed into the intersection, you didn't pull out?" I scribbled that down on my pad. Collaboration for my story.

I could see she was losing patience with me.

"Let me get this, Roger Frasier just happened upon you at the stop sign and just happened to push you in front of the cement truck?"

"Didn't I just say that?"

"Not really, no. Why?"

"So the CEO can steal more of my inheritance. When I was home for spring break, I audited the company books for one of my business classes. I didn't tell anyone I was doing it. Somehow he found out I knew that money was disappearing. I was going to get rid of him as soon as I had my feet wet at the company. He made sure my feet got wet all right but it was with my friend's blood." Her eyes were a cold steel blue. No one would mistake this blonde for an airhead.

"How did he know where you would be?"

"I told him. I didn't think anything about it. After I picked up my car, I dropped by the Herman Steel corporate office. Seth Lynch asked me to drop off some papers to Bertram Switzer. I was happy to go in my new wheels and wanted to see what my office looked like. I was having it redecorated."

I could see she was thinking back. "I didn't see Roger when I was there, but I dropped the papers off and looked in on my office. It was nearly completed. It was being cleaned before the carpet was installed that afternoon."

"Did you see anyone following you?" I leaned in closer to watch her expression.

"No, but he had to have been. I left there and went and picked up Ashley. I was only at their house for maybe ten minutes and we took off. We drove around for a half hour talking about what we wanted to do this summer. Ashley was telling me about a job interview she just had. I wanted to hire her at Herman but she wouldn't hear anything of it. Said she wanted to get a job on her own and then no one could say anything and she wouldn't be beholden to anyone."

Tears started again down her cheeks. "She's not beholden to anyone but God now. That's my fault. How can I ever face her mother? She doesn't even know Ashley is dead yet. If she did she would be at church praying the rosary over and over. God would have to let Ashley into heaven or he would be inundated with Hail Marys. You've never seen Angela Albanese when she is unhappy with one of her children. She grabs her shawl and heads right to church. She prays at the church and doesn't come home to cook or clean until that child has seen the error of his ways. How can I face her?" The tears turned into sobs.

I looked down at my notebook and I had written nothing but Roger on it along with some doodles.

■ CHAPTER 25

My cell phone vibrated on my hip. "Malone."

"Are you watching TV? It's all over. They just broke into the Tiger's game for a special bulletin. You need to get in here and start pounding out some copy. This is big. The network people will be all over this and you better make the *Journal* look good, you hear me Mitch?"

I heard the weekend editor loud and clear and just didn't know what he was talking about. I did know he would be vying for Neil's open slot, now that he was dead. I wasn't ready for the real world to intrude on my exclusive sitting on my couch but I could cover something else if it didn't take too long.

"What is it?"

"That chick in the car that killed that furniture heiress. She's gone missing from the hospital. No one knows where she is. They came in to take blood and found her gone."

"Got it. I'll get right on it."

"What's wrong?" said the object of the current mega story.

"You are. The hospital didn't keep your disappearance a secret. You are breaking news on all four networks. That was my boss. He wants me to get to work and scoop the TV crews."

"You can't print that I'm alive." She grabbed my arm to keep me from leaving.

"I have to print something. Let me go down to the hospital and poke around. See who sounded the alarm. Make sure no one saw us leaving."

"You aren't going to tell them where I am?"

"You're not going to go running across the city, are you?"

She dropped her gaze, hiding the shame I suspected was in her eyes. The doorbell rang. I looked around and then met Dominique's eyes. "I didn't call anyone." She was scared.

It rang again and I looked through the peephole. Mrs. Dobson was on the other side. I motioned for Dominique to go in the bedroom and shut the door. I should have pretended that no one was home but she had cookies on a plate and they looked good.

"Mr. Malone, I know you are in there. Your neighbor said you came home not too long ago. Open the door." I could hear the determination in her voice.

I double checked the living room making sure no sign of Dominique was visible.

I opened the door, pretending to rub sleep out of my eyes.

"Hi, Mrs. Dobson. Shouldn't you be resting?"

"It's Elsie and I had to do something. I can't sit around my house all day thinking about yesterday, especially with the news that that poor girl from the accident is now missing. Do you think something bad happened to her like that guy who tried to kill me?" She thrust the plate of cookies into my midsection, pushed by me into the apartment and started to pace.

"Elsie, this worrying isn't good for your heart. I don't have time today to take you back to the emergency room."

"But what happened to her? I should have told someone sooner. I should have made that stupid deputy see reason. Could someone have hurt her?" She was wringing her hands.

"Sit down. I'm sure she is fine. This has nothing to do with you." I crossed my fingers for telling a lie.

"Don't try to patronize me. Mr. Dobson always said I could tell a lie a mile away and you aren't being truthful with me."

Back to Mr. Dobson. If she was spouting his words, she couldn't be too worked up. Either that or planning on joining him real soon.

"Could you just sit a minute and calm down." I was beginning to get just a little testy but an idea had formed in my mind.

Else did as she was told and sat on my couch. I set the cookies on an end table next to the couch. I sat beside her.

"I'm sure the girl from the hospital is okay. No one has hurt her yet.

She is being taken care of."

"How do you know that?" She had that look in her eye that dared you to tell a lie.

"I know that because I helped her get out of the hospital to protect her."

I saw Dominique's head peak out of the bedroom and I motioned for her to come in.

"Oh, my goodness. You're the dead girl." Mrs. Dobson had gone white from shock. Dominique sped up her pace.

"I'm going to be okay. Please don't worry anymore." I saw the color return to Elsie's face.

She reached over and grabbed the plate she had brought. "Have a cookie, dear. It looks like you could use it."

Dominique did and I cleared my throat. "Take another." I reached over and grabbed a cookie before they were all gone. These were mine and she was giving them away. The cookies were still warm from the oven and chocolate chip. Almost better than a doughnut.

"I'll tell you what. I have to go check out the story about her disappearance," I said pointing at Dominique. "How about you two stay here and keep each other company and watch over each other." I explained to Dominique about Elsie's rapid heart omitting the part about the break-in.

I grabbed my notebook and pen off the table, and my jacket off the back of the couch where I had thrown it after we came in.

"Lock the door and use the chain when I leave." Dominique rose and walked me to the door. In a lower voice for her ears only I said: "Let me check in with my sources and see what's going on. When I get back we can compare notes. You can tell me why Roger pushed you into the intersection and I will see what the police know about where you've gone."

■ ■ ■

I drove to the police station trying to clear my head and pretend I was an objective observer, only gathering the facts. How had I immersed myself into an active police case? Depending on what they had to say, I could be harboring a fugitive.

A cold wind was blowing out the earlier rain, belying it was spring. I pulled up my jacket collar to keep the wind from my face. I quickly swung open the main entrance to the downtown police station and sauntered in. I nodded to the desk sergeant and cocked my head toward a door to his left that reached the inner sanctum of the department.

He nodded and I heard the click of the lock being released just before I turned the knob. As I entered the hallway, yellowed with age and lit by fluorescents, I pondered who to look up for information. The homicide department didn't seem right, nor did burglary or sexual assault task force. I kept going down the hall, discounting door after door. I was nearly to the end with no better answer of who to ask for details when a couple entered the far end of the hallway escorted by a uniformed officer. I wanted to jump into the nearest room and shut the door before they got closer.

The problem was they were the answer to what was going on. I wasn't sure I could look Anthony and Angela Albanese in the face, knowing their daughter was dead and not just missing from the hospital.

"Mr. Malone, isn't it?"

"Yes, ma'am. What's this I hear about your daughter missing from the hospital?"

"She's gone. Do you know where she could have gone? I just don't understand it. They said she might not act normally. That was to be expected from the head injury, but to leave the hospital and not even come home. I can't believe it."

I wanted to unburden myself to her but couldn't.

"How did she get out?"

"No one knows. The security cameras were down for maintenance when she apparently left or something." The officer tried to encourage them to keep going but Mrs. Albanese wasn't having any of it.

I should have remembered the security cameras. I'd have to check on it or was that just a line by the police until they caught the guy, namely me.

"They told us to go home and get some rest. She was out of danger and being moved to a regular room. We would never have left her alone if we thought something like this was going to happen. We got back to her room right after I went to early morning Mass. She wasn't there. I thought maybe they'd taken her for tests but no one knew. No one knows what happened. I don't know how that could happen."

I couldn't respond. I had most of the answers I needed. Mr. Albanese enveloped the small woman into his large bulky frame and moved her down the hall. I watched their backs retreating until the officer opened the door to the lobby and they disappeared. I knew I should move on, but I just stood there having a war with my conscience. Do I call them back and confess that I helped spirit away the girl they thought was their daughter and in reality, their daughter was dead? The parents would go from missing a daughter to planning a funeral.

Speaking of funerals, what was up with the funeral for Dominique? You would think someone would be planning that. Maybe I should make some calls and start asking for details and see what pops. By now the cop was abreast and nodded and continued down the hall. I turned and followed him. I still wanted to get some information from an official source, not just a confused mother.

The officer went into a bullpen area where uniformed officers who didn't have cubicles did their reports. I saw a sergeant I knew and sauntered in his direction.

"Hey, Mitch, how's life in the tabloids?" He laughed at his own lame joke.

"Not bad, Kevin. How's life pounding a beat?"

"Good one." He looked back down at his fingers on the keyboard going back to his report.

"Whaddya know about that missing patient, Kevin?"

He looked up at me and glanced around the room and noted there were only a couple other cops and they weren't paying any attention to us.

"I hear there might be a problem with the identification. The lab boys were on their way to see her and get a DNA sample to test when she went up missing. I think someone tipped her off and she fled."

"Who do they think she is?"

"Don't know. I just heard a bit of scuttlebutt about it." I was dismissed as he went back to his report.

"One more thing, Kevin. Who's handling the case of her identity and disappearance?"

"Bob Johansen from the sheriff's department. Don't that beat it. He never does anything but crashes, but is handling this one personally. Now, I got to get this done before my shift is over. They're clamping down on overtime for reports. Nice to see you, Mitch."

"Thanks, Kevin." I turned and left the room. I had a mission now. Bob had been ducking my calls for a couple of days. Time to track him down.

■ CHAPTER 26

I went to the sheriff's department and was able to get in the side door as a deputy left. I pushed through a fire door and went down a flight of steps. Bob's office was located in the bowels of the basement. On the other side of the building, it opened to the street level and was a garage for working on the cruisers and other police vehicles. Most of this half was storage, evidence and Bob's office.

His door was propped open with a closed folding chair jammed up under the knob. I stuck my head in and Bob was hunched over, staring intently at his screen. He moved the mouse a bit and looked at the data again, frowning. His PC was old with the screen as deep as it was wide taking up half of the desk space.

"Anything good?"

Bob jumped in his seat and nearly sent his keyboard flying when his stomach hit the pulled-out shelf.

"Ah, Mitch. Been meaning to call you."

"Sure Bob, no problem. Was here for something else and thought I would look you up. Want to grab a cup of coffee, my treat?"

"I'd love to but I've got to get this done. Don't let me keep you."

He was back engrossed in his screen. I'd worked with Bob before and knew this wasn't a snub. He was just single-minded in his determination when it came to his cases.

I liked that about him. I sat and waited a few minutes while he worked. After about ten minutes he paused and stretched, rotating his head. He stopped when he spotted me.

"That offer of coffee is still open."

"Thanks, Mitch. I'd appreciate it. Seems I worked through my lunch."

"Need another set of eyes?"

Bob stared at me for a minute. I could see he was making up his mind about something.

"I can't figure out this car crash and now the only witness is up and missing. The more I look at it, the more I think it has to be more than an accident."

"How so?"

"I can't get the simulator to agree on what happened. There are a couple of variables that just don't fit." He scratched his nearly bald head.

"Can I help?" I had done a story a year or two back on his program after it arrived. We had spent a fun afternoon playing around with all features, so I knew how it worked. Basically, it was a big expensive video game that could be used in court.

"Sure, can't hurt."

Bob stood, stretched to either side then moved around his desk. He held out his arm in invitation and I jumped around the desk and into his vacated chair.

The rough details of the intersection were on the screen of the Mapscenes software program. It was basically a computer-aided drawing of an intersection where you punched in known variables and it supplied missing details such as car speed at impact.

Bob was a good crash investigator and I knew he wouldn't be able to let this one rest until he made sense out of it.

He had all the variables but the one I had tried to give him for days—the second car ramming the first. I quickly added the details and as Bob watched over my shoulder.

"You know the victim from this accident is missing?"

I looked over my shoulder at Bob. He didn't ask random questions, ever. I had to be careful.

"I'd heard that. Any idea where she went?" I turned back to the screen adding details about the car and my guesstimate at its miles per hour when it connected with the back of the little red sports car. I was avoiding eye contact with Bob.

"Nope, just vanished. Word is somebody tinkered with the camera system." Bob was studying me intently. I was trying not to sweat.

"Really?" I wished I had thought about doing that. Just proves there was somebody after Dominique and I needed to keep her whereabouts a secret. I didn't like lying, but couldn't see any way around it. If it was the CEO who sent his lackey the first time, he had some pretty deep pockets to fund it—Dominique's money.

I finished adding the information and clicked on the "re-enact" button, and watched the three vehicles move of their own accord. At the end, probabilities came up along with other potential variables.

I could feel Bob leaning in closer over my shoulder, his breath wheezing out. I was sweating but it wasn't from the heat. I didn't want any more questions about how the heiress had gone missing. Did Bob know the dead girl wasn't the heiress? I wanted to probe gently about that. From what the officer had said, I believed he did, but he wasn't sharing it for some reason.

"I'll be damned." The voice was a whisper in my ear.

Bob straightened and grabbed a file off his desk, flipping through the pages until he found the one he was looking for. "If that car was black, that would explain the paint on the back of the red sports car that didn't make sense. What I can't figure out is why there weren't any brake marks at the stop sign."

He shuffled through some more papers. "You put a small resistance factor in for the impact, like a pinball being shot out of the gate, and in this case, the car shooting out in front of the truck," I explained.

"Yes, but what about the lack of brake marks?" Bob asked.

"I'm getting to that. Did you get the report back yet on what the fluid was that I slipped on?"

"Not yet. That was sure a good laugh." He chuckled again as he thought about it.

I cringed. Bob reached over and picked up the phone.

"Fred? Bob here. I sent over a sample a week or so ago from the Pewter accident at Lake Drive and Vista Point. Do you have that analyzed yet?" There was a pause in the conversation and I could hear the voice on the other end but couldn't make out the words.

"It was, huh? Okay. Could you get me the paper on that as soon as possible? Yup, it's going to get complicated in a hurry. Thanks, Fred." Bob hung up the phone and turned back to the screen.

I could see I was in the way, so I stood, going around the back side of the chair. Bob entered the seat from the desk side. He quickly took my place and started adding in other variables to the program with quick efficiency. Some was information about the dark sedan such as body style and weight.

Bob's fingers were moving fast and I couldn't see what he was changing. I waited impatiently and finally he hit the "re-enact." Everything moved easily in what appeared to be slow motion. Afterward, the probability came out at ninety percent.

Bob leaned back in his chair and smiled. "Gotcha."

I gulped. Did he know I had the heiress?

Bob wasn't looking at me, though. "I got you this time. You bastard."

I couldn't wait, I had to ask. "Got who?"

Bob started and turned toward me. "Sorry, Mitch, but I gotta keep this under wraps until I have just a bit more evidence."

He didn't trust me after I gave him the piece that helped him figure it out? That wasn't fair. "Bob, just tell me one thing. What did the report say? You owe me at least that much. I found the substance, if you will remember. I'll keep it off the record." I knew I was pleading, but I wanted to know.

Bob looked at me, and then back at the screen. I stepped back from behind the desk and took a visitor's chair in front of it to give him time to think. I wasn't in a hurry.

My cell phone vibrated on my hip and I knew it was the weekend editor trying to plan Monday morning's newspaper. I had plenty of time yet and he could just wait.

I could see Bob mentally wrestling with his dilemma. I watched, not saying anything.

"Brake fluid. And you didn't hear it from me. Now I've got work to do." He swiveled back on his chair to the screen and started playing with more variables.

"I know who rammed the car." I let the statement fall in the silence of the room. Bob's hand stilled, poised over the keyboard. The silence stretched.

"Will it hold up in court?"

"Yes. An eyewitness."

"Not Elsie Dobson. She is a good witness but her identification of a suspect wouldn't hold up in court from that long of a distance. She is 83."

"No, not Elsie Dobson." If he only knew that Elsie was babysitting the real witness.

"Who?"

"Sorry, Bob, but I just gotta keep some things under wraps," I parroted and I couldn't help the smirk that crossed my face.

Bob smiled back. He enjoyed a good game of chess and didn't take offense like some cops.

"What are your terms?" He left the screen and clasped his hands together, resting them on the desk blotter.

"What are you offering?" I leaned back in the chair, ready for a long negotiation.

"An exclusive when we are ready to announce." I could see Bob was happy with his offer.

"I already have my exclusive and on my timetable." I tried not to sound smug but I knew about the car, the laying in wait, what Elsie saw, and the *coup-de-gras* being the mistaken identity.

"Mitch you have been a part of this investigation and I know you won't do anything to jeopardize it. That's not your style."

I nodded in agreement. Waiting. I wasn't interested in printing too much yet, but I wanted information to help the heiress. Sometimes the best skill in the reporter's arsenal was silence, making sources fill the void.

"Off the record. I think whoever caused the accident also caused the accident that killed the dead girl's parents. I've quietly reopened that case and there are similarities."

I leaned forward. He had shocked me. So Dominique's parents' accident wasn't a mistake. That might help get more cooperation out of the heiress if we could solve her parent's death, too.

"Okay. I can work with that." I started to rise.

"Who is the eyewitness?"

I had my information and I needed to give him something. That's how the information highway worked. I didn't want to tip my entire hand. I wasn't sure Bob could keep a lid on it if he knew Dominique was alive. I needed to give him enough to make the assumption without too much that he would have to launch an official investigation. I knew he suspected the mistaken identities.

"How about the dead girl?"

"Seriously, Mitch, who?"

I said nothing but looked at him, arching one eyebrow.

He arched an eyebrow in return.

"Are we in agreement?" I asked.

Bob hesitated.

"Can you give me any more?" His color was beginning to turn red and he rose out of his chair. I didn't want to lose a good source but I had to protect Dominique.

"If I told you, word would leak out. The person wouldn't be safe. Let's meet tomorrow. You'll have time to check with your sources and I will have time to check with mine. Say two o'clock, Lookout Park."

I kept looking Bob in the eyes, he nodded slightly. He sat back down. I held out my hand and Bob shook it quickly.

"I promise to bring your witness with me tomorrow to give you more information to fill in the gaps. I just have to convince the dead that it's time to start living again. That will be difficult, but manageable for an old smooth talker like me." Bob smiled and I laughed with him.

■ CHAPTER 27

As I drove out of the sheriff's department lot, I contemplated what to print. I wasn't ready to announce that Ashley Albanese was killed and that Dominique Pewter was alive. I also didn't want the Albaneses to find out their daughter was dead from my news story. I wanted that to come from the police.

My next story should focus on Ashley Albanese's disappearance and motives. I reached Michigan Avenue and instead of heading toward the paper I turned in the opposite direction to the hospital.

As I drove I planned my story. The hospital's angle would only be a paper statement. I would add to that a couple of quotes from Mrs. Albanese from the police station, a recap of the accident and I should be done. Then I could return to my apartment and begin doing a full court press for a more satisfactory interview with my little heiress, then major headlines for Tuesday.

Pleased with my plan, I entered the hospital through the main entrance's automatic sliding door. I walked to the elevator bank and hit two to go to the second floor. The hospital always had a designated person to give the media conditions on victims twenty-four hours a day. Unless it was the early morning hours when a lead nurse would give the information, the public relations person on duty would be in the administrative offices by the elevator.

I knocked on the door and pushed it open. My favorite public information officer sat behind the desk. "I'm not going on camera. I would be happy to read the statement to you." There was a pause. "No. Sorry." She hung up the phone.

Patrice was the newest of the staff who hadn't been jaded by the media hounds on the trail of death and destruction. I wondered if this fray would change her open demeanor. She was petite, barely hitting the five-foot mark, with dark, curly hair that framed her face. Her brown eyes looked like a deer before you've caught them in the headlights, still soft and expressive.

"Hi Patrice. Got that apartment decorated yet?"

"I'm getting there. Still looking for furniture. What can I do for you today, as if I didn't know." She wrapped her finger around one of her curls and straightened it out, then let it go. It sprang back into place.

"What's the spin you're handing out today?"

She reached into the top desk drawer and pulled out a piece of hospital letterhead with three paragraphs and handed it to me.

Skimming the standard garbage that said a lot without saying anything, I took my time folding it in thirds and putting it in the inside pocket of my leather jacket.

"Thanks. Now my job is done, I should head back. All the hounds got a copy?"

"I'm still waiting for one of the networks, but their first newscast isn't until ten o'clock so they won't be in for a couple of hours yet."

"What's the scuttlebutt?" I planted one hip on the edge of the desk, going for that nonchalant look.

"You know those sensationalists. Is the family going to sue? Can we have the footage from the security cameras? Did you lose her on the way to get an X-ray? Good grief! And they even wanted to ask such inane questions on camera. I got my orders. No live interviews. It's the statement only."

"I bet they won't leave you alone."

"Oh, please. One pair tried to divide and conquer like I wouldn't figure out the cameraman was wandering around the hospital while the anchor kept me busy. I notified security immediately. They had already found him trying to film the ICU. Hello! Patient Privacy. Haven't they ever heard of the HIPAA regulations?" She spread her arms out with her palms up to the side in exasperation.

"I hope you booted them out none too gently." I chuckled at her story.

"I wanted to, but I let security handle it. They're cranky enough." She dropped her voice. "They got caught with their pants down.

Someone took out the security system and no one noticed. Seemed they were checking on a fire alarm in another part of the building when the girl went missing."

"I was wondering how that could have happened. They can't blame the hospital if someone disables it, can they?"

"Of course not, but you know those media rats. Everything is a big deal."

"Don't I know it? We chase the same stories, but they sure are stupid sometimes. We are at the same places and their TV blurbs are nothing about what really happened."

"Tell me about it. I say one thing and they blow it way out of proportion. I'm not supposed to say anything to anyone. Just hand out releases and give updated conditions. Period."

"That's got to be boring, but speaking of conditions, was the girl who disappeared still in critical condition?"

"No. They had upgraded her to fair. They just kept her in ICU until the police could talk to her. They were coming in the morning. They hadn't been able to talk to her yet, because whenever they came, she was having a test or something."

She pulled on another curl. "Now she's missing and they don't know what happened. I heard the two uniforms who came to investigate when we made the call. They were supposed to interview her. They did not want to go back and face the accident guru. He had given them specific questions to ask."

"What were the questions?"

"The cops were saying they were pretty stupid. "Where did you grow up? Do you remember your first communion? Who's your favorite sibling? Few of the questions had anything to do with the accident."

"Really, that does seem weird." So, someone already suspected the mistaken identity.

"They kept saying old BJ has finally lost his marbles."

"BJ, huh?" Could it be they were asked by Bob Johansen? He was crafty. He would send uniforms to make a person think it was routine. Those could all have been questions to make someone feel comfortable, but I sensed an underlying reason. Or was I just being too suspicious? Did Bob have an inkling that a mix up had been made in the identities of the accident? Had he already figured out my clue?

I let the silence stretch to see if Patrice would add anything. She seemed all out of tidbits. I decided on a different tactic.

"Any idea how she was able to walk out?"

"They're not sure she did walk out. All her clothes were cut off when she was admitted and they didn't find her gown. With the snafu in the system, they think she was abducted for some reason but no one knows why. It's all sinister."

"Wow. Did they make the ICU a big crime scene like in CSI or what?"

Patrice laughed. "I think they wanted to, but the hospital administrator said unless they had reason to believe she didn't just walk out, they couldn't. Something about the greater good for the other patients."

"Hey, can I go up and look around? Maybe I can describe the scene or something."

Patrice bit her lip. I could see her considering it. She wanted to but I knew she was thinking of her last reprimand.

"You could escort me. Make sure I didn't bother any patients or take photos."

"Yes, I will escort you. No funny business." She wagged a finger at me.

"Scouts honor." I lifted my right pointer finger and crossed my heart with an X.

■ CHAPTER 28

W e exited the elevator into a hallway I was familiar with. I spotted the plant I had hid behind when I heard the squeaky shoes. As if by thinking about it, I had conjured the noise. Squeak. I wondered if I was losing my marbles or it was a figment of my imagination, but Patrice turned her head to the sound, too.

"Aren't nurses shoes supposed to be quiet?" I asked half in jest.

"Actually we try but it has more to do with the floors than anything. That's the surgical suites and it's not as critical there as on the floors where patients are trying to sleep." Our conversation had been in hushed whispers. I wasn't sure if it was because we were up on a floor, she was trying not to alert anyone to our presence, or listening for more shoe noises.

We heard the squeak again and it came from the waiting room. I had to see who it was. We walked into a man of about thirty. He was in jeans, gray sweatshirt and shiny black leather loafers, an odd contrast to his otherwise comfortable attire.

He was running his fingers through his hair and he couldn't keep still. He was pacing the floor and every time he changed directions, his shoes released a piercing squeal.

Patrice and I looked at each other and couldn't help grimacing as he reached the far wall and made his turn. He approached.

"I'm sorry. I'm supposed to be trying the biggest case of my career in federal district court tomorrow. I bought a new pair of expensive shoes to complete my successful look. I was breaking them in today when I got the call. If I had thought the Italian leather soles would be so annoying, I wouldn't have worn them. But then I didn't think I would be here waiting to see if my father survives surgery."

"I'm sorry." The statement didn't seem adequate, but it was all I had. Patrice just nodded, her brown eyes mirroring his pain and he seemed to find comfort in her expression.

"Have you been spending much time waiting?" I asked.

"No, he was only brought in this morning after he collapsed."

I wondered if the squeaks I had heard the first night Dominique was here was another pair of Italian loafers. I needed to visit the offices of Herman Steel and see who wore Italian loafers.

I missed the next exchange between Patrice and the troubled man until I felt Patrice grab my arm, startling me.

"I hope you have some good news soon." I allowed Patrice to lead me from the room as the squeaking began anew.

We opened the double doors into the ICU. Yellow crime scene tape stretched across the room Dominique had occupied. I motioned toward it and Patrice shrugged her shoulders. She allowed me to scan the area and then motioned me out the door as we caught the attention of a nurse returning to her center station.

We returned to the elevator banks and started down. I thanked her warmly for her help and she exited on the second floor. I rode to the bottom and headed out of the hospital to the newspaper to write up what I knew—or at least what the public needed to know at this point.

■ ■ ■

I found myself whistling as I walked back to my condo. My latest bit of news on the missing hospital patient went well. My interim editor was particularly happy with the detail and I didn't give anything away on what the real story was. My palms were itchy. I wanted the big story soon. I had to nail down the heiress and figured now was as good a time as any.

As I approached the outside entrance, I wondered if she would still be there. She had disappeared before. If I were in her shoes, where would I go? Mrs. Dobson was there to keep an eye on her and as long as Elsie didn't have a heart attack and needed medical attention, Dominique should stay undercover. I wondered again what Dominique's life had been like. As different as we were, we were similar. We both were orphans now, we didn't have siblings and had few friends. Her best friend had just been killed and well, I didn't have a best friend.

That thought put a damper on my enthusiasm, but it wasn't something I wanted to dwell on. Instead I was mentally planning my latest interview technique for Dominique. I was going to get her all comfy and have her tell me her life story and then work into the last week of her life. I was determined to get the details.

I walked into my apartment and the first thing I noticed was the smell. Potatoes, if I'm not mistaken. Garlic too. It smelled heavenly and I realized I couldn't remember when I last ate. I shed my jacket and walked the few steps to the kitchen. Elsie was at the stove tasting from the large pot whose steam emitted wonderful smells that were making my mouth water. Dominique was looking over Elsie's shoulder.

"Hi." I wasn't used to seeing guests in my kitchen.

Dominique startled a bit but covered it quickly. "I hope you don't mind. I was hungry." She looked embarrassed.

"Mitch, dear, you ought to be ashamed. You have no food in your cupboards." Elsie wagged her finger at me while stirring the pot.

"It smells delicious. How long until it's ready?"

"Only a couple more minutes."

Dominique seemed to have lost her energy and moved back to sit on the couch.

I looked around. My small dining room table was covered in junk mail, bills and week old newspapers. I grabbed out the bills and wadded up the rest, dumping it in the trash can under the sink.

I set the table using my meager assortment of china, okay, Corelle, with the oldest olive green stripe. My stomach growled as Elsie lifted the cover off the pot of stew. I wondered how she was able to pull this off. I wasn't going to look a gift horse in the mouth. What could I add to the mix? I went to the cupboard above the refrigerator and hauled out a bottle of wine, dusty from age.

I wiped it off and pulled the cork. It didn't smell like vinegar, so it couldn't be too bad. It had been a gift from someone I had helped figure out who was ripping his company off every weekend. Turned out the culprit had been the owner's nephew.

I pulled a couple of jelly glasses from my cupboard and filled each, setting them beside the plates. I saw Elsie searching my drawers.

"What are you looking for?"

"A ladle."

"Don't have one." What did I need a ladle for? I rarely ate at home.

Elsie harrumphed. I walked over and my stomach started its whining song. After I pulled plates, Elsie had pulled bowls.

"Let me help you." I grabbed the pan and poured the savory concoction into each of the three bowls and then set the pan back on the stove. It felt good working in the kitchen, helping to get the food on the table.

Else turned off the burner, grabbed two bowls and carried them to the table. She returned to the kitchen and using a dishtowel as a potholder she removed a pan of steaming biscuits from the oven. When she was finished, there wasn't much room for anything else at my small table.

Dominique rose from the couch and I noticed her color recede. She paused a few seconds before moving forward and then sat heavily in the chair I had hastily moved out for her.

"Thank you. I keep forgetting I've been ill."

It was awkward for a minute with all three at the table. I looked at each of them and they looked at me. I dug in and only realized after a couple of bites that they were waiting for me to say grace. I rarely ate at the table and I never said a prayer. I just kept eating.

"This is delicious, Elsie. I see why Mr. Dobson couldn't resist your charms."

She blushed and took a spoonful.

"Dominique helped with the biscuits."

How did a rich orphan learn her way around a kitchen? "Where did you learn to cook?"

"Mrs. Albanese. I spent so much time there during high school and college breaks. She was happy for the help. I owe that family so much." The last said with a catch in her voice. "I keep forgetting that Ashley is gone. It should have been me."

I looked around the table and realized I enjoyed company for meals especially at my own table. It felt right, homey. I knew it couldn't last. I needed answers from the only witness left.

"We have to talk about that. You need to come clean with the cops, too. Why all the secrecy?" I took a bite of biscuit and it melted into my mouth.

"No secret. Greedy bastards are after my money. Simple. One of the oldest motives in the book." Dominique waved the fork at me to emphasize her point.

Elsie gasped. I forgot she didn't know any of that.

I hastily swallowed. "Yes, but who?" I washed it down with a gulp of wine.

"My bet is the CEO, but I don't have any proof." She took a small spoonful and blew on it daintily.

"You saw Roger, right?" I put a little butter on my biscuit.

"Yes, but he is not the mastermind. I want that person." She scooped another small forkful. "I will never be safe until the top person is punished."

"How do you know that?" I took a bite of biscuit.

"Roger wasn't working in a position of power for the company that long. He has only been on the top floor of the pyramid for a couple of years, since my parent's death." She took a small sip of wine and wrinkled her nose.

"Let the cops handle it." I popped the rest of my biscuit in my mouth.

"Lot of good that did. Whoever did this to me, also killed my parents. No one would listen to me then. I will make that person pay." She cut a piece of potato jabbing it with the fork's tines.

I backed off. She needed to eat to get her strength. I took another sip of wine, tried not to flinch. It wasn't good. A little dry for my taste.

"Mr. Dobson used to say that heavy subjects at the table ruined a good meal." Elsie looked at each of us.

I smiled at Elsie to let her know I got the message. Was this what family discussions were like? I got the point Elsie was trying to make but ignored it. I needed more of the story. "Tell me about your day before the accident."

Dominique took a deep breath, swallowed her small bite and cut more of the vegetables in smaller pieces. I started to rise to get out my notebook and pen in my back pocket, but Elsie grabbed my hand and set it back on the table and patted it. I didn't fight her and continued to just listen.

"I went to see my guardian, Seth Lynch. I wanted to pick up my new car. Seth had to co-sign the check because of the amount. I won't come into my full inheritance until I'm twenty-five. My parents wanted me to find a career, not just live off the family money. That was important to them." She took a deep breath and took a bite of food.

It was like that much information had exhausted her. I had to remember she had nearly died a week ago and had a major head injury. She was not healthy. Had she not been in danger she would be under a trained professional's care and not making conversation that was sure to result in indigestion regardless of how good the food was.

I shoveled in another large spoonful. A man's gotta eat.

"I picked up the car and wanted to share it with Ashley. She had helped me pick it out. I think she was more excited than I was. Seth took me over and completed the transaction and then I dropped the papers at Herman Steel. I went to Ashley's house. Stupid. Stupid. Stupid."

"Don't dwell on the bad stuff. Tell me what happened and maybe we can get the bastard together." I reached over and touched her hand briefly. I wanted her to know she wasn't alone anymore.

She nodded. "We left to take it for a spin. I took the same drive I did when I was test driving models at the dealership. The route has lots of curves to test for handling and a flat spot to open it up. I drove a bit and we stopped for ice cream and ate at a small picnic table so we wouldn't christen the car. I wanted Ashley to give it a spin but she was hesitant. From the ice cream stand to the accident, I showed her how everything worked. I had finally convinced her to drive. There wasn't any traffic at the stop sign, so we switched places. Ashley had just put the car into drive."

I could hear the self recriminations starting in her voice. I squeezed her hand again. We were in this together. This was not her fault.

"Ashley was a very cautious driver and I told her to feel the machine's power." She paused to get her breath, control her emotions.

"She was giving me heck for teasing her. She said she couldn't help it she was a safe driver. I laughed and then she started laughing. We were both laughing so hard." Dominique paused to gulp back tears. "Ashley took her foot off the brake and said 'Look, I'm being reckless.'

We laughed. That's when we felt the car bump us from behind. I know Ashley slammed on the brakes. The last thing she said was, 'oh, no.' I don't know if she saw the cement truck or what. I shouldn't have let her drive. She panicked and she died."

"No. You have to quit blaming yourself." I thought about the pool of brake fluid behind the stop sign. What if in her nervousness, Ashley had pushed on the brakes, causing the faulty line to gush out. The lack of brakes had to be all part of the accident master plan. No one would suspect faulty brakes on a brand new car. I debated with myself, but she deserved to know the truth or at least part of it.

"I think Ashley was commenting on the fact you didn't have any brakes to stop you from being pushed into the intersection."

Dominique's head came up, a question in her eyes. I watched the pupils harden. "The bastards!"

■ CHAPTER 29

After Dominique's profanity my interview stopped. Elsie stepped in and started clearing the table and Dominique returned to my couch where she was asleep within minutes. The interview was done.

My apartment was a bit too crowded and domesticated for my comfort. I thought about ways to get proof of who ordered the killing, who was the mastermind. If we didn't catch the guy pulling the strings, then no one would be safe.

Everything seemed to swirl around Temptations. Neil went there and he was dead. Trace Richards met his client there and he was dead. I couldn't prove it, but Neil's companion tried to kill Elsie and he had been there. An heiress who was supposed to be dead had a coworker who hung out at the bar. Temptations seemed to be the common denominator. I'd used the back door twice but I wanted more. I decided a little reconnaissance was called for.

I left my apartment and drove to Temptations. I wanted to make sure the bartender was in on my plan. I didn't think having a drink away to escape the two women in my apartment was a bad idea either.

"Draft," I said, nodding at the bartender as I took a stool at the bar. The place took on a whole different look from this side. My hiding place was good because you couldn't see anything in its recesses. There were only two other people in the bar and I was sure they were doing a drug deal off in the corner booth.

The bartender returned with my glass. This was not the place for refrigerated mugs. I took a drink and considered my options for tonight. Very few tables were close enough to the bar to overhear the conversations.

"Good stuff," I said as the bartender ambled back and collected my twenty. I grabbed his hand to keep him a minute.

He shook it off. "Not interested."

"No, me neither." I stuttered. "I was in here a couple of nights last week. Grace brought me in the back. I'm looking for a guy that doesn't like to be seen and wondered if I could use the back entrance tonight."

"Whatcha want with this guy?" The bartender wiped off some foam that had dripped off my brew.

"I just want to surprise him. He's been ducking my calls. I want to see who he's with."

The guy laughed. "The jealous type, huh?"

Then it hit me. I was talking like a jilted lover. The thought made me cringe. I was strictly heterosexual. I was about to complain loudly and masculinely about my sexual orientation.

"Sure, go ahead and spy. Just don't make a scene. You hear?"

My denial clogged in my throat. I can pretend to be interested in Roger to get access to him. "Promise." I crossed my heart with my index finger. "No scene. I just want to see who he's with."

I took a long drag off my beer and the bartender moved away. A few more and the glass was empty. As I left Temptations, I realized I'd never received any change from my twenty. A small price to pay, the higher price was letting him continue to think I was gay. I vowed to dissuade him of that after I had my hands on Roger.

■ ■ ■

I wasn't sure if I was wasting my time at Temptations. I was banking on Roger being at the bar. He didn't know I had seen him nor did he know that Dominique had fingered him for the supposed accident. Maybe he would meet with Bertram Switzer and I could wrap this up in a pretty bow. Get my life back. Then I thought about dinner. It was nice eating with people I'd come to care about. Yes, I was grilling a source, but the food was great and Elsie even did the dishes. Elsie left as soon as I'd returned but the apartment looked great, shiny even. Dominique had been awake, but was still worn out from her trip to church. I set her up in my bed and told her I was following up on a lead. I'd explain it all to her in the morning. Then I'd put my plan into action.

I knew coming to Temptations was a long shot. It was a Sunday night and no one went to the bar on Sunday. I thought about Roger. He was a strange one. The only place I had seen him was the Pyramid and Temptations.

I parked just down from Temptations on the other side of a warehouse building so I wasn't readily visible but just looking up and down the street. I still had the borrowed camera. I'd never returned it after using it to take the shots of Neil. It seemed like so long ago but was only a couple of days.

I entered the gay bar by the back entrance as Grace had showed me. I let my eyes adjust before I headed to the opening alcove behind the bar. I surveyed the crowd. It was early yet and only a few people were scattered between the tables, booths and bar stools. The door opened, casting the last rays of daylight into the bar. It wasn't Roger.

The waiting gave me time to think about what I knew. I didn't figure Roger for an early bar-goer. He was more of the fashionably late guys to garner all the attention about some five hundred dollar article of clothing adorning his person. He wanted everyone to know how much he made and how important he was. I had already reasoned that he was angling for the top job and getting rid of anyone who got in his way.

I was willing to bet the CEO would be next. Bertram Switzer could be the mastermind trying to get rid of the threat to the empire he ran. Maybe Roger was planning on bumping off Bertram to take over after the dust settled from Dominique's death. Bertram didn't strike me as the murdering type, but I couldn't figure out why he was at the hospital. I still had no proof. Only theories.

The door opened again and Roger bobbed in. I wanted to high-five the bartender but knew I couldn't give away my observation point. I was glad my supposition was correct. Roger was a regular.

Roger nodded to a couple of patrons. This was his "Cheers" from the seventies sitcom and he was "Norm." I wondered if they would be so happy to see him if they knew he was a cold-blooded killer.

He walked up to the bar and the bartender nodded. Roger said something I couldn't hear and the bartender laughed as he made him a gin and tonic with a twist of lime and set it on the bar. Roger added another comment and the bartender chuckled again. I wished I could hear the exchange.

Roger took his drink to a table to the left of the bar that couldn't be seen easily from the door or most of the bar. The corner booth from the night before was occupied. He set his drink down then walked over to another table and chatted for a few minutes, then the other couple laughed. Must be some joke he was making the circuit with. Roger indeed went to nearly every occupied table. He finally returned and sipped his drink, sitting with his back to the wall.

He looked at his watch and kept half-standing to see over the end of the bar at everyone who opened the door. After a few minutes, he raised his drink glass and signaled to the bartender. A waitress I'd never noticed grabbed the drink off the bar and exchanged it for the empty glass.

I took a few photos of him as he drank when his head was turned for both a full frontal shot and a profile shot. He was clearly impatient for something to happen. He would tap the table with his fingers, take a drink, then twirl the class around its base. He'd look at his watch and then begin the whole process over again.

The door opened and he stood nodding in the door's direction. My eyes followed his gaze and I gulped. It was Seth Lynch, Dominique's executor.

I almost forgot the camera until the lens hit my knee as my mouth hung open. I was looking for a mechanic that could have fixed the brakes of a silly college student who wouldn't ask many questions. Boy, I really wanted to hear what they said.

Seth was the mastermind, not Bertram, unless they were all in it together. I remembered the photo in his office. Him working his way through college as a mechanic. He could have fixed the brakes at the dealership. Motive, means and opportunity were shaping up nicely.

I snapped off five or six photos in quick succession.

I crawled from my hiding place keeping low to stay below the counter's height. I worked my way to the far end of the bar where there was a small open area with only a hinged top that allowed the bartender egress to bus tables, if needed. The table Seth and Roger were at was just on the other side of the bar. There was soft music playing and the drone of conversation. This was all the closer I dared to go without being seen.

The bartender ambled back toward my hiding place. He almost stepped on me and nearly gave me away. He quickly recovered. Conducted his business and retreated.

"Why'd we have to meet?" It was Seth's voice, angry.

"I need more money."

"Money? Money so you can buy more rounds of drinks and make everyone think you're a big hotshot. I got you this job and I can take it away." Seth's voice was low, emotionless.

The waitress interrupted their words. Roger ordered another drink. Seth waved the girl away.

"Maybe, but I'm the one doing all your dirty work."

Roger took a long swig then continued. "I have all the blood on my hands. I made the call to the private eye. I met him on the bridge. I pushed him over." Roger's voice got higher with each sentence.

"You're threatening me now?" Seth broke off.

This was good. I had the camera up and was taking shots of the heated exchange. I could see the headline now: "Negotiating murder." I wish I could write and shoot photos but I had to get the proof and those were the photos. I wouldn't be able to forget the words.

The waitress returned and put another drink in front of Roger. He lifted the first glass, gulped down the drink and returned the empty glass to the table. "Keep them coming," he told the waitress, and Seth frowned.

"Keep your voice down. Be patient."

The door opened again and Seth turned from the door but Roger looked up. When he did, I saw Seth slip something in his drink. Seth was so smooth, no fear, no hesitation. I hoped it would appear in a photo, but I wasn't focusing on the drink, only the players.

Roger returned his attention to Seth and took a gulp of liquid courage. The more Roger drank, the more insistent he became.

"If we wait much longer, there won't be much of a company to run. Bertram is running this company into the ground. I'm trying to clean up behind his back, but I think he's getting suspicious."

"Don't worry. We'll have an emergency board meeting next week. I'm pushing the coroner to release Dominique's body so we can have a decent burial for the girl, then I will become the real chairman of the board, not just acting on her behalf."

"Then you'll get rid of Bertram and name me the CEO?" Roger's words slurred together. The alcohol was making its mark.

"Yes, then we will make some changes and bring this company into its legacy as a Fortune 500 powerhouse."

It's a good thing I was hidden and sitting on the ground because I would have fallen in shock. Seth had to be crazy to think he could get away with this.

"What about the girl that is missing from the hospital? She might be able to recognize me and then the accident won't be an accident."

"I've got it covered. The minute she surfaces, she will be out of the picture. She'll be found to have died from her head injuries. Don't worry about that." Seth's tone was hard, unfeeling.

Would he be as unfeeling if he knew it was Dominique and not Ashley?

I had thought I saw genuine warmth the day I talked to him. What a crock. He's had Dominique fooled, too. I had to get back to her. She needed police protection now.

I crawled back to the alcove and into the dark recesses, nearly falling as I stood up with the rapid blood flow back into my legs. I turned around and leaned against the wall for support. I lifted the camera. I wanted more shots of the pair together. I got one of their heads together. Then Seth stood and they shook hands.

Before leaving Seth surveyed the bar, assessing the threat and to see if anyone was paying him any interest. I thought I saw him nod at someone at the bar, but then he left.

I stayed for a few minutes after Seth left to see what Roger would do. He sat and ordered a double from the waitress. I wanted to leave, but wondered about what Seth had put in his drink. Was he tying up another loose end? Roger rose, but grabbed the table for support. The drinks were starting to hit him hard. He weaved and knocked into another table, nearly upsetting all the drinks. He didn't stop to apologize but continued on, maybe heading for the door but it was hard to tell. He didn't make much forward progress, mostly swaying side to side.

He took another step. Then he fell forward on his face and I heard a crack. The hawk nose would never be the same. Roger laid on the floor and conversation only stopped for a moment and no one came to his aid. I felt sorry for Roger. He'd made the rounds like these were his friends. When he'd dropped to the floor in trouble, no one cared.

I pulled my cell and called 9-1-1.

"Need an ambulance at Temptations. Drug overdose. Needs his stomach pumped. Oh, and a broken nose," I added as an afterthought.

I could hear the dispatcher sputtering questions but I disconnected.

I didn't want to wait. I had some major plans to make and a Pulitzer to write.

■ ■ ■

It only took me minutes to reach my apartment and I pulled in. I was giddy like a teenager and couldn't wait to tell Dominique what I had uncovered. Then my steps slowed as I reached the elevator.

Seth had taken the place of her parents. This would crush her. She would truly be losing the last friend she had. That bothered me but I didn't know what else to do about it. Besides, it was about two in the morning and she was probably sleeping. That would be okay. I wanted to get my notes into the computer fast and record the conversation word for word. A shower would be nice. I felt gross from lying on the sticky floor but it had been worth it.

I hit the red up button expecting the doors to open immediately. Someone in my building must have had a late night. I shifted my weight, anxious to share my news. Finally the car arrived and I started my ascent.

I was finalizing my plans as I exited the corridor and moved to my door, putting the key in the lock.

I walked in and stopped cold. Something was wrong. It was too quiet. The lights were all out and I had left a light on in the bathroom in case Dominique had gotten up. Had Dominique left and turned off the lights. She wouldn't do that again, would she? It was pitch black and the curtains were drawn, too. I never drew the curtains. I was on the third floor. No one could see in. I left the front door open to get the light from the hall.

I didn't know if I should go in or run. The run urge gripped me. Then I thought of Dominique. If someone had hurt her or worse…I couldn't think about that. I pulled my cell phone off my hip and rested my finger on the last number of the speed dial. It was the best protection I had. I hit the light switch and nothing happened. I glanced back in the hall and saw my neighbor's door. The hall had power.

The light from the hall was a warm soft glow I wanted to retreat into, but I had to know. I took another step in. I could see the outline of the couch. From what I could see it looked exactly as I had left it.

Maybe Dominique had just blown a circuit or something. I proceeded toward the bedroom door that was ajar. It was getting darker now, the light from the hall not reaching this far. I had to see if Dominique was in the bedroom. I wanted to cry out and wake her but my throat was parched and could only manage an inaudible croak. I inched forward reaching the doorway.

The curtains were closed here as well. Damn the room darkening blinds I'd gotten because I slept until noon when I was on nights. If only I had adjusted to days and had opened the blinds. I pushed the door open. My eyes had adjusted and I could just see the outline of the foot of the bed. I pushed the door open farther and reached to hit the light switch. I was past caring about waking her up.

Nothing. I strained to see the bed and if anyone was in it. There was a lump and I rushed to it.

"Dominique."

I felt myself falling.

■ CHAPTER 30

The pain in my head. It felt like it was going to explode. I wanted to slip back into obscurity. It was so easy. I heard voices and the pain sharpened.

"Mitch, open your eyes, God damn it. Open your eyes."

I knew that voice and it was pissed. I wanted to retreat back into the blessed painless darkness. I felt something on my cheek. Each touch sent a shaft of misery from my head down my back. I started floating.

"Mitch, open your eyes." The voice pleaded, which was odd but required too much agony to figure out. What was going on? I hung suspended and felt the black returning. I fought the pain for a minute, trying to figure it out.

"Mitch, your exclusive, you have to get the story." Dennis' voice. Confusion reigned. Dennis never wanted me to get the story.

I felt my body move, more pain. I was tired. I wanted relief. I felt myself relax, the ache receding.

I was jerked out of my euphoria. It was brutal and it was swift. I was coughing and the pain, the cold. I felt my hands on my face. Wet, cold.

My eyes opened and the light was too much. I closed them again. "Good Mitch, that was good. Try again." Dennis' voice sounded softer, more controlled. What was wrong?

I consciously thought about opening my eyes and the pain didn't intensify as much. I tried to move.

"Stay still. Moving will only make it hurt worse."

It sounded like good advice. "What happened?" My voice was groggy and hoarse, unrecognizable even to my own ears.

"You tell me. What do you remember last?" Dennis' tone was cajoling which belied the urgency I saw in his eyes.

"I came to tell Dominique I knew who tried to kill her." I paused to lick my lips and found moisture. My throat was dry.

"Dominique, who's Dominique and who is trying to kill her?"

I tried to rise up to see if Dominique was in the bed, the pain and dizziness spiraled and I wanted to reach out to the blessed darkness. "Is Dominique here?"

"Mitch, don't move, talk." This was more like Dennis.

"Dominique? Is she okay?"

"No."

I didn't want to know but I had to ask. "Is she dead?" My voice was a croak.

"No, but it's bad. She was shot."

I hadn't been crafty enough. I was responsible. Dennis handed my bathroom cup to the paramedic. It dawned on me that Dennis had splashed me with water to get me to consciousness.

"Lucky for you, your neighbor lady saved your bacon."

I must have looked weird. The paramedic returned with the cup and Dennis took it and held it to my lips. The water was cool and felt good. I felt my body start to respond.

"Listen, you probably have a concussion and a serious bump on your head. The paramedics are going to insist you go the hospital and undergo all kinds of tests. I need to know what you know. Now!" Dennis' green eyes pierced mine. I felt the intensity.

I knew what he was trying to say and with head injuries, there is always a chance you will go to sleep and never wake up. Where to start? My brain was muddled.

I just started talking. It was in bits and phrases. I saw questions in Dennis' eyes and I wondered if I was making sense. I figured the order wasn't important. As I talked, the story started to come easier, more coherent. I was able to concentrate and bring in more details. I was oblivious to the activity around me. I caught movement and I knew Dennis would send uniforms out on errands but it was taking all my energy to keep talking. My burst of strength was waning. I wanted to sleep.

I started dozing a couple of times and Dennis brought me back with pungent odors. Once, I felt contact to my cheek. This time the touch

.ughter.

"Okay, Mitch. I've got enough." He touched my shoulder, which on some level was better than the smelling salts he had given earlier.

I didn't know if I talked for ten minutes or an hour. Time had no meaning.

Something cold was pressed to my head. A light was shined in my eyes. A collar put around my neck which I started to struggle against.

"Mitch, you did good." Dennis' voice was soft. "I have to let the paramedics get you to the hospital. I'll stop by later and bring you to my place. We'll let Colleen take care of you."

I closed my eyes.

■ ■ ■

I awoke to a beam of light.

"Stop that." I moved my arm but felt tied down. I turned my head away.

"Can you tell me your name?" The voice sounded nice but the light made my head hurt.

"Mitch Malone. Leave me alone." I sounded cranky to my ears but I wanted to sleep.

"What day is it, Mr. Malone? Can you open your eyes?" The voice was soft but insistent.

"I don't know. Last I remember it was the middle of the night but it is obviously morning." Light streamed through a window. I tried to focus my eyes and saw a pretty woman in a white jacket, a stethoscope for a necklace.

"That sounds like the Mitch Malone I know." Dennis' voice came from my feet.

"Okay. That's good enough for me." The hand taking my pulse left.

"How are you doing?" Dennis came around to the side of the bed and pulled up a chair.

"Okay, I guess. My head still hurts." I tried to reach up with my right hand but felt resistance as before. I looked down and saw a tube in my arm and a silver clip on the end of my finger. I reached up awkwardly with my left hand and felt bandages.

"How long have I been out?" I took stock. I was in a hospital gown and bed, the sun streaming in my window.

"Not long, maybe six hours."

"How's Dominique?"

"Still critical, but I think she'll pull through. Lucky for her, you were right behind Seth and he didn't have time to do anything before you got there."

"Tell me." I again tried to move my right hand toward my back pocket and realized I wasn't in my jeans. I looked around and realized there wasn't a pen or a piece of paper anywhere in my room.

"Don't quote me." Dennis laughed, knowing I was looking for my pad and pen. "You'll live if you want to write a story."

"Very funny. What happened?"

"Well, my smart friend, you should have called 9-1-1 the minute you realized something was wrong in your apartment. You were just lucky. I was leaving the station and was able to answer my cell phone. You were in the first place I looked."

"I don't remember making the call." I had tried to recall but there was nothing after waiting for the elevator.

"When I answered, I was finishing a conversation with another officer as we walked out. I knew it was you and you'd wait. I heard a strange voice say: 'That should take care of that damned reporter.' I knew you were in trouble and started running for my vehicle. A patrol car pulled up and I gave them the address. As I rushed over to your apartment the phone was still connected. I heard a voice say: 'What do we have here? Dominique. Well, this is an added bonus.' Then came the muffled gunshot.

Dennis paused briefly to get his emotions under control. He then continued the tale I had slept through. "We had paramedics rolling instantly. I couldn't take any more pressure from the publisher if another employee was killed." Dennis paused to laugh. "Those paramedics saved Dominique's life."

My eyes widened.

"I thought you were gone. I took the stairs and ran into Seth coming down, dressed in black, tucking a gun into his waistband. I was pissed. Let's just say Seth has a bit of a concussion too, but isn't getting the medical treatment you are. His is county provided."

"Your neighbor also heard the shot and called 9-1-1. A second unit arrived on our heels. They came up the stairs and took Seth off my hands and I continued to your apartment where you were looking dead on the floor and Dominique was bleeding all over that California King you're so proud of."

"My bed, blood-soaked. Crap. I knew I never should have rescued her."

"You should have told me." Dennis's voice took a hard tone.

I looked guilty. "I learned my lesson." I pointed to my bandaged head.

"I doubt it, but maybe."

"Great, one of the best stories of the year and I'm not able to write it." I was whiny from my guilt and injuries and the fact I didn't get the story. Every rag and news broadcast would have the story before me. Reporters weren't supposed to become the story.

"Yes, I thought about that." Dennis reached down and pulled out my laptop in its carrying case. You better get to work. We've tried to keep this quiet but when you have one of the county's top attorneys in lockup, word is going to get out." Dennis pulled the table that holds the dinner trays and adjusted its height. "Call me when you need some quotes."

Dennis disappeared out the door. I pulled on the zipper of the case and only felt an increase of pain when I strained to plug my laptop in the bank of outlets, gauges and other connections on the wall above the bed.

I got to work. I was only interrupted a couple of times by nurses wanting blood pressures and the endless questions about my name, day of the week and did I know where I was.

The pretty doctor returned and checked me again. I had just finished the story and was anxious to get it to the newsroom. I had checked the internet connection but I couldn't get a free network in this part of the hospital.

"You got wireless internet in the hospital?" I asked the doctor.

"Yes, Mr. Malone, we do."

I hit some keys and a log in screen appeared. "Secured access, right?"

"Yes, we have patients' rights and privacy issues. What did you expect?"

"I don't suppose I could get you to give me access?"

"What's so important?"

"I'm a reporter and I have to get this piece about my injury to the paper. I can't get scooped on a story that got me injured, can I?" I tried to smile but couldn't help wincing with the pain.

"Tell you what, Mr. Malone. I will let you send your story if you promise me you will rest for a couple of hours."

"I promise." I crossed my heart with my index finger.

She turned the computer toward her and tapped the keys. When she turned it back, it was connected to the internet.

"Send your story."

I did and hit the send key with satisfaction.

"All set?"

I nodded and she turned the keyboard away from me. Hit some keys and gave it back. The internet connection was gone. I winced.

The doctor consulted my chart and marked a couple of notes.

"I'll send a nurse back with some pain meds. Now rest." And she was gone.

I, however, wasn't tired and I had a follow-up story to work on.

■ CHAPTER 31

I found my clothes rolled up in a plastic bag in a tall cupboard. I pulled them into the bathroom. I replaced the hospital gown with my jeans and T-shirt, dirty from lying on the floor behind the bar. It was a little smelly but it was all I had. Hopefully I wouldn't be too obvious as a patient who has flown the coop from an overprotective staff.

My bravado didn't last long as I peeked out the door to make sure my beautiful doctor was not going to catch me. I tiptoed out. The pain in my head only hurt a little each time I took a step. I had a new appreciation for what Dominique had gone through when I had sprung her from this joint.

At the main hall bank of elevators, I pushed the 'up' button. I wanted to check on Dominique and no one would tell me how she was doing. The number on the side of the elevator frame said I was on the second floor. I could only think about when she came into the Emergency Room from the accident and her heart kept stopping. I wanted to pray that her heart was beating strong but with the loss of a lot of blood, I knew the odds for a strong person weren't good. Dominique hadn't recovered from her first accident that wasn't and the second was even more evil by a man obsessed with money and power.

The doors chimed and then opened and I was surrounded by a mass of Albaneses who pulled me in and surrounded me.

I wasn't sure what type of reception I would be getting. Did they know I hadn't told them their daughter was dead? That I had spirited who they thought was their daughter out of the hospital.

That was way too complicated for my brain in its current state. If they wanted their pound of flesh from me, I was in no shape to defend myself. I also deserved it. They were a nice family and I lied, withheld information, and then abducted who they thought was their daughter.

Did they even know this was Dominique and not Ashley? The elevator doors shut and it jerked as it began its assent. My back was to the doors and I was surrounded by the dark-haired heads and eyes.

"Hello." It seemed like a lame beginning, but I didn't know what else to say.

Mrs. Albanese detached herself from her husband's arm and stepped toward me. When she was directly in front of me, she reached around my waist and pulled me close, her head only came to my shoulder.

The hug about did me in. I hadn't realized I had a chill until I was enveloped in her warmth. I took a deep breath and thought I smelled cinnamon and something sweet I couldn't quite place.

"Thank you for taking care of our Dominique."

They were thanking me? I didn't get it. My puzzlement must have shown. She unwound one of her arms and patted my check, but didn't step back.

I looked over her head at her husband and he just nodded but I swear his eyes were shining.

"You're not mad I didn't tell you?" I blurted out the only thing that came to my mind.

"No. Dominique needed you. She didn't need us." Angie Albanese looked up at me to make sure I understood. I didn't.

"Dominique is like our own daughter. She spent so much time at our house even before her parents were killed. We grieved for her as well as rejoiced that Ashley was saved. We knew something wasn't right when we saw her in the hospital, but we thought it was due to the head injury. The doctors told us she might not seem herself for a while until it healed."

I saw Mrs. Albanese wipe a tear from her cheek. It must be so hard to lose a daughter. Or maybe it was realizing you didn't lose a daughter and then you did lose a daughter. My thoughts were chaotic and confusing. Mrs. Albanese struggled with control and waved her husband back as he stepped forward. She spoke again.

"When Dominique's parent's died, she withdrew into herself and she was only coming out of it in the last few months. After the accident, we were afraid that Ashley had retreated into the same dark grief that

Dominique had. We tried to give her some space to heal and come out of it on her own. We knew Ashley needed to grieve for her best friend and we understood that when she asked for some time alone. Had we realized it was Dominique who was shutting us out because of guilt, we never would have allowed it. That horrible man, if I ever get my hands on him." I felt her arms tighten around me. Angie Albanese may be small but she had strength in those arms.

"Dominique's guilt had to have been unbearable every time we saw her, told her we loved her. She tried to tell us once but couldn't get the words out. We didn't wait for her to find the right words. We told her to rest and that must have been terrible for her to keep going with the lie. You were there to listen to her and be her friend. You saved her life at least two times." Mrs. Albanese stopped and rooted around in her pocketbook and came out with a tissue and dabbed at her eyes.

Tony gently pulled his wife into his embrace. "What my wife is trying to say is we are heartbroken Ashley is gone." He paused, clearing his throat. Taking a deep breath, he continued. "Ashley leaves a hole in our lives, but we will always have a part of her with us and that part is Dominique."

"We're going to tell her that right now," the youngest Albanese blurted out as the doors of the elevator opened. Everyone stepped out.

"How's she doing?"

"We're not sure. We only found out she had been shot when the officer came to apologize about the identity switch." The senior Albanese's tone was somber. "He let it slip."

"Our pain is deep." Mrs. Albanese wrapped her hands around her husband tighter. "We are grieving for her but it explains so many things. We couldn't understand why she turned from us when we went into the hospital room to see her, rejoicing and praising God that she'd regained consciousness."

"Knowing now that it was Dominique, we understand." Mr. Albanese completed her thought as his wife started to choke up. "She would feel tremendous guilt and would be unable to face us. She was still feeling guilty over not being with her parents during their accident. She was suppose to be in the car but wasn't feeling well. It saved her life."

"We are here to pray for Dominique, to sit at her bedside knowing she is Dominique and give her the strength to survive. We will miss Ashley deeply." A tear slid unanswered down her cheek. Her husband rubbed her arm and shoulder, pulling her in tighter.

"Dominique needs us and she is all alone now. We will be her family. It is what Ashley would have wanted. It's what we want. We will remember Ashley and she will live on with Dominique. Those two were so alive. It will be like having Ashley with us when Dominique is there." Tony's voice was somber.

The elevator chimed again and the doors opened. Only then did we realize we were right in front of the elevator. We had only stepped out of the elevator, but never moved down the hall toward ICU. The doors' opening propelled us in that direction, breaking the mood.

I lagged back as the family surged forward to be with Dominique. When they reached the doors of the ICU, Angie turned back and saw me leaning against the wall. She sent Tony Jr. back.

"I'm supposed to help you. Ma didn't notice your bandage."

"I'm okay, just tired." I straightened to show him.

"Won't matter none." He nodded in the direction of the doors. "Once she sees someone hurting, nothing can stop her. You might as well just accept it."

"Dominique needs her, I don't."

"Don't matter. Ma could take on an army of sick people and will them all to health. It doesn't matter what the patient wants. My advice is just go with the flow and bail when you can. Right now, I won't be allowed back until I bring you. Don't make me hurt you. You will be joining us."

I could see why the mafia was so strong. This Italian family was a bunch of tough cookies led by a little woman who took no prisoners. Dominique was in good hands and I knew she would recover. Angie Albanese wouldn't tolerate anything less.

I allowed Tony Jr. to walk me into the ICU waiting room where his mother greeted me with a short nod of approval. I felt stronger already.

Tony Sr. returned to the room a few minutes later. "They will allow us in a couple at a time. It should be only family but the nurse relented after I reminded her they let us see her before."

I wasn't sure what Tony had to threaten to lower the rules but I'm sure it involved some type of litigation or blackmail about the mistaken identity or just really bad publicity. I didn't want to cross them.

"She is still unconscious but should be coming out of it soon. She made it through the surgery with only one minor scare." His report finished, he walked back over to his wife and she hugged him for a second and then slipped back. Angie reached in her pocket and pulled out a string of beads with a crucifix on the end. I saw her lips moving in silent prayer as she clutched the beads. After a moment she opened her eyes. It was like she'd received a message from a higher authority.

"Mr. Malone, why don't you go see her?"

"I…" I looked into her eyes filled with kindness and an iron will. I had only wanted to see if Dominique was alright. I didn't need to talk to her. I couldn't finish my denial. I turned on my heel and walked toward the door. I looked back. I wasn't alone. The patriarch had followed.

"I'll just make sure there aren't any problems," Mr. Albanese said as he opened the door to ICU.

The nurse looked up when we entered and the second she caught sight of the elder Albanese, she lowered her eyes back to the chart, ignoring our presence. He walked me to the door and looked in the room.

"She needs to hear you are alright. In order for her to summon the strength to heal, she can't be loaded down with guilt. You are the second person to get hurt on her behalf. Forgive her."

I looked up into his face and saw the kind, understanding eyes. I wanted to throw myself into his chest and cry like a baby. But I wasn't a baby. I was Mitch Malone whose biggest scoop to date was lying in that room. I needed a quote to finish off my story. I instinctively reached back to my pocket for my notebook.

Misunderstanding what I was doing, Mr. Albanese pulled me toward the door and closer to him. "It's okay to lean on somebody. It doesn't lessen the man, it makes him human. You might want to remember that when you play cowboy."

He released me and kind of looked me over from head to toe. I could see indecision written on his face. Words were Mrs. Albanese's department.

"Dominique isn't the only one that might have some guilt that requires forgiveness. Confession is good for the soul. You think about that."

He pushed me toward the door with one hand and opened it with the other. I had no choice. The elder Albanese had spoken. I walked to Dominique's bedside, only once looking back. Mr. Albanese hadn't moved. He was a rock blocking the door, but also there if I needed him.

■ CHAPTER 32

Dominique was pale as a ghost and attached to monitors and tubes like the first time I had seen her. I grabbed the railing of the bed, not sure why I was here but knowing the Albaneses were right. Dominique had a lot of guilt to get over.

"Dominique, it's Mitch, Mitch Malone from the *Grand River Journal*." I felt stupid after saying all that. I looked back over my shoulder. Mr. Albanese hadn't moved. He nodded his head. I needed to get on with it.

"I'm so sorry you got hurt. It's all my fault. I shouldn't have left you." My hand reached down and grabbed hers. I wasn't planning on touching her but I couldn't stop. I had to get my message across. Her fingers were cold but not lifeless.

She needed to get her blood moving to all her limbs again. She needed to wake up and become that vital girl I had glimpsed on occasion. She had a multi-billion dollar company to make a Fortune 500. She had so much to live for.

"Dominique, I don't want to worry you but the Albaneses are all waiting for their turn. I can't be long. They love you, Dominique. They don't have to be here… but they are. You are a member of their family and they will not leave you alone. You don't know how lucky you are to have them."

I raggedly sucked in air, refilling my lungs. Something was different. Dominique had squeezed my hand. She was holding my hand now. I looked at her face but her eyes were still closed but I thought I saw a bit of color in her cheeks.

"Dominique." Her eyelashes fluttered. She was coming out of where she had been.

"That's it, girl. Open your eyes."

I recalled the blue sapphires that had shined in mischief at times or looked with determination to get whoever had killed her friend. Those emotions weren't strong yet, but they would be there. Mrs. Albanese would see to that.

"It's so good to have you with us again and no, I refuse to sneak you out of the hospital this time. You are truly safe."

She smiled a little, then stopped.

"Does it hurt?"

I could see the pain in her eyes but she refused to acknowledge it. She tried to say something but her mouth was dry and her lips chapped.

"It's okay. I'll come back and we'll compare notes. The nurses and the doctors are going to want to check you out now that you are awake. Maybe they will even give you some crappy hospital food for dinner. Maybe I can get Elsie to cook something for you."

I paused and stared at her a moment. I felt weird, emotional. I felt like crying.

"Get well," I choked out.

I slid my hand from hers and felt bereft as I left the room. By the time I reached Mr. Albanese who hadn't moved, I was exhausted.

"You did good. Now I think it's time you went back to your room and rested."

I wanted to argue but I just couldn't. I wasn't strong enough. I allowed him to lead me to the elevator and back down to my room. I didn't know how he knew where it was. I was just glad to see my hospital bed. He took off my shoes after I sat down and covered me up with the thin blanket. I slept in peace.

■ ■ ■

"Mitch, time to wake up."

I kept my eyes closed, trying to remember where I was and who belonged to that perky voice. I opened them slowly and when I saw the hospital room everything flooded back. The perky voice belonged to a beautiful doctor in blue hospital scrubs. I wanted to move over and have her join me. Then I realized I was fully dressed in my hospital bed.

"That's a good boy." She shined a light in each of my eyes and quickly removed it.

Great, I was blind now.

"Mitch, can you tell me where you are?"

"The hospital. Our Lady of Mercy Hospital."

"Excellent. Why are you here?"

"I got hit on the head and my friend Dennis made me come."

"Another correct answer." She grabbed my arm and took my pulse. The blood pressure cuff went on next.

"How is your head?" She pumped the ball and inflated the cuff watching the gauge.

I thought about it. My head hurt but it wasn't throbbing like it had earlier. She released the valve and the pressure in my arm diminished and she ripped off the cuff.

"My head hurts a little, but it is more of a dull throb."

"Good. It looks like you're going to be kicked out then."

"I can go home?"

"I don't think you will be going there." Dennis had just entered. "That's a crime scene for a while longer. Besides, I promised Colleen she would get a crack at you for a few nights. Sean and Kelly promised they would be very quiet so Uncle Mitch could rest. Colleen's happy to have you if only to keep the twins in line."

I enjoyed Dennis's preschool children but they could be a handful. I also liked his red-headed wife who could keep the hardened detective from becoming obsessed with his job.

"You can leave. I'll have the discharge papers ready whenever you are." The doctor left the room.

I noticed Dennis was carrying a bag. "Whatcha got?"

"I didn't think you would enjoy hospital food so I brought you a little sustenance." He pulled the table over to the bed, moved my computer off to the side and set the bag down, pushing it in my direction.

I opened it and saw a pint of chocolate milk and two long johns. "Are these from Donna's?"

"None other."

I was ravenous. I picked out one and bit it, letting it melt in my mouth. Both doughnuts and the milk were gone in record time.

I looked up at Dennis with a sheepish expression. "Did you want one?"

"No. I already had one. Knew I couldn't pry one away from you once you knew I had them."

"Thank you. I do feel much better." It was true. My energy was returning and the fog in my head receding.

"Let's spring you from this joint. You have an exclusive to write."

I'd forgotten the story. I must have been hurt worse that I thought.

"We can set up in my den and announce the latest bad guys are behind bars with your handsome source in the police department providing details."

"You're going to invite that cute little officer on nights to stop by?"

"I can see the doughnuts did the trick and you are feeling better. Time to hit the road."

■ CHAPTER 33

As soon as we arrived at Dennis' suburban digs, I locked myself away in the den and went to work. After an hour, Colleen came in with a bowl of soup, a sandwich and a glass of milk.

"You feeling okay, Mitch?"

"Yup. My headache is nearly gone. My stomach started growling just a few minutes ago. This smells delicious."

"Nothing special but chicken noodle is the kids' favorite."

"Let them know it's mine too and thanks for sharing."

Colleen waited for me to start eating. After making sure I didn't need anything, she retreated and I went back to work.

After another half hour, I just finished and determined what details I needed to confirm. Dennis walked in and sat across from me.

"So is Seth in custody?"

"Yes. Will be arraigned on Tuesday. Charged with two counts of attempted murder. Not sure what all else the prosecuting attorney will come up with. Additional charges are pending." Dennis looked at me with an I-out-foxed-the-fox grin. "How's that for official sounding?"

"Great. Now what about Roger?"

"Lying in a guarded room at the hospital. He ingested a lethal dose of GHB, the date-rape drug, but thanks to an anonymous caller, he got his stomach pumped quickly instead of being treated as too much to drink. He's charged with attempted murder and leaving the scene of an accident for starters. Other charges may be added. We don't have everything wrapped up with a bow yet, but he is making a deal against Seth." Dennis got to his feet and walked around the desk to my side. "May I?"

"A good reporter never lets anyone read his copy, then they won't buy the newspaper," I smiled at him. "But, in your case I could make an exception."

I rolled the chair back and let him see the screen.

"Not bad for an amateur detective," Dennis said after a few minutes.

"What's the sheriff's department's spin on the mix up in identification?"

"Not so much a spin as protecting Dominique while the department investigated the attempted murder." Dennis moved back. "Also need to add that this has been a joint investigation with the Sheriff's Department."

I moved back to the screen and added the joint investigation. I looked at him to see if there was more.

"Bob Johansen knew about the identity switch from the day after the accident. Added to that, he was suspicious of the parents' accident. Keeping Dominique 'dead' for a few days allowed him to quietly investigate the motives behind the people in her life. He came up with Seth rather quickly and was drafting warrants to search his files. That was a bit dicey with him being Dominique's attorney and all."

"That explains why Bob was ducking my calls. I knew it couldn't be because he was mad at me or I printed too much information. I never print too much."

"Yeah, right. You always print too much information." Dennis punched me lightly on the shoulder. I winced.

"This time I have the bumps and bruises to prove it and on my head no less." Then I yawned.

"Looks like the bumps and bruises are winning. Can you send it via the Internet to the paper or do you need to go there?"

"I can send it from here." I opened up the wireless window. I moved aside and Dennis typed in the username and password to put me on the World Wide Web.

I emailed the story to Ken the night editor who had begged me to get rid of Neil. I'd forgotten about Neil.

"What's up with the investigation into Neil Speilman's death?"

"That's at a standstill. We found the boy you saw and he is the same boy taken into custody at Elsie Dobson's but we can't find any motive for him to kill Neil. He was in the room and swears he didn't see anything. Neil was leaving for the evening and the boy was to take a taxi home in the morning."

Whatever happened to my camera, I wondered. I needed the card out of it to see if my photos were good enough to show who was meeting with whom.

"What is it? You have something?"

"Maybe another follow-up and more charges, if I'm right. I have to get that camera. Last I remember, I left it in the Jeep. What happened to my Jeep?"

"Nothing that I know of. It wasn't part of the crime scene. Where did you leave it?"

Crap! How long had it been in the visitor spot? My noisy neighbor would have had it towed by now.

"In my garage. I'm not sure it will still be there. Can we go check?"

"If it clears up the Speilman homicide, I'll pay the impound charge. Damn publisher is working the police chief over about solving it and I'm tired of getting my ass chewed. Let's go."

We headed for his front door and just before we closed it, he turned and yelled.

"Mitch and I are running an errand, be back soon."

Within minutes, we were in the garage of my building. My Jeep Cherokee was where I had left it. My neighbor must have been out of town or something. Dennis pulled in next to my vehicle. I pulled out my keys from my jacket pocket, surprised I still had them considering I'd been knocked out, the ambulance ride, my clothes taken and then me putting them back on. Sometimes the luck was just with you.

I looked in and the camera was under the front seat where I left it. Another stroke of luck that it hadn't been stolen. I pulled it out and climbed slowly back into Dennis' car. I was feeling better but not really up to driving. Fast movements brought the pain back to my head. I liked Dennis' taxi service.

As Dennis drove, I reviewed the photos from my last night at Temptations. These would be great for the front page to go with the story. I kept going back to my first night in the bar. There was something there. I remembered but never got back to it. I slowed as I paged through the photos. It seemed surreal to be looking at Neil in animated conversation with the boy toy. Neil was a pain in the ass but he didn't deserve to die. I would miss all his cell phone calls. Well, I wouldn't miss his overzealous time management of my day. I just wanted him out of the *Journal's* newsroom, not leaving this world.

There it was. Neil was in the middle of a conversation when at the moment I clicked, something caught his attention. I couldn't see what it was.

I went back a couple of frames and in one where I was focusing on the boy toy, there was something in the background. It was hard to see in the one-inch camera screen.

Dennis pulled into his driveway and before he had the family van in park, I was out of the vehicle and halfway to the front door, despite the throbbing in my head. I had the biggest story all along.

"Wait for me." Dennis hurriedly shut off the car and followed, jogging to catch up.

I opened the door. "Colleen, we're back," I yelled. The sound of my own voice made me wince, but I was intent.

I gingerly slid into the desk chair and nearly rolled past my computer. I hit the power button to bring it out of sleep mode and slipped my camera card into the slot. I opened Photoshop and went through the photos until I found the one I wanted.

I opened it, then changed the view to make it full screen. Someone was in the booth behind the boy toy. I enlarged the image further concentrating on the face and then enhanced the photo to take out some of the graininess from the low-light shot.

I was staring at the screen. "What are we looking for?" Dennis got impatient when I was onto something and didn't share. He was standing behind me but wasn't savvy about photos.

The enhancing was completed. Bingo. I leaned back in the chair and let Dennis see the image.

"I'll be damned! This might give the investigation a new twist."

Seth was sitting in the booth and I hadn't noticed. I had been so focused on getting the goods on Neil and returning to nights and the routine I liked.

I clicked to a photo a few frames later.

"See here. Neil is looking over the boy toy's shoulder. He sees Seth and realizes who he is. Maybe Seth is meeting Roger again and he puts two and two together. Maybe he had the boy toy be the bagman for the blackmail. That would be motive." If I had looked at the photos earlier could I have saved Dominique from a bullet? I didn't want to think about Neil. Maybe if I had taken him up on his dinner invite, I would have seen him for the blackmailing snake he was.

"Have you searched Seth's office and car?" I asked.

"We're working on warrants for his office. It's sticky because he's an attorney with other clients and their privacy must be protected."

"Any cell phones?"

Dennis's eyes lit, realizing where I was going. "There was one in his car. I'll have to compare that number to another phone call. Another nail in Seth's prosecution."

I thought for a minute about Neil and his constant requests for dinners and drinks.

"I wonder if Neil was riding you so hard because he hoped to find other victims to blackmail," Dennis echoed my thoughts.

Another piece slipped into place. I wondered if Ken was being blackmailed and why he was so intent on getting Neil to move on. I had never seen him so desperate. I'd have to have a talk with Ken some night when the news was slow. I bet there were several at the paper Neil had his hooks into including the publisher who hadn't batted an eye at the pink masthead.

■ EPILOGUE

I walked off the elevator onto the top floor of the Herman Steel pyramid. It had only been a month since I'd left Dominique with the Albaneses in the ICU. She'd made a miraculous recovery, being released into their care after only five days, according to my follow-up, but I hadn't visited or spoke to her. I'd been back on nights the following week. Back to my routine, covering crime in the city of Grand River.

At the end of last night's shift, Ken and I finally had that talk. He admitted that Neil had been blackmailing him. Found out he'd had an affair with another reporter and threatened to tell his wife if he didn't come up with $1,000 a month. After the confession, Ken suggested a story on the newest CEO of Herman Steel.

I agreed to leave my nights for this and had called this morning to get an appointment. The woman with the pleasant voice only needed my name to schedule the appointment for this afternoon. I looked around and noticed a much warmer feeling to the offices. The cold sculptures were gone and in their place were watercolors of Lake Michigan.

Purple irises were in vases on coffee tables and the outer guard's desk. The nameplate read, Helen Brown, and looked old and battered, both the nameplate and lady. The receptionist with the legs was nowhere to be seen.

She stood and held out her hand. "Thanks for taking care of Dominique."

"You're welcome." I was a little embarrassed by the gesture as I pulled my hand back.

She picked up the phone and pressed a couple of buttons. She set it down and walked me to the office that had housed Bertram Switzer.

She opened the door and then stood aside to allow me to enter, closing it after me.

I stopped suddenly and sucked in my breath, not believing my eyes. I wanted to let out a wolf whistle. It wasn't the view of the downtown and the natural light that warmed the room, but the vision of health and happiness behind a large library table desk.

Dominique stood up and pulled on her tailored navy jacket, straightening it. She flipped a strand of blonde hair off her shoulder and it bounced down her back. The smile on her mouth radiated out from under her sparkling blue eyes.

"Mitch Malone. It's great to see you."

"Same here, heiress. At least the title fits you now. You look like the picture of health." I stepped closer to her. I wanted to grab her hands and squeeze them to make sure she was alive and breathing. Instead, I stopped at the desk, my hands hanging limply at my side.

"I owe you so much. I wasn't sure you would ever come to collect on my story. Helen had standing orders if you ever called or arrived to give you whatever you wanted."

"What is the story with Helen? Not quite your style?"

"My style? I'm not sure I have one. I have a lot to learn. This is not as easy as it seems. Helen is helping with that. She was my father's assistant. Bertram had relegated her to an assistant in the marketing department. She has given me so much of my father, how he ran things, how he based his decisions. It's almost like he's with me."

I could see the survivor's guilt was manageable. She was trying to move past the weight of sadness to remember the good times and the memories. She was beginning to heal.

"That's great. You really look happy. Speaking of Bertram, what happened to him?"

"For print?"

"Maybe."

"Let's sit." She motioned toward a large leather sofa and matching chair near the window.

"He came to see me just before I left the hospital. Right after your big exposé ran. It was sad really. He had no idea what Roger and Seth were up to until the car accident. He genuinely liked my father and didn't see how Roger was manipulating him with bad information. He trusted Roger. After my death, he started looking deeper."

I nodded. I wasn't sure what my story would be out of this. I didn't want to break the mood to pull out my notebook and take notes.

"He resigned as CEO. He told me he would stay until I had found a replacement. I told him to leave on his own schedule and I already had a replacement. He was gone the day I reported to work. I think he knew I was the replacement and he just couldn't face it."

"Tough break for him, but why was he at the hospital?"

"I'm not sure, but I think he knew Roger was up to something. The accident was too much of a coincidence. I think he was watching over me, as Ashley, trying to protect me but didn't know how." She paused and licked her lips. I knew Dominique was beautiful from the photo Roger had given me, but the real thing was so much more. I could barely take notes as she talked. She broke eye contact and I glanced down at my pad. I needed to write something down.

"Seth pressured Bertram into taking over after my father died and gave him Roger to help. Bertram was set up to take the fall for all of the murders. Seth had Roger plant papers in the safe. I bet Bertram would have been found dead by his own hand with a note saying he couldn't live with himself and with what he had done. But that we will never know." Dominique raised both hands, palms out to punctuate her point.

"Seth was smooth." I didn't tell her I thought it was Bertram as well.

"Yes, he was. He duped me too. He was always there for me. Ready to help." She sighed. "I'm trying hard not to dwell on the bad. Mrs. Albanese won't allow it." She chuckled, clearly at peace with the diminutive woman's rules.

I nodded, knowing the force of that small woman who was more than the leaders of most third world countries. "Why are you here, Mr. Reporter?" Her eyes sparkled in mischief.

"I wanted to see how you were doing and the best way is to do a profile on the new CEO. So here I am." I patted my notebook for emphasis.

"Fire away. There are not many media types I would trust, but you've had my back and done it well. What would you like to know?"

"What was it like facing your first board of directors meeting asking them to appoint a recent college graduate to the CEO chair."

"My knees were knocking, but I knew I could do the job. I had studied for years to be able to do this. The company is in my blood and I will do my best to succeed. I assured them if the company wasn't seeing financial gains within the first year, I would step down."

"Do you think you can increase profits?"

"Yes, part of what I saw when I studied the company's books for a class was some skimming. I wasn't sure who had authorization for what, but I was suspicious. Our accounts receivable policies weren't created for electronic banking. Bringing the accounting department into the new century alone will help our balance sheet."

"Spoken like a true CEO." I smiled at her.

"Surprisingly, it hasn't been that bad. The business decisions are easy. The difficulty is what to say when Roger comes up for sentencing in two months. I'm glad he pleaded guilty and will be testifying against Seth, but how do you forgive the man who was responsible for your best friend's death?"

"I don't know." The silence stretched for an awkward minute. I didn't have another question immediately. Dominique was a true heiress saving the day.

"Let me tell you what I'm thinking about doing. I'm planning on funding a scholarship in Ashley's name. The first recipient will be Stacey Richards. I understand she has given up on being a private detective, but is thinking of joining the police department when she finishes her criminal justice degree next year."

"That is great news." I had wondered what had become of Stacey.

"I'm also creating an internship program at Herman Steel for students who want to get some practical experience before leaving college."

"I think Ashley would like that. How is her family doing?"

"Good. They miss Ashley as much as I do, but we're coping." I hated to see the sadness in her eyes and searched for a change in subject. Again, she was the better person.

"Mrs. Albanese and I went to visit Elsie last week."

I must have turned red. Dominique grabbed my hand and squeezed gently.

"Elsie understands. Besides, she is too busy to worry about one sorry reporter who doesn't call or visit."

I must have looked both surprised and guilty.

"Mrs. Albanese took one look at her and hauled her off to church."

"I didn't think Elsie was Catholic."

"She's not, but she has something far better, love. I haven't told anyone this yet, but I plan to build a neighborhood center adjacent to St. Bonaventure to work with kids that have working parents, to keep them off the street."

"That sounds generous." She was handing out her money like candy.

Dominique punched my arm. "You are a hopeless cynic. They currently have an afterschool program and Elsie is the favorite grandmother of about twenty kids."

"Really?"

"She bakes cookies all day and then doles them out with hugs and advice. She's even gotten under the skin of some of the toughest would-be thugs. She's amazing."

"That she is." I nodded, thinking about how she had gotten to me. I hadn't forgotten her advice, just not found the right opportunity and until I did, I didn't want to face her.

"Between Elsie and the Albaneses, I don't feel so alone. I've been staying with the Albaneses but will be moving into my own house just as soon as I close on the deal."

"Really? Where does the city's newest and most sought after CEO live? The Rock Creek Estates?" I was happy now we were on to safer subjects. I didn't want to think about my feelings for Elsie or Dominique.

"With all those stuffed shirts? Not on your life. I brought a run-down place in the Albanese's neighborhood and will be fixing it up. Just down from the community center."

"Sounds ambitious. Will you have the time?"

"I will make the time. I don't want this job to consume my life. That is what happened to Seth. He let the money cloud his judgment. He liked what the money could do. I want to do something with the money that I like and will make a difference."

Her words made me look at my own life. Is that what I was like? Consumed with the job? No. I had others and I didn't want to dwell on it. I had a story to write.

"That sounds wise and very much like your mother." I didn't add that what I knew of her mother came from Seth and I wasn't sure he could be believed.

"I'm not a saint. As a matter of fact I plan on stepping out of my shell, but you will have to be surprised about that."

"What kind of reporter would I be if I didn't try and get it out?" I teased.

"You can try, but my lips are sealed." She pulled her thumb and forefinger across her lips to seal them but the light danced in her eyes.

We talked some more about her goals and plans and then I knew I had to leave. Dominique was ready to take on the world and I had to find the next big story. It was waiting for me and I couldn't let a future Fortune 500 CEO dissuade me from it.

I was Mitch Malone and I was back on the beat, and, most importantly, back on the night shift.

■ ABOUT THE AUTHOR

W.S. Gager has lived in West Michigan for most of her life except for stints early in her career as a newspaper reporter and editor. Now she enjoys creating villains instead of crossing police lines to get the story. She teaches English at a local college and is a soccer chauffeur for her children. During her driving time she spins webs of intrigue for Mitch Malone's next crime-solving adventure.

Visit the author's website at http://wsgager.com/

W.S. Gager is also a frequent contributor to the publisher's company blog at http://otpblog.blogspot.com/

Also from Oak Tree Press...

Night Watch
by Mary Montague Sikes

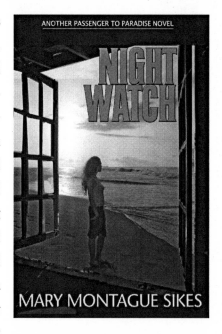

From the moment Lily's plane lands in tropical Trinidad, things go awry. She planned for rest, relaxation and photography, but instead faces mistaken identity, a gun running operation and danger. Her transportation to her lodging does a no show, and she is mistaken for someone named Katherine by Kyle Warren. Putting the unsettling feelings of her trip and recent deaths of her parents behind her, Lily enjoys the ocean view from her room only to see the familiar figure of the man from the airport watching men stealthily unloading cargo from a small boat. Over the next few days, Lily's resemblance to another puts her in danger and Kyle's attempts to protect her further complicate the uncanny memories and feelings that she may indeed know him from the past. With her life in peril, Lily discovers a deep kinship with her doppelganger and a growing attachment to Kyle.

The Pot Thief Who Studied Ptolemy
by J. Michael Orenduff

The pot thief is back, but this time Hubert Schuze' larceny is for a good cause. He wants to recover sacred pots stolen from San Roque, the mysterious New Mexico pueblo. An easy task for Hubie the pot digger. Except these pots are not under ground – they're above it— in the top-floor apartment of Rio Grande Lofts, a high-security building which just happens to be home to Susannah's latest love interest.

Hubie's legendary deductive skills lead to a perfect plan which is thwarted when he encounters the beautiful Stella. And when he is arrested for murder. Well, he was in the room where the body was found, everyone heard the shot, and he came out with blood on his hands. Follow Hubie as he stays one step ahead of building security, one step behind Stella, and one step away from a long fall down a garbage chute.

Ask for these and other books from Oak Tree Press
at your favorite retailer

or buy from the publisher's online shop
at www.oaktreebooks.com

Breinigsville, PA USA
28 June 2010
240711BV00002B/1/P